# REINCARNATED WRATH

# REINCARNATED WRATH

## BARBARIAN PRINCESS™ SERIES BOOK 03

### MICHAEL ANDERLE

LMBPN

DISRUPTIVE IMAGINATION

Copyright © 2021 LMBPN Publishing
Cover copyright © LMBPN Publishing
A Michael Anderle Production

LMBPN Publishing
PMB 196, 2540 South Maryland Pkwy
Las Vegas, NV 89109

Version 1.00 December 2021
ebook ISBN: 978-1-68500-624-2
Paperback ISBN: 978-1-68500-625-9

# THE REINCARNATED WRATH TEAM

**Thanks to our JIT Team:**

Peter Manis
Diane L. Smith
Zacc Pelter
Jeff Goode
Angel LaVey
Paul Westman

*If I've missed anyone, please let me know!*

**Editor**
SkyHunter Editing Team

*To Family, Friends and
Those Who Love
To Read.
May We All Enjoy Grace
To Live The Life We Are
Called.*

**— Michael**

# CHAPTER ONE

Blazing heat glared from overhead. Anywhere else in the world, folk would be curled inside layers of furs and wool to keep the cold away, but the farther south they traveled, the less impact winter appeared to have on the elements.

Cassandra had heard dozens of explanations. Some had to do with how the earth was curved. Others said there was magic involved—a magical shield that grew weaker the farther south you went. Of course, that didn't make sense given that she'd traveled south far enough to where the weather grew cold again. Folk who believed in the magical shield had no answer other than that she must have been confused in her travels and turned north again.

It was interesting to know there were things out in the world that she didn't have the answer to. Some people likely knew—folk who dedicated their lives to studying the secrets of the universe, for better or for worse. She patted her horse on the neck. It was probable that she would never understand why but in the end, she didn't need to. Her world had enough mysteries to solve of the kind she knew how to answer.

"I told you so."

She turned to where Bandir was seated on his horse. Drake-Hunters didn't hold the same aversion to riding as their DeathEater cousins, fortunately. She knew well enough that there were few barbarians like the DeathEaters, almost to the point where they needed a new definition. Something other than merely barbarian.

"You told me so?" she asked and tried not to yank too hard on the reins so Strider could lower his head to munch on some of the grass growing by the side of the road.

"I told you it wasn't worgs. Or wargs, for that matter."

"What are wargs?"

"You know, men who can cast their minds into beasts to control them from afar," Tandir interrupted and tightened his grasp on his ax. "I've never seen one myself, but it's said that tribes deep in the mountains of the north cast their minds into eagles and use them as a way to track their prey in the icy wildernesses."

"I heard there were druids who could do that," Cassandra muttered. "But they live in the jungles out west. They are able to look into the minds of the creatures all around the forest, although I've never heard of any who can control the beasts."

"It might have been shapeshifters too," Tandir suggested.

"None of the attacks happened while the moon was full." His brother scowled at him.

"They can change when the moon isn't full too, you know."

"Well, yes, but they cannot resist changing when the moon is full, which means attacks would have happened when the moon was full. Every full moon."

She hated that they knew so much about the hunting habits of these creatures. They had tracked the group for going on three months. It hadn't been time wasted, of course, and in their travels, they had found ways to help the folk they encountered here and there. Knowing there was a threat to the travelers around the eastern road, however, had nagged constantly at the back of her mind.

Now they finally had a good chance to stop them from attacking again. It had been interesting to track the beasts since they left camps and droppings behind that appeared to be those of humans—or humanoids at least. The tracks they left, though, were the padded prints of wolves.

There had been questions of what they were precisely and in all honesty, she had never seen folk riding wolves like that. The beasts were particularly large and stocky and capable of carrying the weight of a human, but it didn't look like a comfortable ride.

"Why don't we strike now?" Bandir asked, hefted his mace, and pointed in the direction where they knew the group would be lying in wait for the caravan traveling the road. "Put the element of surprise to work in our favor?"

"If we attack them now, they'll still be in a defensible position. We wouldn't be able to circle and approach from the high ground behind them in time to stop the ambush." Cassandra pointed her spear at the open area their quarry would have to traverse to reach the road. "But once they are committed to their attack, their attention will be drawn elsewhere while they are in an uncomfortable position to defend against an assault. Surprise will still be on our side but this time, we will cut through their flank instead of engaging them while they are waiting for someone else to come along."

"I merely hate waiting for the battle." The younger of the twins shook his head and nudged his horse forward a step. "Besides, wouldn't this tactic put the caravan at risk?"

She did appreciate that he was trying to think of the good of the people they were protecting to justify his lust for battle. While she didn't believe it for a moment, the fact that it had occurred to him at all was a step in the right direction.

"They've been warned of the dangers and will expect the attack on this stretch," she answered and slipped her spear into the slot that kept it on her saddle. "It was the least we could do before we left them behind to scout."

"Three days of scouting and following only what the bare rock could tell us." Tandir settled into his saddle, reached for his waterskin, and took a mouthful. It was more of a nervous twitch than any indication that he was thirsty. "And now we wait for them to attack. I stand with my brother on this."

"And it's a good thing we do not hold a vote on such matters. If we did, you would have us charging up the hill to their position while arrows and spears rain on us the whole way."

Their enthusiasm was appreciated, though. There weren't many in the world who would travel the barren roads with her in search of brigands and monsters to kill to ensure the safety of others.

Well, there were a few, but they would have demanded far more coin for the effort.

"What do you think will be riding the mounts?" Bandir asked.

"We don't have long to wait to find out," Cassandra answered.

"Well, yes, but there might as well be something for us to do to pass the time. I still think those wolves are too small for real humans to ride."

"It would be interesting to see a very small pack of barbarians riding the damn things," Tandir muttered.

"Is that what you guess? Half-pint barbarians?"

"I thought maybe a group of halflings who call themselves barbarians, to be honest."

"It could be goblins," she suggested. "Not many I know would be willing to travel in the sunlight without an orc or two lashing their heels. But if they managed to train a pack of mountain wolves to their purposes, it would allow them to attack and withdraw without ever spending too much time out in the sunlight."

"Goblins don't like the sunlight," Bandir disagreed. "And

halflings like to stab from behind in the dark before attacking anything headlong. I say humans."

Cassandra was right about one thing at least—the attack would happen soon. She could see the cloud of dust rising down the road, the sign of the caravan's approach, and it wasn't long before she heard the yipping and howling of the canine mounts being gathered for the ambush.

"How much shall we say?" she asked and squinted toward the caves their quarry had chosen for a camp.

"How much?"

"We are passing the time. We have all said what we think will come from those caves. We might as well make things interesting. Three silvers?"

"Three?"

Bandir nodded slowly. "I could stand to make three silvers."

"You would make six, you idiot," his brother snapped. "Three from me and three from the Barbarian Princess if you're right—however unlikely that might be."

"Right, six."

"It's agreed then," she whispered and continued to watch for movement as the caravan came into full view.

They were using mules and donkeys to pull the heavier loads, but the smaller wagons were being drawn by goats. She'd never seen the like before, but it made some sense at least. Goats were notoriously hardy and able to eat almost anything, which was a benefit in the deserted areas of the world.

That added to the milk they produced meant the group always had some source of food wherever they traveled without needing to resort to eating their beasts of burden. She'd even heard of people who resorted to drinking the milk and blood from horses when things grew desperate but thankfully, she had never needed to.

Milking Strider would not result in anything she wanted to drink, even in the throes of desperation.

"Here they come," Tandir warned.

Rocks began to roll down the hill, evidence that the group had begun their attack as the caravan approached. There was one downside to traveling with mules, donkeys, and goats. Nothing ever went quite as quickly as they wanted it to and for Cassandra, it was about damn time that something happened. She had baked in the sun for far too long.

Howls erupted from the caves—only one at first but quickly followed by dozens more. All echoed through the hills and mountains around them, clearly meant to instill fear in their intended targets.

It was effective. She could hear the braying from terrified beasts that wanted to advance no farther along the path while they heard the sounds of predators nearby.

But it benefited them as well. While Strider shifted nervously between her thighs, the warhorse was used to the sound of death and destruction all around him. She couldn't have asked for a braver companion.

The charge had begun and the creatures streamed down from where they had been hidden. They traversed the steep drop from the caves with expert precision while their riders held on for dear life.

Although they were a good distance away, nothing in the world looked quite how goblins did with long ears and massive eyes, at least when attached to their smaller skulls, developed over long centuries of living underground where light and sound were scarce. It was no surprise that they disliked living in the open where the sun hurt those eyes. Now that they were attacking, it was their work to stop them.

"Damn it," Tandir muttered.

"It's for the best." Cassandra grinned and nudged Strider into a trot. "You two would have wasted it on drink and whores. You might as well let me pay for the first of the drinks."

"Is that a promise?" Bandir asked.

"If you survive."

They moved out from where they had hidden in a crevice in the rocks. Horses were considerably less nimble in negotiating the rocks than the wolves were, which meant they had to wait below where the ground leveled out for them to attack effectively.

The beasts still hadn't caught their scent. They were likely whipped into a fury and focused on the easy targets waiting for them. The fighters among the caravan were already out and waiting, although there was no telling what their rusty spears, axes, and plank shields would do to help. Still, it was better than no defenses at all.

"DrakeHunters!" the twins shouted, drew their javelins, and rushed to intercept the charge.

They came in from the marauders' flank, which gave them the opportunity to attack with some advantage as well as providing a clear view of the full number of their enemies.

Cassandra counted thirty of them, all told, although she had a feeling that had more to do with the number of wolf mounts they had available. Goblin tribes tended to wander through the mountains in the hundreds.

The fact that they were goblins had another benefit she hadn't considered before. In the daylight, the damn things were all but blind. They would no doubt rely on the wolves to guide them to where their prey waited and use sound and smell to give them a direction to attack from.

And they wouldn't notice that they were being attacked from the flank until their mounts warned them.

The beasts only noticed that danger approached them from the side when the first of the javelins struck to kill two of them and crush their riders as they fell.

Five or six skidded to a halt and looked around to determine what was attacking them. She pushed Strider toward them instead of the main party and raised her spear as a battle cry surged from her chest.

It wasn't anything in particular, merely the need to shout her defiance and aggression to her enemies as she plowed into the group. Her spear drove through the throat of the closest wolf and it stumbled down the hill before she withdrew her weapon when arrows flew in her direction.

To the naked eye, the bare skin revealed by the armor she wore would have led anyone to believe that the arrows carved from flint and rock should have wounded her, but all she felt were the dulled impacts before they were pushed to the side. Her amulet still worked to drive the projectiles away from her skin.

Cassandra shifted her spear to punch it through the chest of a goblin as its wolf mount turned to try to attack Strider, perceiving the horse to be an easier target.

The assumption was corrected when the gelding reared and crushed its skull with a powerful hoof strike. She adjusted in the saddle to prevent herself from being thrown as she brought herself around to push a strike from one of the goblins' wickedly curved sabers to the side and drive the spearhead through the creature's open mouth and into its skull.

As they turned to engage the new threat, the charge was dragged to an immediate halt and with perfect timing, the two barbarians launched their assault from a little higher in the path. Four more of the goblins and their mounts were felled before they realized that they were being attacked from a second angle, and she was determined to take advantage.

Somewhat isolated from the rest of the fight, she hooked her spear to her saddle and took up the small recurve bow she had practiced the use of over the past few months.

Her inspiration had come from another barbarian archer, but the twins had little to offer to help her train. They were better with their javelins, but if there was ever a time to put her new skills to use, this was it. The goblins already looked like they were considering simply turning back to the safety of their caves and if they escaped again, it would be more months before they finally had the beasts pinned in a decisive fight.

She wouldn't let that happen.

Cassandra fitted one of the arrows to the bowstring as Strider pushed forward to where the goblins tried to overcome the twin barbarians. They had already lost a good third of their troop but it would take more than that to stop them from attacking the road ever again.

Her first arrow flew wide of its intended target and into the rocks nearby. The second was a little more encouraging. It buried itself into the shoulder of one of the wolves and made it trip and fall. Its rider tumbled into an ungainly sprawl and cracked its skull on a boulder the wolf had attempted to jump onto.

"Come bring your face to my arrows, you ugly shit," she muttered and drew another arrow from the quiver mounted on her saddle as the injured wolf turned his glare on her instead of the twins.

It looked like a wolf from a distance, but there was something off about it. The snout was shortened and almost flat against the rest of its head, which allowed its mouth to open like a snake's. Its eyes were odd too, with streaks of gold and red that reflected the light.

These were creatures raised in the darkness as well, and she could see scars marking its fur to turn it white. Some were the results of battle but most of them appeared to have been carved into their skin in a ritualistic manner by their goblin riders.

The realization almost made her regret having attacked them —until with a snarl, the wolf bounded toward her. The arrow already nocked to her bowstring loosed and sank into the beast's skull, punched through, and sent it off course. It slid down the hill amidst a small cloud of dust.

"Come on, Strider," Cassandra whispered. "Our friends need us."

She slipped the bow into its harness. Three arrows were already more than she could spare given that she only had fifteen of them to begin with. That was enough practice with the weapon for now, she decided.

The twins had cut through another five before the rest of the goblins decided they'd had enough. They were lightly armored and armed and showed no intention of openly engaging anyone in fair combat. The group liked to attack by surprise and kill the weak and unprepared before they retreated into the safety of their caves. That appeared to be what they intended to do there as well.

The barbarian princess wanted to cut them off from that retreat, and the twins were of a similar mind. They truly had come into their own. While they still showed signs of their upbringing in their desire to charge directly into any fight that was silly enough to present itself to them, there were clear signs that they had listened to her when she spoke of tactical approaches to combat, and they applied it to their fighting as well.

"Cut them off!" she shouted and motioned the twins to the path the wolves tried to take to the caves. "If they reach their camp, we won't be able to pursue them."

Tandir nodded and pushed his horse a little faster to intercept the group that ran from them. A dozen wolf-mounted goblins fleeing from three fighters seemed a little silly, but given who their adversaries were, perhaps not that insane.

They had a reputation to live up to these days.

From what she could tell, however, they wouldn't get there in time. Cassandra nudged Strider forward another step before she drew her spear again. She didn't like having to use magic in a fight like this, but it appeared it would be necessary. If the rest of the goblin tribe rushed out, they wouldn't have the opportunity to cut these off from their retreat, and if more wolves were in there waiting for them, it would be the end of their advantage.

And the beasts were much better at navigating the terrain than horses.

Reputation or not, there were still only three of them.

She raised her spear and pointed the tip at the rocky outcroppings above the cave the wolves were trying to reach.

"Let's see how you like it when I use the terrain to my advantage," she whispered, focused on one of the larger and more precarious outcroppings, and let that focus flow out through the weapon. It warmed in her hand for only a moment before the flash of light launched away from the spearhead and flickered like a falling star toward the rocks.

It didn't quite make the impact she expected—barely a crackle—but before she could call the power for another strike, the rocks began to shift. They moved slowly at first but increased speed and momentum as more of them began to slide and tumble free.

"That went better than expected," she muttered. A handful of the mounted goblins reached the entrance before they saw what was happening above them.

The rocks plummeted with a dull roar and easily crushed those caught in the avalanche. Those that weren't caught had to jump away before they were swept from the perch and down the mountain with the rest of the rocks.

Only a handful managed it.

Perhaps it wasn't fair to use magic, but thirty mountain goblins attacking a mostly unarmed caravan wouldn't have been fair either, and they didn't seem too distressed about it.

Cassandra reached the top, grasped her spear, and stared at the five that remained. They shouted something at her. She assumed they were cursing her but held their mounts back from attacking all the same.

"I am the Barbarian Princess," she offered by way of answer and twirled her spear in one hand before she pointed the head at the nearest goblin. "Which of you five would dare to attack me?"

Before they could answer the question or show any sign that they understood what she had said at all, two javelins cut two more of them down and killed the riders as well as the wolves.

"Three of you," she corrected when the twins rushed in from the other side.

They didn't bother to send only one. The three that remained gave their wolves free rein and attacked as a group. She turned the spear into a backhand and tossed it like the twins did with their javelins. One of the wolves fell as she drew her sword, ducked under a spear thrust at her chest, and slashed the goblin that had attacked her across the stomach. Strider reared again to crush the smaller wolf with his hooves.

The third failed to realize that Tandir was charging at him and the barbarian's mace shattered his skull before his horse trampled the wolf and crushed it underfoot. He would have barreled into Cassandra and Strider if he hadn't finally dragged his horse to a halt.

"You almost hit me there," she told him and eased Strider a few steps away before she realized that the man was squinting as he tried to see what was happening around him. "Damn it. You looked directly at the blast again, didn't you?"

"Well, we might not have if you warned us about what you were doing," Bandir answered and appeared to be half-blind as well.

"Aye. How are we supposed to not look at our enemies while we're in pursuit?" Tandir agreed.

"How—why did you throw javelins if you both had trouble seeing?"

"Well, the goblins that survived made a right noise and we could attack them based on that."

"And if you had wound up attacking me instead?"

"We would have heard you," Bandir asserted with a firm nod and looked like his vision was slowly returning to him.

"Aye. A bit of a screamer you are, boss," his brother added.

"Shrieker, to be honest."

"A downright howler."

"Shut it, both of you." She growled when she noticed the pitying look they exchanged. "Collect your javelins. We'll see if the caravan still needs help."

# CHAPTER TWO

Cassandra's blast had littered the winding track leading down the mountain with rocks. As a result, they had to negotiate the path with care.

Night was falling and the caravan had begun to set up camp for the evening by the time they reached the bottom.

"Why do you think they stopped there?" Bandir asked. "If I was leading them, I would want to put some time and distance between the damn goblin tribe and myself. There's no telling if they'll rush out after dark."

She shook her head. "Their pack animals won't travel any farther. Besides, goblins aren't brave creatures by nature and they'll hurry away from where so many of them were killed. They will probably simply hide deep in the caves and expect us to press them the way orcs would."

"Where do you think they got the idea to raise wolves to ride?"

"Worgs," Tandir corrected him. "They look like wolves but not quite. You see that in the eyes and the snout."

Cassandra nodded. "It might have been something only this tribe did. Or it could be something goblin tribes are doing more often, which does not bode well for the dwarves who share the mountains with them. We might need to send warnings to the dwarf cities to make sure they won't be surprised by packs of wolves attacking them through the goblin tunnels."

But it was a matter for another time. They had done the work they were hired to do and the area did not pose many other dangers. Most bandit troops had left the region to avoid being attacked themselves, which meant it would be a smooth trip for the caravan the rest of the way.

She hoped it would be, at least.

The caravan master approached them as they dismounted and he laughed loudly.

"And here I was, doubting the stories of the Barbarian Princess and the DrakeHunter twins," the man said. "I will never doubt again, but I didn't expect you to bring the whole mountain down on the creatures."

"It'll be a while before the goblin tribe attempts to attack travelers on this road again," she answered.

"We saw most of the fighting from the ground. It was impressive."

"Remember that when the time comes for the guild to collect the coin you owe us," Bandir commented and checked his weapons. "We've had problems with folk trying to sneak away from paying what they owe because we did not do the work in the way they wanted it to be done. Or simply because they did not want to part with the coin."

"Believe me, many would be more than willing to drop what coin is necessary to open this road. Numerous caravans want to use it to travel through the region. The refugees we are escorting are only a few of the many who would want to reach a civilized location to start over. Those fleeing the remnants of the troops who used to fight under the banner of Grimm the Cruel would appreciate a safe road for them to travel."

She nodded. It had been a problem. Grimm had planned an invasion, and those she and her little troop had managed to kill were merely a drop in the bucket of an army of those who willingly followed a man who called himself the Cruel. His army was suddenly left with no one to lead them or pay them.

Somehow, she wasn't surprised to find that he had been the type to arm and lead goblin tribes, but she had not expected it either.

"We've worked to make Draug's Hill and Torsburch burgeoning trading cities for the region," Cassandra commented as they were led to where the rest of the travelers had begun to prepare the evening meals. "It's not quite the most civilized corner of the continent but it has improved."

"Are you in command of Draug's Hill?" one of the refugees asked and looked at them as they joined one of the campfires.

"I wouldn't say I am in command of it," she answered and took a seat when it was offered. "I've worked with those who are and fought alongside them as well. Many people are looking for a new home in the region, and both Torsburch and Draug's Hill are full to bursting. Draug's Hill was once an abandoned fortress of ill repute but now, a burgeoning community has begun to till the land and has found all kinds of opportunities that would let them grow and prosper with help from the dwarf stoneworkers who remained in the region."

She felt as though she had told this story countless times. Numerous folk looked for new homes and new opportunities in the area, and with the rumor of a Barbarian Princess who protected the land, they flocked in. The reality was a little less soothing, of course, but it was still a decent enough location for them to start homes and businesses. While there were enough monsters and raiders to make living there perilous, it was no more so than anywhere else outside the borders of the empire.

And even inside, depending on how close to the major cities and trade routes one happened to be.

"So...you are the master of Draug's Hill?" a refugee insisted.

"Aye," Bandir asserted quickly, although he quieted once he

caught the glare she directed at him. "Well...in a manner of speaking."

"In no manner of speaking," she corrected him. "If I had responsibilities coming from any authority in the place, do you think I would rush out into the wilds like this?"

"Well, Karvahal certainly does listen to and respect your judgment. When we go there, he finds a way to drop most of the troubles of leading his people on you." Tandir shrugged.

They weren't exactly wrong about that. He was a young man and not quite prepared for the practice of leading his people as a chieftain and so found ways to delegate the responsibility to those he trusted. It was a skill many leaders had difficulty acquiring, but he needed to learn how to take on the role himself.

"All right, I suppose it could be said that I have some manner of leadership when I am inside the walls," she conceded.

"And outside. You saw the little town the dwarf is starting to build where folk have started to live and trade from. What was the dwarf's name again?"

"Sifeas," Cassandra reminded him. The twins were as bad at remembering names as Skharr was. Maybe that was something all barbarians had in common. Perhaps it was a skill she would have to acquire for herself before too long. "He's all but set up headquarters in Draug's Hill. Many of the traders have begun to find reasons to work from both towns. Some might even say they're sister towns, a sign of civilization here."

"It won't be long before the empire decides to take over whether we like it or not," another refugee commented to grumbled agreement from the others.

They weren't wrong. Eventually, the empire would decide there was enough coin coming through the region to justify taking over, whether the folk in the region wanted it or not. It wasn't like they could summon a big enough army to stop them. The only reason why the empire had not spread this far was the fact that an army large enough to take over the small towns and villages would require more effort than the region was worth.

If the attempts to settle there continued, that would change but maybe that wasn't such a terrible thing. The new emperor seemed a decent enough fellow—certainly decent enough for Skharr to accept a proper position under him, which was something she had never expected to see from the man. It was an unsettling thought. The world truly was changing.

"All that to say," Cassandra stated and interrupted what was becoming a heated discussion about whether the empire's arrival would be a good thing or not, "Karvahal is the real chieftain of Draug's Hill. I am someone who is occasionally trusted for advice."

That seemed to make sense to them, although the discussion had already moved on to other topics. A sense of celebration had threaded the group and she couldn't blame them. They had headed off to a new land with new opportunities and now, the greatest threat to their safe arrival was done away with. The food was hot and a handful of the travelers produced cheap wine for the evening meal. It wasn't much but was enough to lift their spirits even more.

Perhaps it was time for her to settle somewhere like Langven had. She could still head off and fight those who needed to be fought but in the end, traveling continuously like they did would end with them dead somewhere. There was nothing to say that finding somewhere to call a real home would help with that, but it couldn't hurt. Still, she was too busy saving folk and fighting this foe or that monster to be concerned about ruling anything, much less a whole damn town.

Langven had his Ebon Pack to look out for and who looked out for him as well, and from what she had seen, he was becoming a person of influence in Torsburch. She couldn't think of anyone better for the job, despite their many differences. His pack had quickly become the largest collective force of mercenaries and it brought a solid amount of coin into his coffers too. She and the twins had enjoyed a little of their success, which allowed them some time to rest in Torsburch, find food and supplies, and make repairs for their travels.

She was snapped out of her thoughts when the caravan master approached, carrying steaming bowls of food and some drink for them to partake in.

"You know we brought our own supplies, yes?" Cassandra asked.

"We wouldn't mind hot food offered by others, though," Tandir said quickly before she could turn him down outright.

The larger man laughed and placed the food and drink down for the three of them. "We have some to share. There was some debate as to whether we would need to find an alternate path that would take us longer to reach our destination, so we packed more than we needed just in case. Now that we need not divert, we have enough to share."

"Be careful with offers like that," she warned. "Barbarians are as notorious for their skill in emptying larders as they are for felling monsters."

"Speak for yourself," Bandir muttered through a mouthful of bread.

"I am."

"Having the Feller of Grimm among us should be enough to inspire our little caravan to share," the man said, running his fingers through his thick brown beard.

"Feller of Grimm?" She frowned at him.

"Oh. Some folk have called you that. Not least of all those troops of his who are pillaging these lands, although whether it is an insult or a compliment varies. But besides that, knowing that you are associated with the vaunted Ebon Pack does do much to instill these people with some semblance of hope."

Cassandra smiled when she realized that a few of the younger men in the caravan were commenting on her choice of attire. If the truth be told, she would have been a little more comfortable in her leathers, but the Barbarian Princess needed to make a statement when in battle. Perhaps a little more was required. As the morning sun rose, she would certainly need more protection from it.

"I cannot say that life will be easy once you find yourselves in your new homes," she answered. "But you will be offered a fighting chance."

"It's more of a chance than what these people have come to expect at all from this place."

She shrugged. Hope was an interesting thing, both when it was present and when it was absent. She'd said enough to temper their expectations but if they intended to push on, they would need hope to keep them going and far be it from her to deprive them of what little they had. A fighting chance was truly more than most people could expect, even in the more civilized corners of the continent.

With that said, Cassandra took the bowl of steaming soup that smelled like real spices had been added and the bread that had been provided. The broth was thick with oats, dried meat, and even a few root vegetables that packed well for longer journeys and made a filling meal. She had been surprised to see how they prepared their bread, though.

There was no need for ovens. Instead, they laid the flat dough over metal bowls that were placed upside down over the fire and the heat made it rise without needing any yeast. It was surprisingly tasty and an interesting alternative to the waybread that most other caravans carried with them for the long journeys. The traditional fare was filling enough but hard to stomach, especially after weeks of eating little other than dried meat and waybread.

She soon cleaned the dregs from the bowl with the bread that remained and leaned back in her seat with a small, contented smile.

"It's better than what we ate while doing our scouting," Bandir commented once the caravan master moved on to check on the rest of their camp.

"In fairness, we couldn't light any fires," Tandir reminded him as they settled against their packs. "Eating cold food in these deserted parts of the world does make it difficult to enjoy meals."

The barbarian did have a point, but Cassandra had no desire to complain. She had a full belly and was seated at a warm fire with the heat of victory still in her limbs, all while knowing they were only a few days away from the closest they had to a home in the region.

Life could be better, of course, but it could be far worse as well. It was best to enjoy the good things while they were able to.

# CHAPTER THREE

Draug's Hill was a rather unique place and not only because of the hauntingly empty chambers in the tunnels beneath, although she still carried some vivid memories of them and the creature that had lived there.

It had taken a fair amount of work to repair the hole they had made in the ground to attack Grimm's forces from behind. The dwarves had put their effort into it to seal the tunnels and make it appear as though they had never been there in the first place.

Still, the whole place looked like a ruin. This was unsurprising given that it had been exactly that for generations. No matter the skill of the stonemasons, it would take years to repair the gate, the crenellations, and the wall itself to make it look like a proper keep. And that didn't even include the state of it inside. No wonder folk had spilled out to live in the small town that was developing at the base of the hill.

They had done more than enough work to start making the area livable again. Water was being drawn from the earth to water the fields where she could already see the fruits of their labor starting to burgeon. It was mostly wheat or barley from the looks of it, but smaller plantings of vegetables were already being gathered and what appeared to be small paddies where rice could grow were created where the water puddled.

Everyone was ambitious, but each farmer produced what they knew. Alongside the crops, goats, pigs, and chickens had already started to earn a living for the settlers in the area.

Of course, the town was still mostly undefended and if there was an attack, they would have to abandon their homes and retreat to the keep, leaving everything to be raided and burned by any party that came across them. The fortress was already well-defended by Karvahal and his men, and the reputation that it was also defended by the Ebon Pack meant that the smaller raiding parties had avoided coming into view of the keep's watchtowers.

Cassandra didn't know how long that would last. Perhaps there would be time for them to bring logs in from the nearby woods to erect a palisade and take advantage of the spring water that seemed to flow in earnest in the region to create a moat that would help to keep all but the most powerful and most desperate raiders from causing them trouble.

Skharr had said before—although she couldn't remember the context for the statement—that defenses did most of their work by giving attackers pause and encouraging them to find weaker prey to attack.

Still, even as a work in progress, it was the breath of fresh air the refugees needed and a small cry of joy erupted from the group when they came into view.

A handful of the defenders were alerted to their arrival almost immediately, and five of them were already on horseback and riding out to meet them.

She could appreciate Karvahal's need to be careful over who he allowed to enter the area, and she pushed Strider to a trot ahead of the caravan to meet the riders on their approach.

It was gratifying to be recognized almost immediately, especially as the twins joined her a few moments later, along with the caravan master.

The young chieftain was at the head of the small group and he scrutinized the approaching caravan carefully before he turned his attention to her.

"What ragged band of misfits have you brought me this time?" he asked as she dragged Strider to a halt next to his horse. There was a gleam of humor in his eyes as she took his outstretched hand by the wrist and shook it firmly before she turned to look at the group.

"Traders and refugees for the most part," she answered. "The traders bring food and tools, and the refugees appear to be hard workers prepared to begin life anew in these parts."

"Are you sure? I can't put it past you to bring assassins and spies into our midst."

"That only happened once and it was an…understandable misunderstanding."

"Understandable? The shits almost killed you and took control of the fort before Grimm even fucking arrived!"

"It all worked out in the end, didn't it?"

Karvahal grinned and shook the hands of the twins before he studied the caravan master. He had no horse of his own but made do with a mule to keep up with the other three.

"I am the master of this caravan," he declared after he'd cleared his throat a few times. "I can vouch for the good intentions of the people I have been leading. None of them are assassins or spies."

"I appreciate your word, friend," Karvahal answered. "But it is unnecessary. The Barbarian Princess vouching for the safety of your people is enough for me. Welcome to Draug's Hill."

With how full the settlement had become, Karvahal would have been well within his rights to turn the people away. He could have sent them to Torsburch where they might have found more space to settle in, although the locals would be a little more hostile.

Still, she doubted that the barbarian chieftain would have

simply taken their word on the new arrivals, and it wasn't long before she could see why. More than a few armed men and women were present, mostly human although there were dwarves and even some who appeared to have elvish blood in them. It was interesting to see the different types who enlisted under the Ebon Pack banner.

They were all armed, but a handful of them was set up with desks and sheaves of paper and looked and acted like the guards she often encountered when entering a walled city. She could generally simply ride past them as a paladin. Of course, things had not been so simple during her time as a barbarian princess but she hadn't been one to complain.

It wasn't like she had entered many walled cities to begin with.

These mercenaries quickly gathered the refugees who wanted to join their little community. The traders did not need to remain for too long and merely provided a statement on what they were selling and to whom. A small market square had been established in the center of the little town where those who did not have immediate sales for their produce could ply their wares to the locals. Cassandra doubted that they would find many who could pay coin for what they offered, but many could barter for their wares.

A few traded directly with the dwarves and even the Ebon Pack, bringing in food, drink, and anything else they might require. None would stay for long, unlike the refugees.

There was more to determine from the folk who would remain for a longer period. She could understand that, especially since Karvahal was right. She had brought in two separate groups of assassins and spies when they first settled there and while all had turned out well, people had died because of her mistake. It was an unsettling feeling to know that she could no longer trust her instincts, but maybe she didn't have to.

Questions followed questions and filled the sheaves of paper.

Langven had chosen the people who had done this before, likely those who had acted as guards in other cities. It was probably a way to keep themselves ready for any kind of attack by subjecting any who might have deceit in their hearts to a polite but relentless interrogation.

It was a time-consuming but effective method. Those with a determined intention to cause the town harm would not be stopped, but it would certainly put them under considerable pressure. If they showed themselves to be anything other than what they said they were, it would be grounds to remove them from the town. For any who were on their own, that was tantamount to a death sentence.

Still, it looked like the newcomers were being greeted with open arms by those already living in and around Draug's Hill. As the process continued laboriously, the children already living there began to approach and immediately formed friendships with those who were with the new arrivals.

A couple of the newcomers began to tell the story of the battle they had seen. They vastly exaggerated the tale, especially when they discovered that the children already living in the town also had stories of the Barbarian Princess' exploits.

Cassandra wasn't sure if she liked the fame but it was interesting to hear a rendition of how she brought a whole mountain down on the giant wolves and goblins that were attacking from the voice of a child.

Once the refugees were cleared to enter, they were offered food, water, and fresh clothes while an area was assigned for them to live in. Houses were already being built by the dwarves in anticipation of more folk coming to live there, and no one could plan a city like they could. Draug's Hill showed all the signs of being a strong location for folk to settle in after months and maybe even years of being driven from one place or another, caused mostly by Grimm's expansion through the region to the north.

She couldn't help a small smile when she saw Langven ride from the keep alongside Karvahal. The two had worked together consistently to ensure that the region was safe for new arrivals. They had encouraged the arrival of skilled craftsmen and farmers, not only to help build but to establish trade outside the settlement that did not rely on the violence of those who raided in the region.

He smiled in welcome when he saw her and the twins seated at the fountain in the center of the market square and he rode up to them.

"It's nice of you to join us," he called, dismounted smoothly, and handed the reins of his horse to one of his men who stood nearby. "Have you brought in a fresh group of assassins and spies for us to sift through?"

"Karvahal already made that joke," Tandir muttered from around a mouthful of chicken soup with bread. "Have you two been comparing notes?"

"It is the kind of joke that will never grow old," Karvahal answered with a grin.

"Well, I'm sure you felt a little bored with all the peace and prosperity you've inspired in the region," Cassandra answered as Langven sat next to them. "If I did bring in someone who could stir the pot, I'll expect you to thank me for making your life a little more interesting."

"You always make my life interesting whether you intend it or not," Langven answered, took half of Tandir's loaf of bread, and popped a piece into his mouth. "You and the twin bastards. It's why I'm always happy to see you arrive as well as relieved when I see you leave."

"Watch us leave a lot, do ya?" Bandir countered.

"Not you."

"I think he likes the look of my ass over yours, brother." Tandir chuckled.

"Aren't you twins?" Karvahal asked.

"Yes, but I spend less time in the saddle than he does. It means there is more tone and form to mine, while his is flattened."

"I believe I have you both beat in that regard," Cassandra commented and winked at Langven.

The twins looked at her and nodded slowly.

"She makes a good point."

"Aye."

The mercenary captain looked away, but she could have sworn she caught a hint of a flush on his cheeks. It had disappeared when he turned to look at them, however.

"Have no fear. I appreciate all three of your asses equally." Langven paused to take another bite from the bread as the last of the refugees were finally guided to where they could start setting their homes up while the sun was setting.

Perhaps a little more time the next day would be needed to properly establish themselves for their new lives, but Cassandra could see how they would have a strong chance at a real future in the region.

"You had a little trouble on the way in, from what I heard," Langven muttered as the four of them watched the sun setting in the west. "Was it the same creatures that gave the other folk trouble while they traveled here?"

She nodded. "They might have fought under Grimm's banner once upon a time but they fight for themselves now. Well, those that survived."

"And here I thought you weren't the type to leave any alive in these battles."

"I didn't intend to, but after I dropped the mountain on the fuckers, it wasn't like I could head on in after them."

"So it's true? You did bring the mountain down on them?"

"Well...I made a few precariously placed rocks fall and they caused an avalanche that covered the entrance to the tunnels they were using."

"I see." Langven leaned a little closer and pushed some of his brown hair from where it had fallen over his eyes. "Answer me this honestly. Were...they shapeshifters?"

"What?" Cassandra coughed on her sip of water. "No, of course not. They were goblins riding worgs."

"Damn. I had a bet with a few of my men that they were men who knew how to change themselves into wolves when the fighting started."

"There were no attacks at the full moon," Tandir reminded him. "Shapeshifters can change whenever they like but are more aggressive when the moon is full."

"Ah. Yes, I should have thought of that. Goblins, though? Riding worgs? I've never seen the like."

"Nor I, but it makes sense, especially if they were fighting for Grimm." She shrugged when he looked sharply at her. "He was the type who would have found a way to make them a little more useful when outside their tunnels."

Langven frowned. "Why would Grimm want goblins if he had a standing army already waiting?"

"I've thought about that," she responded. "Both my logic and my intuition suggest that he planned to fight a war on two fronts to take the dwarven mountain cities while he staged his invasion at the same time."

"That does make sense. And it would have been an ingenious way for him to supply his forces if they stayed close to the mountains."

"Right. It in turn means he would have organized the goblin tribes in numbers enough to take the dwarf cities. From what I heard, they have the numbers but they hate each other almost as much as they do the folk they share the mountains with. Only someone with a great deal of will and who can inspire fear in the creatures would be able to organize them into any semblance of a fighting force."

The mercenary captain scowled as he considered this. "And

now that he's dead, they parted ways and likely slaughtered their gathered numbers to a point where they pose little threat."

Cassandra raised her water skin. "We can only hope."

"In the meantime, my pack has encountered fewer raiders and marauders over the past few weeks."

She smiled. "You almost sound disappointed."

Langven chuckled softly. "Not quite disappointed. But a real fight is a good way to keep my people engaged. If things are settling more, we'll have to find another way to keep them paid. For the moment, though, coin is pouring in from guilds. It may be a little less from this region, but there are many issues in the surrounding areas that call for our skills and experience. We've seen more work opportunities as escorts for the caravans that come this way that might provide smaller chunks of coin but are more reliable."

"Trade brings the best coin," she agreed. "And the safest too, as it turns out."

"I'll have to take your word for it. It's the first time caravanners and traders have trusted the Ebon Pack to escort their people. We've been associated with brigands and raiders in the past."

"You were brigands and raiders in the past," Cassandra reminded him.

"Well, yes...but that is beside the point. These days, we are known as proper mercenaries, trustworthy and the like. With everything settling, I would say that having a good strong stream of revenue flowing in is a rather good thing."

"Settling? Since when does a mercenary like you want anything to settle?"

Langven drew a deep breath, finished his bread, and brushed the crumbs from his hands. "It was an odd thought for me as well. But when I stand on the battlements and see our fields being tended and homes being built, my only thoughts of swords and blood turn to how I might use my skills and knowledge to keep this place safe."

"Our fields?" Cassandra narrowed her eyes. "Have a care, Langven, or folk might think you sound like some kind of feudal lord."

He cleared his throat and looked around for anyone to rescue him from the conversation. None presented themselves and he turned back to her. "Well...I suppose... I didn't mean that—"

"It's not a terrible thing, mind you. Folk like you and I might thrive on the madness that is war and battle and skirmishing across the known world, but we are not in the majority. Most folk, even most soldiers, want the world to be at peace. They want nothing more to worry about than the troubles brought on by the weather and the world at large without the concern that their fellow folk of whatever race might wage war on them."

"Not all of them."

"Well, no, obviously not. A few civilizations would be lost without something to fight and something or someone to antagonize them. Barbarians especially. But again, we are in the minority. If you consider the greater good, peace must always be the goal. Settling down must be what you are fighting for. People need stability and protection if they are to build a new life, and I think you could be just the man for it."

"Interesting." Langven leaned back and focused on the setting sun again. It filled the sky with bright reds and vibrant oranges as the golden disk began to slide behind the mountain ranges. "Would you not be interested in such a future? Being a barbarian princess and all, you might be considered a better candidate for ruling these folk as their feudal lord. Or...lady, as it were."

Cassandra shook her head slowly and scowled. "I do not believe that to be where my life is heading, at least not for the moment. There is too much contention in my life, too much time spent running around, and too much requiring my attention. I'll admit that I do enjoy it."

"Aye. I cannot say I miss the worst of it, though. Scrounging food on the road, the heat, the cold, the aches and pains that come from being on the saddle all day—or worse, on my feet. Hours and hours on the march."

"Of course. And I'll complain about each and every ache and pain in my bones from now until the gods reclaim the heavens, but for the moment, I cannot help but feel as though life would truly be miserable if I were restricted to one place."

Langven paused to beckon to one of his people. It looked like a small feast was being prepared to celebrate the new arrivals and the young woman stopped in her tracks and allowed him to take a skin of wine she was carrying before he waved her on her way.

He pulled the cork from it and sniffed the contents before he swallowed a deep gulp, winced as it went down, and passed it to Cassandra.

"That bad, eh?"

"Cheap wine is better than no wine. For the moment, at least. Come the morning, a splitting headache might prove my words wrong."

She shrugged, took the skin from his hand, and swung it up to sample it. It was a little too sweet with a sour aftertaste that was representative of most cheap wine but for the moment, it was better than none at all.

"Why would remaining in one place be so miserable for you?"

"I'm not sure." She handed the wine to him. "If the truth be told, when I was a paladin and fought the various denizens the gods wanted me to, followed all their rules, and bowed my head in humility to stuffy old men who forgot how to trim their beards, it always felt like a stifling way to live. I never thought there would be anything else for me in the world, and now that I've found the world opening up to me...well, I would not want to find myself restrained until I've discovered why I was allowed such freedom."

"I understand that, I think." Langven sipped the wine, corked it again, and let the skin slide into the cool water of the fountain.

She could agree with him on that matter at least. Cheap wine was somehow better when it was cold, and the water coming up from the streams underground was like ice. "I remember the days when I was released from my...previous duties."

"And we've never discussed what those duties were."

"It will take more than a little wine to crack into what I did before my days with the Pack. Still, when I was released, I scoured the world for any coin I could find and spent it as quickly as possible on as many vices as I could afford and repeated continually. Freedom was mine for the first time in my life, and I wasn't sure what to do with it. So what did I do? I merely did it all. Eventually, I would find what I wanted to do. That was what I told myself, at least."

"And you joined a loyal group of men that now helps to establish you as a lord over this fucking land."

The captain chuckled and shook his head.

"What's funny?"

"I'm only...laughing at the notion of me as a lord. With... proper etiquette and following the rules of lordship where I need to. Buying purple silk from the fabric traders to make myself proper attire for when I'm summoned to rub elbows with the other lords and ladies."

He was right. It was an interesting idea and even merited a laugh or two.

"Your Ebon Pack playing the part of your knights and men-at-arms." Cassandra lifted the wine from the water, checked the temperature, and slid it in again. "As hilarious though it may be, you might become more used to the idea—you and Karvahal. He's already the chieftain and while young, he is more than capable as a leader. Between the two of you and your skills, you would transform this whole area into a safe and prosperous place for people to live in."

"You sound like you've considered it seriously."

"And you haven't? I can only assume that what you did in the past had much do with proper lords and ladies. You might have even been a knight yourself before you broke free of it all. You have a strong idea of how such situations are settled, and I know the people of Torsburch and Draug's Hill already see you as the person to turn to when they find themselves in trouble."

"What do you think? That I should charge them taxes for the privilege?"

"It's something to consider. At least when they're all settled and growing fat off the land. Coin will pour in when your men escort caravans and traders, but there might be something more to be found. Especially if the local businessfolk have a mind to keep you interested in maintaining a strong military presence in the region."

"I was joking." Langven growled in protest. "Why aren't you?"

"Because reality is a cold-hearted bitch who will rear her ugly head for us in this place before too long." She decided she wouldn't wait for the wine to cool any longer and lifted it to her lips. "You might want to find yourself a handful of cold-blooded bitches ready to fight against her at your side."

"Why would I want that? I have you and your twins to help me."

Cassandra tilted her head and looked at where the barbarians had begun to show some of the children a few dance steps she assumed were traditional among DrakeHunters. The slow, sweeping steps made them look like they were on the prowl and hunting for something.

"They are bitches and yet not quite cold-blooded."

"I suppose we agree on that, at least."

# CHAPTER FOUR

It hadn't been the long night she had anticipated. She had nothing against wanting to join the festivities, but she'd been too tired to participate with too much enthusiasm.

Langven had been right, though. The sweet, cheap wine had a bad way of making the head throb. Thankfully, she had only shared that one skin with him and he'd ended up drinking most of it. Still, it had been enough for her to feel like a cat had shat in her mouth, and she was left with nothing but the throbbing reminder that she hadn't enjoyed the night the way she probably should have. They were all in a situation where they could be dead before they had another chance to celebrate, and she liked to think that she would have been able to find reasons to enjoy the night.

She pushed from the bed she'd found. Karvahal always said there would be a bed and a roof for her and the twins whenever they needed it, but given how many people were coming in regularly, she could understand that the situation might mean she had to share that bed or roof with those who had a greater need for it. In the end, she didn't mind sleeping under the stars as long as it wasn't raining.

Fortunately, it didn't rain in the region during the winter. They saw heavy storms in the summer, but they were still a few months removed from that. It certainly made traveling easier.

Although still early in the day, movement around the fort told her that she wasn't the only one awake. The sun hadn't yet peeked over the horizon but there was enough light for work to begin. She ascended the walls and looked over the hamlet people already were starting to call home.

Inside the walls, buildings were quickly being repurposed, with enough ruined structures to provide stonework to make houses and even larger halls for where there might be a guild or a dwelling for the chieftain to live if he felt inclined to change his somewhat spartan living situation. But the ruins were still there, a reminder of what this had been for so damn long that it practically radiated from the walls themselves—a tomb.

No patrols were active on the walls as yet, but small fires glowed in the towers where guards were on constant watch all around the hill. They made sure that any troop of raiders or army approaching would be seen well in advance of reaching the town below.

"You're up early."

She turned as Karvahal climbed to the battlements as well. He looked like he had engaged in a little too much wine but wouldn't let that interfere with his work as chieftain.

"Speak for yourself," Cassandra answered and gestured for him to join her. "You look like you would be thankful for a few more hours of sleep. And enough water to drown a shark."

"Well, needs must when folk expect you to be up with the sun to attend to their problems. I already have a handful of my people complaining about the newcomers stealing from them although thankfully, it appears as though all the items that disappeared were found again in the possession of the complainer. Still, I assured them that the guards would watch over the town while they slept. I suppose it'll happen more often as more people join us. And we might even find ourselves with a few real thieves in our midst before too long."

That seemed reasonable enough, although she had expected him to make another snide comment about her bringing criminals to join their little abode. Maybe he was a little too tired or affected by drink to think of it in time. She knew it would come sooner rather than later.

"How do you feel about being back here?" he asked, sat on a stool, and looked down between the crenellations.

"I think the men you have positioned on the towers might need to turn their fires out if they plan to notice anyone approaching in the dark of night."

Karvahal turned in his seat, looked at the tower, and scowled deeply. "I'll have a word with them about that. But I think you know exactly what I was talking about."

"Do I?"

"You were as much a part of bringing Draug's Hill to life as I was. Maybe more, although I'll never admit it. A chieftain who has been with the people since before you came along certainly does need to maintain certain…illusions."

"You weren't chieftain before I came along."

"Which means the illusion must be maintained that much more. These people expect me to make the correct decision every time, and I need to speak with the kind of authority they will come to respect for that role. It comes as a street going both ways."

She laughed and nodded. "All right, then. I suppose I'll have to maintain this illusion of yours. I cannot have you thinking of me as a threat and wake up with a dagger at my throat in the middle of the night."

"I would never do that. You know me well enough. Besides, the folk here love you as well and they would riot if you were killed."

"The promises of kings, emperors, and chieftains, Karvahal."

It was his turn to laugh. "I don't think I am that conniving a chieftain. And I need you, threat or no. You had a hand in building all you look at now, and we might need that hand of yours before too long."

Cassandra shook her head slowly, gathered her thick blonde hair carefully, and twisted it into a bun on the back of her head. "Unless there is some great calamity or enemy rising up that we know nothing about, I doubt that you or the people here will have much need for me in the future."

"What are you talking about?"

"I don't like the thought either but in the end, this settlement has grown beyond what I can do to help it. The best I can do is continue to make life hell for any monsters or raiders that might find their way here, but from what I hear tell, between your men and Langven's Pack, you already have that well in hand. I imagine this might be what a parent might think when seeing their child grown and ready to face the world without them."

"Are you talking about me or Draug's Hill?"

"Both." She grinned at him and leaned on the cool stone battlements.

Karvahal nodded slowly and tilted his head thoughtfully. "If you do not see yourself here, where would you go? If you don't mind my prying?"

"After my time dealing with the issues nearer the capital, I am drawn more and more back west—and maybe even to the worship of Theros, although I don't know if I can go back to being a proper paladin."

"I thought you were his barbarian. Although I'm not sure... what that means, precisely."

"No one does. And that is the fun of it. Everyone knows what to expect from a paladin, even if they happen to follow that royal ass Janus. They will always have a lawful and peaceful mind and approach death and danger only as a last resort to save their lives or those of the innocent. People know that well enough, and the smarter ones know how to take advantage. No one quite knows what to expect from a barbarian of Theros, and I do enjoy being able to keep folk on their toes."

"I can see the appeal to that. Added to the fact that most do not know what to do when any other kind of barbarian encounters them. Especially one dressed in your particular battle attire."

"Oh, that is certainly one of the appeals. I couldn't ever run around in that outfit if I was a paladin."

Both of them laughed this time and the sound echoed across the walls and down to the hamlet below where people were already starting their work for the day. The sun inched slowly higher and it would not be long before the heat beat down on the battlements. Even if she was somewhat better off without too much drinking the night before, she had no intention to bake out in the sun if she didn't need to. That was something she did not enjoy from her time on the road.

"If you're this removed from being a paladin, why would you want to return to where you could be drawn back into the situation you made such an effort to escape from?"

He was a sharp one. Cassandra had unwittingly fallen into the same trap that most of the people who encountered barbarians and even orcs did. Just because they didn't quite have the same grasp of the common tongue as others, people doubted the intelligence of the person they were dealing with. Skharr had pushed that further and deliberately sounded like an oaf to make sure people's assumptions of him were confirmed.

She had a feeling that most barbarians had keener insight into what made folk do the things they did, and it was interesting to be consistently surprised despite the fact that she, of all people, should have known better. Maybe her prejudices needed a little more effort to push them aside.

"True, I might leave some of the freedoms I've come to enjoy behind," she muttered and sat beside the young chieftain. "Still, time has worn down my anger at Theros, cooled it, and allowed me to think clearly about how I might benefit from wearing a paladin's garb again. Besides, leaving it all did little to help correct the reasons why I left in the first place—the corruption and the deviance from the elders. I would be in the best position to do something if I worked from the inside in a position of authority."

"If you ran before, you knew of the problems and made a point by turning away from them."

She looked to where most of the sun was already visible, shook her head after a moment, and turned away from it. "I don't know. Maybe I didn't believe I was capable of making that kind of change in a system that has been in place for centuries. At the time, I was still recovering from a dragon attack that almost killed me, and I had all kinds of conflicts in my head, very few of them good. Now…well, look around you. Draug's Hill, once a ruin with rumors of ghosts and monsters, now looks like a burgeoning town watched over by stout fighters in a mighty fortress. Maybe now there is a chance that I will succeed where I once saw no reason to try at all."

Karvahal leaned forward a little. "Where exactly do you plan to go?"

"Verenvan, most likely. I don't think I can stand another trip to the capital city, and those are the two options for someone like me, I think. The best options, anyway."

"What is that city like?"

She shrugged. "It's massive. A little too big and starting to spill out. It's at the delta of a river and at a major crossroads for trade, as well as being one of the few ports in the region that is open all year round."

"What would close a port?"

"Ice. Many of those in the region are closed when winter reaches its peak, but Verenvan remains open for trade despite it all. That makes it one of the largest trading hubs in the empire. Towering walls were built all around the city, and half of it is where the richer citizens live. Less than a quarter of the whole population live in lavish mansions and rich estates while the rest of the population is crammed into the other half and spill out into the marshlands closer to the river."

"I would like to see a city like that one day."

"Hells, if another barbarian made an appearance there, you might have to fight to get out from under all those who want to drag you into their beds for a night of passion."

"Truly?"

"At least from what I hear. Barbarians are a rare delicacy in the region."

"You talk as though I would be eaten alive."

"In some ways, maybe."

He chuckled softly. "Now I want to visit a town like that even more."

"You might discover that they eat you alive in more ways than one. Skharr told me that he was very nearly killed a few times while there. Rich folk make it a very dangerous place to live."

"That...does temper my excitement somewhat," he admitted. "When do you plan to leave us, then?"

Cassandra sighed. "I have not decided yet. I would like to make sure that what we built here will sustain itself. More than anything, it means I need to address the concern that rose from the source of the threat of Grimm. Theros warned me of a dark god named Karthelon who inspired the bastard to do what he did, and we've heard of a great force of fear in the north that has driven the raiders and marauding beasts toward us. There is nothing tangible yet, however, and nothing that would indicate that Karthelon plans to move against me directly. Still, I fear that this is more cause for concern than relief. I do not believe that a dark god like that would forget or forgive me for my offenses against him."

She paused and focused on Langven who approached and trudged slowly up the steps to the battlements. If Karvahal looked like he needed a few more hours of rest, the mercenary captain looked like he needed at least a week. He was a mighty warrior but a barbarian he was not, although she assumed he had been drawn into a drinking game with the twins and lost far more than only his coin in the process.

"Whatever in the seven hells is causing this infernal clanging in my head?" he whispered, "I would see it dead and eight generations of its family joining it in the grave."

"If you have that much hatred for the wine grapes, you might reconsider consuming them in the future," Cassandra commented and beckoned for him to join them.

"Consuming them is my way to kill them as quickly as possible." Langven sat heavily, leaned against the crenellations, and rested his head against the cold, hard stone. "It's also the most efficient. Slashing them with a sword will not do much more than spread their vile seed. By consuming them, I take their power into myself and kill as many of them as possible."

"You could simply eat the grapes," Karvahal reminded him. "There would be less chance that they would leave you with the pounding head that drives you to kill them in the first place."

"What would be the honor in that? I must beat them at their most powerful or there would be no point in consuming them."

"Aside from suddenly gaining the ability to sing 'The Seven Little Wenches and the Orc Companion' while dancing to all the moves dictated by the great bard Volantes," Cassandra pointed out.

"You….saw that, did you?"

"No, but I've seen you drunk before and I happen to know that it is the first song that comes into your head and the only song you know how to dance to."

Langven nodded slowly. "It is a damn good song."

"Aye. A true masterpiece, especially the part where the bard starts to compare the size, heft, and shape of the seven little wenches' tits."

He laughed at that, although he immediately regretted it, placed his head in his hands, and groaned softly. "I was woken by my affliction. What the hell are you two doing up here this early?"

"Talking, mostly," Karvahal answered.

"About how your watchers in the towers won't see anything with a blazing fire not five feet away from them?"

"That too." The chieftain cleared his throat. "It looks like our princess here might be planning to return to Verenvan. She might even return to the role of paladin for her god."

"Well, that would be a fucking crime. Unless they suddenly allow paladins to run about in the kind of attire you've made your own as the Barbarian Princess."

All three laughed, although Langven groaned in pain again.

"I've not made any decisions as yet," Cassandra clarified. "But the concept is starting to hold more appeal to me."

"Is this about what Theros told you? About the dark god who might pose a few problems for the people in this region?"

"I've looked into the matter." She suddenly tired of talking. There was no koffe for her to use to wash the pain of the morning away, but cold water from the underground streams would certainly help. "It's rumored that there is a temple in the north."

"We all love to hear rumors," Karvahal muttered. "Did you hear about that one where a gorgon lived under Draug's Hill?"

"Aye," Langven answered. "I also heard the tale of how some barbarian princess or another killed that fucking gorgon. It must be fictional. Barbarians have no concept or semblance of royalty among their tribes."

"True enough." Cassandra shook her head. "The rumor is that the temple is situated in a place where Karthelon's fury shattered the earth to its core. It was the site of a great battle of good against evil, but I have a feeling the truthfulness stops somewhere before the point where angels descended from the heavens to fight on behalf of the mortals present."

"It sounds like a pleasant location." Langven sighed, closed his eyes, and rubbed his temples. "I assume there are magical waterfalls with talking fish that grant wishes."

"Fishes don't like waterfalls," she corrected.

"How would you know?"

"I…don't. I merely assumed."

"Well, the talking fish that grant wishes do like waterfalls."

"Anyway," she said hastily before he could go on about what wishes he would want granted by the fictional talking fish, "they also say they offer sacrifices of mortals and beasts to Karthelon there, and that if the pit didn't reach so deep into the ground, they would have created mountains of corpses from those killed in the dark god's name."

"All I hear are reasons to avoid it like your life depends on it," Karvahal commented.

"I happen to agree with our good chieftain here." Langven scratched his chin, still unshaven from the night before. "Avoiding it certainly feels like the best way to avoid being turned into one of those sacrifices."

"There are more rumors. Whispers that offerings are made on the first altar using stones that Karthelon himself stood upon naked, soaked in the blood of the dead before his ascension to godhood."

"You and I need to have a long, detailed discussion regarding the people you hear these stories from and why they tell them," Langven all but growled and narrowed his eyes. "Because I want to find out if there are any more stories on how the other gods ascended and to find out if there is a way for me to join them in immortality. Most importantly, I want to make sure that you are not seriously considering paying it a visit."

"I think I need to go there."

"Why?"

"To ensure that the ends left untied in this area do not whip around and slap you all across the face," Cassandra answered smoothly. "Not literally, of course, but…you know what I mean."

Langven and Karvahal both looked more somber now and exchanged a glance before the former nodded slowly.

"I think I do."

# CHAPTER FIVE

She knew they wouldn't agree with what she suggested, but it was certainly something for them to consider in the future. While she trusted them to deal with most of the threats they would face in the region, there was no denying that she had the most experience when it came to the deities that haunted their world.

Although Cassandra doubted that she would be much good against a real god. All the knowledge she had was that it was best to keep one's head down and avoid the attention of the gods. As suggestions went, it was rather useless in her current situation, all things considered. She had already secured the attention of Theros and if Grimm had not made idle boasts, she had killed the son of another. It meant that she already had their attention, for better or worse.

If she could have a conversation with Theros about how to prevent a dark god from giving her trouble, she would at least have somewhere to start—maybe a sword, a dagger, or a spell that would be able to protect her or at least ensure that Karthelon's attention was directed at her instead of Draug's Hill. Or

Torsburch, although she cared considerably less for the festering hive of vice and villainy that Langven liked to call home.

Both the captain and the chieftain needed to head off, as the business of running a mercenary company and a growing town made continuous demands on them.

That was one of the reasons why she did not want to be in any position of authority. It was a kind of freedom as well, as people always assumed that paladins would take charge of whatever situation they were in and that they would know what to do.

And they were mostly right on that account, but it was still an exhausting way to live. She didn't feel up to the responsibilities of running much of anything now, and she assumed Langven felt the call even less.

All she needed to get done for the day was wait for the twins to wake up in whatever pile of hay they'd collapsed in before they discussed what needed to be gathered for the trip to Torsburch.

They hadn't dug too deep into the stores they'd purchased for the trip thus far, which meant they would not need to use much of the coin they'd earned for the trip back.

She wondered what the twins would do if she wasn't around. They were rather well-known these days and could probably make a solid amount of coin working in the defense of some lord or another on the border of the empire if they wanted to.

Langven would be more than happy to have fighters of their skill and renown join his pack and add a few extra fangs to their number. Tandir and Bandir would likely not want to be confined by the life of a paladin or even by being associated with one in good standing. It was something she would need to discuss with them before any decisions were made.

While she was in a position of authority over them, they made her work for it.

Cassandra collected some water from the fountain in the town center, took a few sips, and closed her eyes. She enjoyed the cool refreshment and gritted her teeth against the ache in the back of her head that it caused before she took another sip.

It wasn't long before the cup was drained and she scooped up another. Familiar curses from the twins told her they were already awake. Neither looked quite as bad as Langven did. Maybe that was because they were younger, or barbarians simply went through the process of drinking copious amounts without as many of the downsides.

"Where did you go off to?" Tandir asked as he joined her at the fountain and unceremoniously dunked his head into the icy water, He emerged spluttering and shook himself dry while dampening those around him.

"I didn't feel up to the evening's festivities," she admitted as Bandir followed his brother's example and left both of his companions dripping wet. "I found a bed and slept in it."

"An empty bed?"

"I didn't have to kick anyone out of it beforehand if that's what you're asking."

"It's not." Bandir nudged her side with his elbow. "Come on, then, princess. No one leaves an evening feast early unless they have some other entertainment calling for their attention. The kind that is better enjoyed in private."

"Sadly, no," Cassandra admitted. It had been a while since she'd had that kind of entertainment, although she couldn't think of a reason why for the life of her.

"Oh, she thinks we don't know," Bandir whispered.

"Know what?"

"That you absconded with Langven before the night was out."

She narrowed her eyes. "The last I remember, the two of you were exchanging bawdy songs and tales to music and dancing with the good captain hours after I left."

"Oh…that's right."

They exchanged a look and cleared their throats before they sat on the edge of the fountain.

"I hope you slept well, at least," Bandir said, desperate to change the subject. "Pleasant dreams and the like."

"I don't remember any dreams, which means they were likely not terrible. But I still woke with a pain in my head. What about the two of you? I assume you did not find empty beds to fall into for the evening?"

"Not...beds, necessarily," Tandir admitted.

"Say no more. But try to avoid angering the locals. I'd rather not have to convince them to not run the two of you out of town. Or worse, march you down an aisle to the tune of Madia's Maiden's song with a spear at your backs."

"Whose song?" Bandir frowned.

"The...song they usually play during weddings, you idiots."

"Oh. Right."

"I can't imagine what it would be like to have a little one to care for, though." Bandir shook his head. "I might have to build a homestead for the tiny ones and give them plenty of room to play on the furs of my hunting trophies. And I'd likely have to build a small room for Tandir to live out his days as a sullen bachelor."

"Fuck yourself."

"Don't you remember that witch who cursed you to walk the earth with nothing but ash and dust springing from your loins?"

"She cursed both of us."

"Did she?"

"Aye, you were the one who fucked her."

"So I was. Damn madwoman, but she made for a memorable night."

Cassandra shook her head. "Why...why did she curse you two?"

"She thought she could have both of us as her acolytes," Tandir explained. "My brother here lied and agreed to it as long as they consummated the arrangement that very night. They did so without telling me and the next morning, as we were gathering our packs to continue our journey, she comes out of her home and curses us for our disloyalty."

"It sounds like you deserved it." She took another sip from the tin cup before she washed it in the flowing water of the fountain. "Although more than a few men I know of wouldn't mind being cursed with no children for the rest of their days. And women too, now that I think about it."

The twins looked like they were considering it for a moment, but her attention was drawn to the sky. They had looked at a bright, sunny day complete with the unbearable heat that all too often assailed the region, but a gust of cold wind had her immediate attention.

While the sun was still rising, it was obfuscated by a thin layer of clouds that chilled the dry weather a little. Ripples of wind cut across the grasslands and made everything much colder as well.

"It's about time we had something to break the heat," Bandir whispered, closed his eyes, and let the wind blow through his still-wet hair. "I was afraid we would have another scorcher to deal with."

"It's not uncommon given where we are," Cassandra pointed out. "Having clouds and cold is an oddity, though."

She felt like she was being paranoid and imagining curses where there were none, but having her mind on Kathelon that morning immediately led her to believe something more was behind the sudden shift in the weather.

There weren't many gods out there who could call storms down directly on a whim. That required more power than even they were capable of. Most of them, anyway. Influencing weather was another thing altogether.

Hells, she knew of a handful of mortals who were capable of such tricks and could call in wind that would cause it to rain after a few days. A few of them were paid by local farmers across the empire to ensure that rain and dry weather came at the right times so that their crops would be allowed to grow and flourish.

But she must be imagining things. The weather behaving abnormally was more common than finding a being capable of causing clouds and winds to form.

"We can only hope this weather fucking holds," Tandir said and rolled his shoulders. "A nice chill is exactly what I need for the trip to Torsburch."

"About that..." Cassandra spoke quickly. "There is something I need to discuss with the two of you before too long—regarding our future."

"Or lack of one. You never know when one of those fucking goblins will get a little lucky with their fucking arrows."

"Still, assuming we are to survive..."

Her voice trailed off when she heard something in the air and had to tilt her head to make out what it was. It wasn't the screech of a bird, at least none that she'd ever heard.

A horn, she realized suddenly—the horn Karvahal's men in the towers used to raise the alarm when something endangered their little settlement.

"Shit," she snapped. Both twins responded much faster and rushed away to where they'd left their weapons and armor. She moved behind them, thankful that she'd left the work of stabling their horses and checking their supplies to the barbarians, or she would have likely left both in the fortress. Having to rush up the hill and down again when something was attacking sounded like a painful waste of time.

She was already wearing her armor, although she touched the amulet hanging around her neck to make sure. Her spear was the first weapon she collected before she strapped her sword smoothly to her hip and retrieved her bow and quiver. She mounted Strider and heeled him almost immediately to a gallop out of the building they had improvised as stables until something better could be built.

The townsfolk were already hurrying to where they could be protected by the walls of the keep but it was a slow process and forced those troops who could be spared from the defenses to move out to where the scouts indicated the danger was coming from.

She shouldn't have been surprised to see the twins already rushing in the same direction without paying attention to what dangers might have awaited them.

They raced ahead and away from where the Pack would be able to keep them protected. She shook her head grimly and increased her pace. They had been trained better than that, which meant something else drove them to put themselves at the very center of the fight.

"Sons of whores," she snapped, directed Strider to break into a run after them, and pushed the warhorse as fast as he could move across the open grasslands.

He was faster than the horses Bandir and Tandir rode, but they were already beyond the planted fields and out in the wild territories before she caught up with them.

"You fucking idiots!" Cassandra yelled when they finally reined their mounts to let her reach them. "If you want to get killed out here on your own, you should have warned me and I would have left you to do it alone!"

Both looked excited but something else drove them now. They were practically frothing at the mouth.

"Drakes!" Bandir exclaimed and pointed at the sky toward the mountains. "We've got drakes coming in!"

A cold sensation settled in the pit of her stomach as she turned Strider to see if what they said was true.

It was hard to see them at first and it looked like they had used the clouds to avoid being detected early on. Now that the chance to attack the town unawares was no longer an option, they began to dive to where they could see easy targets to attack and probably assumed that the three who were isolated from the rest of the group would be simpler to kill.

They might have been right about that, but Cassandra would make a point of ensuring that they were a tough meal to chew.

"Split up and divide their attention," she snapped and hooked her spear to the saddle. There were at least two drakes, but it was difficult to determine if more were hiding in the clouds.

With a quick upward look to gain a better idea of where the monsters would attack from, she pushed Strider into a canter, moved in the direction of the creatures, and drew them away from Draug's Hill as much as she could.

"Shoot at the wings!" Bandir suggested. "It's the weakest point in their skin and if you get them right, you'll stop them from flying."

She nodded as they finally veered away from where she was riding and drew the attention of one of the drakes, while the other appeared to adjust its dive toward her.

Cassandra drew an arrow from her quiver and retrieved the bow as well before she looked into the sky and tried to avoid being blinded by the sun as she waited for the beast to advance.

The first arrow flew but arced downward well short of its target. The second reached a little closer and forced the drake to twist to avoid being struck.

It was clear that she wouldn't have time for another shot. She tossed her bow aside and hoped she would have the presence of mind to find and collect it later, then armed herself with her spear.

Her first impulse to impale the creature when it swooped to attack her was quickly pushed to the side. Even if she was able to catch it, the speed at which it traveled would likely kill her anyway if she was so close.

With that in mind, she tossed the spear up, caught it smoothly in a backhand, and looked at the drake again. She could barely see its eyes as it swept around to try to target her from the side, almost low enough that its claws were at Strider's head height to give her the one opportunity she would have.

The spear launched from her hand. The twins' instruction had certainly helped, and she watched it fly true and drive hard into the creature's wing, high up and close the shoulder.

It screeched, twisted away again, and immediately went out of sight, but she felt the impact behind her as it landed heavily.

Without thinking, she vaulted off the saddle, drew her sword, and raced to where the creature had fallen. It wasn't difficult to find since it had kicked up a cloud of dust with its impact and subsequent struggles.

The beast continued to move within the flurry of debris and she didn't want to give it the opportunity to go to ground or maybe pull the spear out and take to the air again.

It wasn't quite a dragon, she decided. There were many who said dragons were creatures with six limbs, usually four for walking on the ground and a pair of wings that allowed it to fly. That was certainly true of the older dragons, but drakes were practically the same to her mind. The only difference was that they were smaller.

And they possessed four limbs, as these did. Some drakes only had four legs and were bound to the earth, but these had wings instead. It slowed them when they weren't in flight, but she could see the one she'd grounded used its wings like a second pair of legs and walked awkwardly while it screeched and howled in pain.

When it saw her approach, the noises turned to roars of anger and it tried to rush at her. The limb she'd wounded slowed it, but it was still remarkably fast. Cassandra dove to the right as a head about the size of her torso jerked through the empty space where she'd stood moments before. The long, knife-like teeth snapped around nothing instead of her body.

She scrambled onto her feet immediately and screamed a response as she swung her sword high. The blade pounded hard into the creature's skull and it fell heavily when it was unable to pull back in time.

The rest of the body sprawled and hampered any attempt it made to lash out at her with its tail, and she arced her sword onto its snout this time to force it down again.

It must have been painful but it was far from a deadly wound, and she needed to end it quickly. She bounded smoothly over its head and stretched to where her spear still protruded from the point where the wing met its shoulder.

It had gone in deeper than she thought her throw would have pushed it, which likely meant the weapon had been driven in when it crashed onto the earth. Still, it took almost no effort to draw it out and caused another shriek of pain from the beast. The wing came up and she felt the claws scrape over her back.

They didn't cut through but her amulet warmed against her chest as she was thrown off her feet. She rolled over her shoulder and before she could stand, the creature rushed forward to try to catch her while she was at a disadvantage.

She pushed to one knee, planted the base of the haft instinctively into the ground, and shored it up with her boot while she aimed the head at the drake as it tried to attack her.

It bent, but the blade cut through the thick skin around the creature's throat and the harder it pushed, the deeper the spear penetrated until it came out the other side. The beast finally relaxed and its eyes lost their light as it sagged against the weapon that propped it up.

Something seeped from the wound—not only blood but a thick green liquid that dripped with less viscosity. Droplets formed and they hissed and smoked when they came in contact with the grass and melted the green away.

"Acid spitters, eh?" Cassandra scowled, kicked the creature over, and drew her spear out, careful to wipe the acid from the weapon on the body of the drake. She turned and was relieved when Strider approached her at a trot. The horse likely had no interest in battling the creature alongside her—although he was a brave beast and would have if she needed it—but now that it was dead, she needed his help to get to where the rest of the fight was happening.

She gestured for him to follow her to where she'd dropped her bow before she scanned her surroundings. It looked like the twins had luck as good as hers and had felled their adversary and now hacked it eagerly to pieces. They were nowhere near the head, which meant they were only too aware of the dangers spewing from the front.

"Oy!" Cassandra called, picked her bow up, and secured it to its place on her saddle before she mounted. Neither paid attention until she uttered a piercing whistle that made them look at her.

Rather than try to explain, she pointed her spear at the town, where other drakes began to swoop toward Draug's Hill. They would have to wait until the danger passed before they could divide the teeth and claws.

They seemed to understand, at least, mounted their horses, and turned to ride to the town.

Thankfully, most of the civilians appeared to have already been evacuated to the keep, although a few still trudged up the winding path. Movement from the town's buildings proved to be three or four dozen fighters, mostly from the Ebon Pack, who positioned themselves to put up a decent fight.

As the drakes began their descent, the archers were waiting and looked like they were more prepared for the option than she had been. They launched a volley at the attackers in a small wave.

The drakes tried to swerve to avoid being hit like they had done before, but there were too many arrows and three dropped from the sky. Two landed outside the town but one crashed into one of the houses the dwarves had constructed. There was no reason to be surprised when she saw that the keen stonework withstood the impact with a monster.

Another volley caught two more, although she couldn't see if they were dead or merely wounded. She turned Strider to where one of them had fallen outside the town's limits.

It moved, even though it was peppered with a half-dozen arrows, and it looked like it was anxious to find something to take its rage out on. Cassandra wouldn't give it the opportunity and she swerved Strider out of the way of its snapping jaws to drive her spear through its skull. The weapon cut through like it was nothing and the drake sank into the dirt again as she rode past it to where archers rushed away from those that were diving.

Ten more were still in flight. She had never known flying drakes to hunt in packs that size before and from what she could see, the younger, smaller creatures were downed first and swarmed quickly by the troops on the ground. The larger ones, however, appeared to not feel the bite of the arrows that struck them.

That certainly sounded right. Still, they were acid spitters. They couldn't breathe fire or ice on their prey from the sky and would need to finish the people up close. A few of them dove to snatch a few of the Pack and carry them high before they released them to plummet earthward. She didn't follow the descent but could hear the screams and the thuds that silenced their cries.

Fortunately, most seemed like they were able to avoid the creatures and delivered arrows and javelins to the monsters that continued their attempts to sweep down and catch them. Another drake pounded into one of the buildings before the others decided that their airborne assaults wouldn't earn them enough kills.

"Shoot for the wings!" Cassandra called and pulled her bow out. "Shoot for the wings and it'll bring the bastards down!"

"Says who?" one of the pack shouted at her from one of the flat rooftops.

"Says the fucking DrakeHunters!" she snapped in return, raised her bow, and let an arrow fly. She scowled as it sank into one of the creature's necks instead of the wings and failed to do anything other than get stuck in the thick scales.

That appeared to focus the attention of the defenders and their arrows were now aimed at the wings. As expected, the appendages were more vulnerable to damage and were already stretched by the wind that held them aloft. A few more of the creatures fell as holes and tears appeared in their wings.

Strider wouldn't be much use in the confines of the town and even worse, would likely be more of a target to the creatures as they tried to come in lower to avoid the arrows that were now aimed with a little more purpose.

Those that had fallen were still alive—some of them, at least—and they screeched and spat their acid, which appeared to have a reaction with the slabs of stone that were used to build their little town, making it easy to see where the creatures were from the clouds of smoke that rose in the area.

Cassandra guided her horse to the stables and made sure he was not an easy target to the drakes still in the air, although she took a moment to gather the weapons that were on the saddle before she sent him in with a slap to the rump. She turned to where Langven rode with another troop of soldiers who ducked low in their saddles to avoid being attacked.

"What in the hell were you doing out there?" he shouted and slid from the saddle. It looked as though they had the same idea she had of wanting to keep the drakes from killing their horses.

That didn't seem like the kind of question she needed to answer while they were being attacked, and she turned her attention skyward for a moment before she looked at the mercenary captain again.

"Your archers should be under cover to force the creatures to land. While they are still in flight, aim for the wings, and prevent those on the ground from attacking."

Langven nodded and turned to spread the instructions to the rest of his men.

"And Langven!" she called before he was out of earshot and waited until he faced her. "They spit acid. Tell your men to stay away from their fucking heads."

"Appreciated," he called and hurried to instruct the first group of his mercenaries.

They needed to be careful dealing with an attack like this, but they couldn't afford to take too much time to kill them or the creatures' attention would be drawn to the keep where most of the civilians were hiding. Sending them to the walls might have proven to be a good idea, although there was no chance that she would risk the lives of the people who trusted Langven and Karvahal with their safety.

The captain shouted orders, and Cassandra beckoned to the twins who had hidden their horses and she directed their attention to three of the larger creatures that had begun to circle one of the larger buildings. She assumed it was meant to be some kind of barn where food could be stored, especially given that it was somehow elevated to stop pests from getting in. She had no idea how since the whole building was made of stone, but the dwarves involved in the building were some of the best. If there were any tricks for how to keep a stone building off the ground, they would know them.

Still, it looked like the drakes circled for a reason and she noticed five of Langven's archers trying to find a way to avoid being picked up and dropped from high enough to turn their bodies to mush.

If there was ever a place to start their attack, it was there. The twins hefted javelins and she raised her bow to unleash an arrow that sliced through one of the creature's wings. It had flown in low and tried to find a good place to land and grab the men trying to avoid it. As the arrow struck, it screeched in pain and dropped onto the roof. It was large enough to make the ground shake with the impact, and the archers flung themselves over the edges of the rooftop, clearly deciding that any injuries they sustained from the drop were preferable to facing one of the drakes in melee combat.

Which meant the onus was on her to kill it while the twins dealt with the other two.

"Fucking hells," she muttered, found the ladder the archers had used to reach the roof, and climbed it as quickly as she could to reach the top. The beast stamped around, uttered soft screeches of pain, and likely called to the others for help.

They were all busy dealing with the Ebon Pack, which left the creature alone with her.

The rooftop was flat, possibly intended as a secondary storage location or maybe a place for the people to gather in the sunlight off the ground while the harvest was brought in. Either way, it had enough space for her to climb onto it without coming within ten feet of the creature that seemed torn between pain and distress and an aggressive desire to join the fight.

It didn't notice her at first, and Cassandra fitted another arrow to her bowstring and let it fly. It was the easiest shot she'd had all day. The drake made very little movement and she was practically in spitting distance. The arrow hammered into the back of the creature's skull but failed to punch through skin or bone and immediately alerted it that a fight had come to it instead.

"You are an ugly bastard," she whispered, dropped her bow, and hefted her spear. She watched the beast as it circled cautiously to look at her. It hissed and gave her a clear view of its teeth as well as what appeared to be acid pooled in the back of its throat. She didn't know how far the creature could spit and she didn't want to find out. Still, if it could be spat the way other drakes threw fire, she would have already sizzled in a puddle.

It didn't appear to understand her insult but was more than willing to attack. Despite being wounded, it lunged forward and lashed out with its teeth first to force her away from the ladder. She sprinted along the edge of the roof, watched her step as best she could to make sure she didn't fall, but remained largely focused on the tail that swept around to take her off her feet.

Her timing, thankfully, was perfect, probably because she somehow counted the beats in her head before she dove over the appendage and rolled over her shoulder and smoothly to her feet. With a gasp, she realized that the beast was waiting for her. That was likely a common tactic for it when it faced something on even footing—lunge forward and make it jump out of the way and into the path of its tail, which would stun its prey and allow it an easy attack.

She barely avoided the fountain of acid spat at her. It didn't go very far, only three feet or so from the creature's mouth, but it had been intended to drench her from head to toe. It was likely more dangerous than the teeth, and she grimaced as a plume of acrid-smelling smoke rose from the stonework it had made contact with.

But the most important fact, she decided, was that the drake's mouth and throat were empty when it turned to face her again.

"It seems like you have only one load to give a lady." She laughed and tossed her spear from one hand to the other. "I wish I could say you were alone in your troubles."

Maybe it simply needed some time to gather more of the acid from its body but for the moment, she still had the claws and teeth to focus her attention on. One of the wings swung violently to knock her from the top of the building. When she ducked, the beast's claws dragged across her back. They were stopped by her amulet, but not by much.

These beasts were full of unpleasant surprises and the other wing swept forward in an attempt to prevent her from advancing while it was relatively vulnerable. She pushed toward it, thrust her spear into where the wing was thickest, and sliced through skin, muscle, and bone almost without effort.

Another screech ended in almost a howl. She could practically hear the creature's anger that she was both still alive and had the temerity to fight it. Maybe drakes like this preferred to pick their prey up from dangerous mountain trails, drop them from impossible heights to break any armor that they might have, natural or not, and drag the kills to their nests.

Which begged the question of what they were doing there.

It was one she would have to reserve for later. She shoved hard on the spear until it emerged on the other side before she dragged it out, took another step forward, and waited for the jaws to snap at her. It was predictable so she was ready to drive the spearhead through its skull from the mouth. The blade punched through easily, came out the other side, and severed its spine and its connection to the world of the living.

"I hope you had a wonderful afterlife planned," Cassandra muttered caustically, yanked her spear out, and kicked the drake for good measure.

It looked like the others were being taken down one by one. The twins shouted and began to sing a song she assumed was a part of their tribe's tradition of hunting drakes. She smiled in response but sobered quickly when she realized that they had been lucky. Someone had seen the beasts before the attack and gathered the folks who couldn't fend for themselves, and it had still almost been not good enough. She didn't like the idea that something would be able to attack them so unexpectedly and efficiently like that in the future.

Something cold touched her almost like a hand on her shoulder and she snapped around, half-expecting there to be more of the monsters for her to kill. The drake lay prone and very dead, but the eyes were open and stared at her.

It was an uncomfortable feeling but not uncommon on the battlefield. Still, there was no reason to endure it if she didn't have to. She approached and stretched her hand to close its eyes over the cold stare.

With a reflexive gasp, she snapped her hand away like it had been burned when something moved in the creature's massive golden eye. The slight flicker might have been her imagination but she was sure it was there. She tightened her hold on her spear, narrowed her eyes, and stepped forward when she saw the movement again.

Two eyes glowered at her from within the beast's one. They were set in a dark face, with a smile that curled unnaturally and displayed rows of needle-like fangs that gleamed where the sun struck the drake's dead gaze.

"This is only the beginning."

The voice felt like it emanated from the back of her head and sent chills down her spine.

She grimaced and drove the spear through the eye to make sure that whatever the monster on the other side was, it would have to find another way to communicate.

"I'll see you," she whispered in response and dragged her spear out. "Soon."

# CHAPTER SIX

Considerable work had gone into making Draug's Hill livable again, but that was only made possible by the skill of the original builders. It had been left to run to ruin for decades and possibly even centuries, but most of the foundations were still intact, which set the groundwork for it all to be repaired over a few years instead of decades.

She knew the dwarves would make a solid mint from their labors over that time as well, and it was a good thing Karvahal and Langven had both found large stores of coin used by Grimm and his forces, likely to keep his men in line while they were on the road. Or perhaps the despot merely enjoyed traveling with a fortune of coin on his person, but the reasons were irrelevant. All that mattered was that they had the skill, means, and resources necessary to turn Draug's Hill from a ruin into somewhere folk could live comfortably.

They had already started on the hall inside the fortress. It looked like the area where Karvahal had made his home while other alternatives were under consideration, but they could always make him a home somewhere inside the building. There was certainly enough space.

His living quarters had been sectioned off with wood and stonework, but it left the main hall of the building intact with a massive central fireplace built around a series of stone chairs. A fair amount of work had gone into making a table that surrounded most of the fireplace. This gave the people seated on the stone chairs access but still allowed others to move between the fireplace and the table. All in all, it was a proper feasting hall that had been designed long before anyone knew what they might have needed it for.

Rather than seat the small war council that had been assembled around the feasting table, another smaller round table had been brought in with normal chairs instead of the chunky throne-like official ones.

The drakes had been dealt with, but Cassandra now knew for a fact that they were merely the opening salvo of a war someone intended to bring to their doorstep. The leadership had wisely decided that they needed to discuss what their options were.

She had been called in, along with the DrakeHunter twins. Sifeas, who had been busy drawing the carved stones from underground and had not heard the alarms, was summoned by Langven and Karvahal, as well as a few of the locals who had been elected by the people living in Draug's Hill as their representatives on matters of great import. There hadn't been much need to call them in until now, but she had a feeling that it would not be the first time she met with the man and two women.

If there was ever a time for her to learn their names, it was now. She knew she needed to get better at remembering names or finding out those she didn't know. Folk expected that from people in positions of authority, but she still had difficulty telling which of the twins was which. There must be a trick that helped with such things but for the moment, she needed to apply her mind to it.

Still, if she stared at her two companions, the differences between them became a little clearer. But on the days when she felt particularly confident that she could tell the two apart, she would make a mistake and it would all crumble again. They were likely fucking with her as a way to pass the time, but how the hell could she determine that for herself?

She shook her head and forced her attention to the discussion that had started while she couldn't decide if she should ask the newcomers what their names were.

"I've never seen drakes attack in those numbers before," Tandir said in answer to a question from Karvahal she had missed. "They don't attack in packs, for one thing. They do mate for life but the only time that you would see more than two adults hunting if is they were raising their young and teaching them to hunt."

"How many young do they generally have?" one of the village women asked. She looked like she was out of her depth but still tried to rise to the responsibility that had been laid on her shoulders.

"One egg is the rule. They occasionally have two. I've never seen more than three."

"And yet we had about twenty of the shits spewing acid on the town and my men," Langven pointed out and folded his arms. "There must be something else at play here."

She'd already told him of what she'd seen in the drake's eye, and while she understood the healthy skepticism he showed at the idea that she'd seen a literal god in the eye of a dying monster, it still failed to answer the questions they had on the matter. They had to know what had driven the drakes to attack them and whether it would happen again.

"Cassandra mentioned that there might have been some influence from Karthelon in sending the drakes," Tandir commented and folded his arms to mirror the captain as he raised an eyebrow.

Trust the barbarian to choose the direct approach as well.

Langven would have wanted to keep that from reaching the rest of the townsfolk. While he did not quite believe it, there was no telling who did and who would spread the word to the rest of the populace. Still, she felt this was better. Most lords and kings liked to rule as far from the commoners as they could. Keeping the people involved and trusting them to make the correct decisions for themselves and for the rest of the town was another way to go about it.

It was always possible for something to go wrong with that as well, but she was learning that more came from trust than not telling people anything. There were ways for that to go wrong too.

"What about Karthelon?" one of the town elders asked with a frown.

"It is said that Grimm was his son," Cassandra explained. "I assumed there would be some repercussions from killing his son if it were true and I...saw an image of him in the eyes of one of the monsters I killed. He spoke and said this was not the end of the attacks. More would come."

There was a moment of silence in the room as the group of elders exchanged glances before the second woman leaned forward.

"If word spread of this into the village, there would be a panic."

"And should there not be?" the man responded. "If a god is attacking the village, they would want to find another place to live."

"If it is true," the first woman responded immediately, "and folk decide they want to leave and find another place to live, what is to stop the god from attacking them while they are on the road? Here, we have a fortress to keep us safe if and when an attack should come."

They appeared to finish their discussion and they turned to the others in the room.

"What do you think should be done?" the man asked, his eyes a little wider than before.

"That would be up to you," Karvahal answered. "You represent the people and you carry the responsibility to decide. We will stand by whatever choices you make. I think Cassandra would be more than willing to escort any who have a mind to leave."

"But again, there is little I can do that compares to having a wall in place between you and the creatures that want you dead," she reminded them.

"We should tell them," the woman with the thick brown curls that adorned her head like a crown answered. "We cannot hold people here against their will, and lying to them about the possible dangers would be like that, no?"

This response was far better than Cassandra had expected it to be. Perhaps these people had been chosen for the job for a reason.

"Besides," the man added, "you were here to protect us when we needed it and there is little reason to abandon you all now. There are dangers all across the continent. At least here, we know something can be done to help the defenses if needed."

She realized that he was one of the people who had been with Karvahal since before the attack on their town. He had likely stood in the ranks and helped to fight Grimm's first attack in the other abandoned fortress.

The two women nodded in agreement.

"You've made our troubles yours for a long time now. It's about time that we help with the load," he stated firmly.

The woman with short black hair nodded in agreement. "We might not be warriors, but running away at this juncture would merely make everything we have fought for until now be for nothing."

Langven sighed and his eyebrows knitted together as he considered the possibilities. "The coin we made from the battle against Grimm would be enough to justify our maintaining a presence here. I'll be able to rotate fighters from the pack in and out to make sure there is a consistent patrol between Draug's Hill and Torsburch. If there are more attacks in the future, you can be sure to have troops here to reinforce those Karvahal can muster."

"There is still the matter of what might come in the future," Cassandra reminded him. "You cannot keep your pack here indefinitely and people are fighting to build a life here. They cannot be expected to live in fear in these parts. If Karthelon wants me, I should find a way to distract him from unleashing his ire at me on the people of the town."

That seemed to quiet the goodwill the elders seemed to have directed toward her. They had to consider the question of if and how this was her issue, and if it would not be a problem for them if she had not been involved.

They might have been ruled by a despot like Grimm the Cruel, of course, but the question remained as to whether that was better than being killed by drakes.

Langven chuckled softly and shook his head. "So we should ignore the fact that you've fought for these people long before they arrived at Draug's Hill? And simply move past how they would have been slaughtered by a witch who served as a Herald for a man who might or might not have been the son of a god? Even if we did, we should remember that there is much this god might hold against us as well.

"We fought against Grimm as much as Cassandra did, and if she hadn't been the first to kill the little bastard, I might have made an attempt—or Karvahal or anyone else for that matter. This god has as much anger toward us as he has for our barbarian princess. That said, if you were to offer yourself to the bastard to prevent him from sending more drakes against us to make Draug's Hill an example to the rest of the world, there is no guarantee it would work."

She smiled. It was nice to know he would stand behind her even if no one else did—barring the twins, who would probably think of it as a real fight. His reasoning was sound but it failed to address the question of how they could stop the attacks from continuing.

"We might find their nests in the mountains and set fire to them," Bandir suggested. "That will make them follow us and we can draw the attacks away from Draug's Hill."

"Karthelon would merely find something or someone else in their stead," Karvahal answered. "I think the princess intended to suggest something that would put a stop to the attacks at the source."

She had spoken to him about it and Langven as well, although she could already tell that he did not like the idea of her heading into the mouth of the beast in an attempt to stop him. It wasn't like they had much in the way of choices, however. He didn't need to like it.

"So you plan to…what? Brave the god in his lair and punch this Karthelon in the mouth?" Tandir asked and inclined his head. She was sure it was him since he tilted his head like a pup when he asked questions, although she knew for a fact it was because he could hear virtually nothing with his right ear.

She was almost completely certain.

"I know where to find him," Cassandra asserted firmly. "He might want to torment you all, but I have it on good authority that his focus is on me and we can use that to our advantage as well. I will seek him out in his temple and do what I can to defeat or thwart him—or at the very least, ensure that his wrath is spent anywhere other than Draug's Hill."

"It's madness." Langven growled his approbation.

"I can understand wanting to draw his attention," Sifeas agreed, "but there must be another way than walking like a lamb into his temple and all but asking to be slaughtered."

Other voices joined the dissent like she had expected, although none of the elders spoke. They likely did not know what to add to the commentary. On one hand, they were well aware that she had put a great deal of effort into keeping them safe and having her in and around the town would certainly help with that in the future. At the same time, though, if she were to find a way to stop the attacks altogether they probably could see no reason why she shouldn't attempt it.

Perhaps they didn't think it in so many words, but hints of guilt were visible in their faces as they looked away toward the door as if to avoid the discussion. She deduced easily that they wanted her to take the responsibility and consequences of stopping the attacks and hated themselves for thinking that way.

"Enough!" Langven roared and quieted the room immediately before the discussion became more heated. "I think we can all agree that sending Cassandra to duel a god on her own is not an option."

"Well, she won't fucking go alone," Tandir protested and looked outraged at even the idea of being left behind.

The captain scowled at him for a moment. "That…was not the point I tried to make. By all accounts, the place you plan to attack would not be easy to reach, much less infiltrate. Karthelon would have taken control of what remains of Grimm's forces, and they'll hold their position and wait for orders in and around the temple.

"These are troops who willingly served a man who called himself the Cruel, so we can assume they will not stand idly by when presented with an opportunity on their doorstep to kill and destroy. Any approach you might choose will be watched by bloodthirsty men and monsters that will be only too glad to bring your head to their leader. Assuming they don't have orders to bring you in alive, of course, since the god will no doubt suspect that you might attempt this."

The group appeared to agree, even the elders, who nodded but looked terrified to be included in decisions of this magnitude. One of them had Cassandra's attention, however. The older woman with dark hair had old, deep scars that marked her skin and most of her left arm was missing, although it looked as though she had been fitted with a wooden replacement.

"I know of the place of which you speak," she said and her gravelly voice carried through the chamber and immediately drew the attention of everyone in the room to her. "My people were herders in the area. We moved our goats and ponies from pasture to pasture but never brought our herds to the Depth of the Wastes.

"Our animals would not come within leagues of the place even if we wanted to, but the warning came from those who survived the culling when the priests of Karthelon used foul sorcery and steel to break us. They would drag our people to a great wound in the face of the earth they called the Utter-Pit. Those captured were joined by others and all were dragged down the craggy sides to the entrance of a temple with gates on the edge of what was touched by the sun. Something great and terrible awaited them inside, known only by the rasping breath that smelled of rotting flesh. Inside...a pile of stones—primitive compared to everything else, but... A fear and terror there killed with knives of shadow."

Cassandra could see the weight of reliving what had happened in the woman's eyes. There were no tears but something caught in her throat as she recounted the events.

"How did you survive?" Langven asked. "You speak with the voice of someone who has been there in person."

She nodded slowly and met his gaze firmly. "Aye, I was there. Women and children were preferred for the sacrifice, but those men who were brought sacrificed themselves to distract the priests while I and my three sisters tried to guide the rest out. They were killed to a man, and we managed to reach the edges of the wound before we were cornered again. Even the children realized that death was preferable to whatever awaited us in the temple, and we threw ourselves from the edge.

"I was caught by a drake before I reached the bottom, and it flew me to its nest to feed its young. I killed the beast with a discarded bone from another recent meal, which I thrust into the beast's open mouth. The bile it spewed cost me my arm. I managed to escape into the mountains where another tribe found me. I have managed to survive ever since and while I have never spoken of it, I have hoped always that such horrors were behind me."

Her tale was followed by silence among the others in the room. Cassandra felt the weight of the warning in the back of her mind and everything in her said there must be a better way to attract the attention of a god.

She could probably persuade Theros to involve himself in the fight. Gods could stop other gods—or that was what she had come to understand, at least. And even if he could not interfere himself, there should be some help he could offer on the matter.

But sitting around and waiting for the gods to solve all her problems was not in her. The barbarian princess straightened her back and nodded.

"Well, at least now I'll know what I face when I get there," she whispered and tried to hide the tremor in her voice. "It is appreciated."

"When we get there," Bandir reminded her. "You need folk with heads on their shoulders on this kind of assault, and we all know you left yours behind long ago."

"Aye," his brother agreed. "There can be no other reason for a woman to charge into battle with naught but her undergarments."

Cassandra grinned. "Well, I hoped as much but I did not want to assume. You two will have to choose your battles."

"You do well enough to choose battles for us, thanks." Tandir nodded.

"You cannot go," Langven insisted. "I understand madness and truly, the only reason why the three of you are still alive is by making sure your enemies will never be able to anticipate what you will do next. But the line must be drawn at pure suicide."

"The only way to keep me here is if you decide to lock me in a cage," she answered.

"Do not tempt me."

"I'm not. We are going. The only choice we have to keep the people of Draug's Hill safe is to find out where the threat is coming from and eliminate it at its source. None of us can stand here and say we'll be able to fight the monsters indefinitely, and what happens if another army comes along? If they besiege the town for months and starve us out? What happens then?"

Something dark and angry flared in Langven's eyes. He was a good man but he needed to tap into the part of himself he accessed whenever he charged into battle. They all did. It was what ordinarily drove him to protect his men, stand by them, and fight alongside them, and she knew he saw her in the same way.

He wanted to protect her or head directly into battle with her if necessary. She knew he would join her and the twins if he did not have responsibilities to attend to. It was likely the only reason why he tried so vehemently to stop her, although he probably didn't know it.

More importantly, he knew she was right or he would address her in the tone he knew commanded authority. He used it when giving orders to his men. Instead, it sounded like he was pleading with her.

Every part of her wished she could do as he wanted.

"Very well." Langven hissed a frustrated breath. "May the gods help you."

"The right ones, anyway," Tandir answered with a grin.

# CHAPTER SEVEN

The mercenary captain had said his piece. He wasn't the type who enjoyed repeating himself and certainly did not like to hear the sound of his own voice unless he was singing. Even then, Cassandra assumed he appreciated having a few drinks before he started.

And likely needed a drunk audience as well.

But he would not repeat his warning to her. She could see that in the way he almost avoided her and the twins once he realized he could not dissuade her. More decisions were made, and she knew the warning had gone out to the people of Draug's Hill.

A handful decided they would not wait for another attack and they traveled out with the Pack group that returned to Torsburch with Langven's new orders. He had undertaken to ensure that his troops were in constant movement in the area. They would take work that would bring coin in while they ensured that nothing caused the residents of either town any harm.

It was the responsibilities that kept him there. The Ebon Pack respected him enough to follow him on the new path they were taking away from being one step above the raiders that pillaged and killed anything that moved in the region. Slowly but surely, they were being forged into a force that kept the locals protected and at peace. If he left, they would likely return to the ways that made more coin for them in the short-term but would lose all the progress they had made thus far.

That was important as well. Maybe even more important than the quest she would go on.

"He understands that this is something that needs to be done," she whispered and brushed Strider's coat carefully. "I'm not someone folk in these parts look to for leadership. I'm the weapon he can direct at the threats to the people, but he's the one they listen to. He has to understand that, right?"

She was beyond expecting any answers from the gelding at this point. Skharr and Horse had a bond she could never hope to replicate, but it was still a pleasant experience to have someone she could talk to, even if the conversation was a tad one-sided. Maybe that was what made it so appealing, although she wasn't sure if he appreciated it. The paladin who trained her had said that horses liked the sound of human voices, and getting a horse used to the voice of the paladin who rode them was an important step in the process of bonding them.

So even if Strider showed no sign of answering, they still bonded somehow.

"I have no idea what the seven hells we would do otherwise," Cassandra added, patted his shoulder gently, and made sure he was dry and comfortable before she put the saddle over him. She was careful to check before she tightened the cinch. He had a habit of filling his belly with air and waiting for her to begin adding the saddlebags before he exhaled and everything fell as the saddle slipped.

A horse with a sense of humor—exactly her type if she wasn't in a hurry. Maybe it was his revenge for having to listen to her for hours while they traveled together.

"I know you don't have any ideas about this but in the end, it needs to be done for the right reasons. The twins have no real weight to add. They will do this because they want a fight and following me seems to bring those that are worth fighting. They will grow up one day but for now, they are like children. Massive, hulking, powerful children, capable of killing almost anything that walks and breathes on the earth, but still. For the people who make the decisions, it needs to be done for the right reasons. I'm not doing this because I want to pitch myself into battle against a god. It must be because it is what is best for the people in Draug's Hill. And I truly do believe that is the case."

"Do all barbarians talk to their horses or only the princesses?"

Cassandra tried to jump from the stool she'd settled on to make sure Strider hadn't filled his belly with air. Her boot caught a loose patch of hay and she fell. Thankfully, he was less surprised by the new arrival than she was, or she might have been trampled by her horse. Of all the many terrible ways to die, it was easily the lowest rung.

She regained her feet quickly and scowled when the beast nickered softly and tossed his mane. Langven stepped in front and grasped Strider's bridle to stop him from panicking.

"Are you all right there?" he asked, unable to stop a smirk from appearing on his face.

"You startled me, is all," she answered and brushed the hay from her clothes before she straightened. "I was…uh, preparing Strider for the ride ahead."

"And unburdening your heart to him as well, by the sounds of things."

"Well, there is that."

"Will you answer my question?" he pressed.

"Question?"

"About whether all barbarians talk to their horses or only the princesses." The mercenary captain paused and scratched under Strider's chin. "I always heard there was a connection between princesses and animals. They are able to speak to all kinds of creatures that others have no inkling into the minds of."

"It sounds like a story that princesses might want to spread."

He chuckled softly. "Aye, true enough."

"I'm not sure if it is a barbarian tradition, however. I know of one barbarian who speaks to his horse, and the reaction from the beast seems to indicate that a conversation happens between the two of them, but I was never able to tell for certain. Still, it felt like a good way to hear my thoughts out loud instead of letting them live alone in my head. And an old captain of mine said that speaking to your horse is a good way for him to become used to the sound of your voice so he feels comfortable with you as a rider."

Langven nodded. "I was told the same. I have no idea if it is true, but I do agree that it is a good way to hear yourself talk. I've…never been much good at speaking to people."

"Your men listen to you readily enough."

"I…well, yes, I suppose I might have learned how to speak to soldiers and appeal to what drives them and makes them who they are. I can speak at folk but speaking to them…it was never something I excelled at. I suppose it's how I came to this place—a land where all rejects are allowed another chance if they are willing to fight hard enough for it."

She liked that. A land where history mattered not. As long as one proved themselves to be a valued member of their community, what happened in the past would stay there. Maybe it meant that killers were allowed peace they didn't truly deserve, but those who did deserve it would be allowed some semblance of it as well.

In that moment, Cassandra allowed her mind to return to what she had said to Strider and realized that Langven had probably heard all of it.

"About what I said—"

"I heard it." He raised a hand to stop her. "And…well, yes, I know you're right although I wish you weren't. And even

knowing it, I would still try to stop you. You are important to...
To...what we are accomplishing here."

It was her turn to smirk, fold her arms, and study him closely.
"Important..."

"To what we are accomplishing here."

"That's not entirely true. I was when it was under threat but
now that something must be built, it needs builders like you—
like Karvahal and Sifeas too. I've never been one for building. I
destroy everything I come into contact with and thankfully, I've
mostly encountered those who need destruction so others can
build. There is no need for me here. Is there?"

His eyes narrowed. She hadn't hidden what she meant too
carefully and so he could certainly hear what she asked beneath
the obvious.

"I wish I could go with you," he whispered and lowered his
head.

"But you can't. You have your responsibilities, as I do. While
they might send us to different places, maybe one day, they'll
bring us to the same inn. Or tavern."

"In Torsburch, more than likely."

"Where I can hear you sing about the Seven Little Wenches
again."

He laughed and shook his head. "I do know a few other songs,
you know."

"None that you can dance to." She grinned.

"Well then, someone else might have to sing and you can do
the dancing."

"I think that might be worse than your singing, but I suppose
it might be worth a try."

He extended his hand and she took it at the wrist and grasped
it firmly. "Stay alive, Cassandra."

"I'll do my best."

He held her wrist a little tighter as well before he lowered his head and backed away. At least Strider got an extra parting pat before he left the stable. She didn't need to think about this. There were more important matters to fix her mind on, and if they wanted to remain alive long enough to meet again, she needed to focus.

Cassandra made sure he was out of the building before she turned her attention to the horse who stood placidly in the stall.

"He wanted to tell me something. And I wanted to tell him something too, now that I think about it. Why can't things ever be simple between two people?"

Strider had nothing to say, but the way the beast stared at her suggested that nothing was complicated. They merely needed to find a way to stop worrying about what did not need to be worried about.

Either that or he was tired of her wasting his time with chatter he could not understand and it was long past time she saddled him and started on their journey.

"You're right. You're right," she muttered, cinched the saddle, and began to attach the saddlebags. "Why would a horse care about human problems anyway? It's not like it'll get you any more hay than you already have. Or apples. Another horse I know likes apples. Do you like them?"

As always, no answer was forthcoming. She reminded herself why she'd stopped expecting one every time she asked the damn beast a question.

When the bags, supplies, and weapons were all loaded, she mounted smoothly, clicked her tongue, and nudged the gelding with her heels to indicate that it was time for them to be on their way.

It looked like the twins were ready to go as well. They waited for her at the edge of town and exchanged glances. They must have seen Langven enter and exit the stable.

"Not a word from either of you," she snapped and raised a hand before they could speak. "I might not like the idea of traveling alone, but I will accept it if I have to kill you two."

"Do you hear that, Bandir? She does fucking care."

"It would do her well to find another way to express her truest feelings about us, though. Else she might find herself traveling with folk who don't understand what she's saying under all that foul language and assume that violence is the idea."

"Well, if that were to happen, I would kill them too," she retorted as they followed her down the road. "It'll be a long enough trip to the ass-end of the world without you two assuming you know something you know nothing about."

Both chuckled as they fell into step with her.

They were on a journey to the Utter-Pit. She didn't like the sound of it or the fact that they would likely enter an area of the continent where magic had seeped into the stones.

Dark magic, she reminded herself with an inward shudder. It was the only kind that required the sacrifice of living creatures. The village woman who had been to the pit could recall few definite details but traveling north toward the mountains seemed like a good place to start based on the little information she had provided.

That aside, control over a beast to be able to manifest what she had seen in the drake's eyes would require a presence close to where the creature called home. The barbarians insisted that the mountains to their north were the most likely terrain in which the drakes would build their nests.

"There should be another small settlement once we reach those cliff faces," Tandir muttered. "But nothing after that on this side of the mountains. Nothing that's been mapped, anyway."

"Since when do you know how to read a fucking map?" Bandir asked and leaned closer to look at the paper his brother studied.

"Since I…well, since before you thought I could."

"That doesn't make any sense."

"It doesn't have to make sense. All that matters is that I'm smarter than you."

"And that means I'm the stronger one. Which means you won't be able to read a map if I've gouged your eyes out."

Cassandra closed her eyes when a dull ache started at the back of her head. It would be a long journey. All she could do was thank Karthelon for making sure the temperatures were cooler as they traveled.

---

Tandir scowled as he pronounced judgment. "It's not much of a settlement."

His brother snorted. "I'd barely call that an outpost."

The barbarians were right, of course. It had been a long day of riding and although the cooler air had helped, it wasn't by much. The grasslands opened in front of them and the wind whipped through the region without any barriers. It was a pleasant break from the heat when the sun beat down on them without interruption but less so when clouds covered it. Either Karthelon still wanted to use it to mask another attack or he had summoned enough clouds to make the weather last for a few days at least. Cassandra had been wrapped in a cloak for most of the day but the twins appeared to be unaffected by the weather.

Now that they had reached the end of their day's journey, it was disappointing to see that what had been marked as a settlement barely met the lowest standard.

A handful of farms were scattered around the region along with a few hunting cabins. The latter likely profited from the gazelles and other creatures that called the grasslands home. Some might have claimed a few lions as their kills as well. She had heard from a few of the locals that their meat wasn't something they could sell but the furs were bought all over the world if one knew where to ply their wares.

Still, this outpost was intended as a trading location for most of the nomadic tribes that roamed the grasslands. They didn't like to be seen and moved constantly but occasionally needed something that could not be foraged or hunted, so were willing to barter.

But calling it an outpost was certainly a stretch. One larger building made from wattle-and-daub with a hay roof appeared to be where the trading was done. A well and a small tavern were the only two other structures in the area, which meant there probably wouldn't be much in the way of trading for them. Still, they did have some coin, and if they had to travel well beyond where it had any value, they would exchange it for what could be eaten or worn when the temperatures reached the extremes.

"It's a roof over our heads and a warm meal for the night," Cassandra told them and nudged Strider forward on the road. They began the descent of the hill that allowed them to catch a last look over the region while night fell quickly around them. "It might be the last of the former that we have in a while."

The twins nodded but made no further comment and they approached the buildings in wary silence. It didn't look like they were expected, and the few people who lived there regarded them with what she could only call suspicion. Nervous glares were cast at them and children were ushered away from the road and out of sight.

She could understand their apprehension, of course. This far out, there were many dangers to consider. Newcomers could be scouts for a larger party looking for riches that did not always come in the form of gold or jewels. A vibrant slave trade flourished on the other side of the mountains, and children generally commanded the highest prices.

Hopefully, with Draug's Hill being only a day's ride away on horseback, the Ebon Pack would find a way to ensure the safety of the people living this far out as well.

Cassandra brought Strider to a halt outside the tavern and the suspicious glares of the locals followed them as they walked slowly to where the owner of the tavern ushered his family out of sight.

"Who might the three of you be and what is your business here?" the man asked once doors were closed. Whispering could be heard on the other side. "Two barbarians by the looks of you. We don't see many of your kind in these parts."

"I am Cassandra, also known as the Barbarian Princess," she answered and stepped forward before the man delivered an insult that would require her to stop the twins from cracking his skull open. "These two are Bandir and Tandir, the DrakeHunter twins and my close companions. We ride from Draug's Hill and hope for a warm meal, something to drink, and a safe place to lay our heads before we continue our journey. Our business is our own."

The man's eyebrows raised and he tilted his head to study the twins before he refocused on her. "Of course! The Barbarian Princess and the DrakeHunter twins! My apologies for not recognizing you sooner, but I thought—"

He stopped and his eyes widened as he realized that what he was thinking could prove to anger the three newcomers.

"Speak your mind, sir," she replied and gestured to the twins to take a step back. "We mean no harm to you or yours."

"Oh…well, I thought you three would be larger, is all. Tales speak of the Barbarian Princess being seven feet tall and the twins towering over her as well. There is also…"

The way he cleared his throat as his gaze drifted lower indicated that he had expected other attire.

"It is my battle garb, sir, and pray you never see it for yourself. It generally means that I intend to fight you or those who might do you harm."

"Of course. I meant no offense."

"And no offense was taken. Do you take coin for your services or do you require something to barter?"

"Gold and silver are readily taken, Your Grace. Copper coins are a little more difficult to prove the value of, but we will take them from you, of course. There is no doubting your...uh, we do not—"

She raised her hand. "Say no more. We have silver to pay for whatever hot food you have that tastes the best. Do you have rooms available?"

"None. Well, we have stables I keep clean and set aside for those who might need to sleep here, but most of our visitors bring their own homes with them if you take my meaning."

"The stables will be perfect. I have a feeling we will be aching for a roof over our heads before too long. How much?"

"Three silver coins, Your Grace."

Cassandra dug in her pouch, pulled out the required coins, and placed them on the counter. "If you have any supplies for a long journey available or if you know of any who do in the region, we would be glad for it as well—and more than willing to pay, of course."

"I will check my stores. If they are light, I know of a few hunters who have been drying meat from a recent hunt that will be precisely what you need."

She smiled as the man rushed into the kitchens with their coins in hand and called for food to be prepared.

"Your Grace?" Bandir asked.

"It's what civilized folk call their royalty in some places," Cassandra explained. "Bandir, tend to the horses and see they're stabled and fed properly. Tandir, hold one of the tables before the regulars take all the good ones."

"And what will you be doing...Your Grace?"

"Fuck off. I'll try to find out anything from our innkeeper about where we plan to travel. Go. Now."

They chuckled softly as they hurried to do as instructed. The innkeeper returned with his family as well. There was no need for them to hide from the Barbarian Princess, after all, and the two young girls watched her closely, even though they had work to do.

"Sila, Mels, off you go," their father chided in a soft voice before he turned to their guest. "I've instructed my sons to help your man to stable the horses and fill the stable you three will use with fresh hay as well—clean and no lice."

"It is appreciated." She leaned forward with another silver coin peeking through her fingers. "I have a mind to know a little about where we will travel. A man in your position will have heard tales from the nomads who call here, would you not?"

He leaned forward, nodded, and spoke in a conspiratorial tone. "Aye, Your Grace. I know a little of what happens. And I hear a fair amount more, although rumors are not what you might call reliable. These nomads might be fine hunters and herders but they have a taste for the fantastical if you take my meaning."

She didn't, and she didn't much care either. "My companions and I must journey toward the Utter-Pit. What do you know of the place?"

The man's eyes widened and he inched back. It was very evidently not a comfortable topic of discussion. She could understand why too, but a glimmer of hope remained as the man's focus remained greedily on the coin she had in her hand. It appeared there wasn't much silver readily available around these parts since one would be hard-pressed to find any establishment that allowed three people to be fed and housed for three silver coins.

"I have little to say other than to warn you to remain the fuck away from that cursed place," he whispered and shook his head. "No good can come of it."

"Can come of what?"

An older woman appeared from the kitchen. She looked a little too old to be the innkeeper's wife, and from the familial resemblance and the same pattern of silver in their black hair, she was probably the mother, aunt, or older sister.

"Never you mind, Mother. Get back to work."

"I'm not your slave to be ordered about. Serea can cook well enough and my wrists are swelling from stirring the pot. Now stop your gossiping and tell me."

"Myself and my companions plan to travel to the Utter-Pit," Cassandra explained. "We would like to know anything about it before we start our journey there."

"I assume my boy here already warned you about how cursed it is." The woman waved her son off to the kitchens in her stead. "Dark magic is there and the folk who spill from it are not the finest, although they know better than to raid the only place cooking food for them in three leagues."

"You've served Grimm's soldiers here?"

"Aye. They did'na pay for it either but there was not much of a choice for us. At least I can see you're doing what they did not."

"I'll pay more for any knowledge that might profit us."

"You're determined to go there, then?"

She nodded and the old woman extended her hand. It seemed she wasn't as trusting as her son and likely a little wiser too.

"Keep north from this point and you won't miss it," she answered and palmed the silver piece smoothly. "And if you do... well, the fall will alert you 'fore you travel too far. There's nothing more to say about it that you likely don't already know. It's the site of all manner of unspeakable things."

"So I've heard. Directly north?"

"Well, I assume you'll need to avoid the mountains in your path, but if you hold with the sun setting at your left hand, you'll find it eventually. It isn't that difficult to miss, although folk find it much easier to avoid."

Cassandra nodded. She could have guessed as much from what they already knew of the place, but it was interesting to see the old woman's lack of terror, especially since her son seemed almost too afraid to speak on the matter before his greed interfered. Maybe she was old enough to know that fear of it wasn't productive and certainly held no benefit for her life, especially if she was intelligent enough to avoid going near it.

Why would an old woman who had likely seen dozens coming and going from there care about another adventurer on their way to a dangerous area?

Still, it felt like she could have spent the coin elsewhere. Not that it mattered. They were not short of it and as things stood, it was always best to know everything about where they were going than not. They couldn't eat silver and fighting with gold was a losing proposition.

Drinks were already being poured and served when the twins took their seats. It was certainly not the finest inn they had ever found on their travels but it was far from the worst. A good night's rest under a real roof would do them good for the events to come.

"What did you find out about the Utter-Pit?" Bandir asked as he leaned back and took a swig of the chilled ale poured for them.

"Aside from having the oddest of names, I suppose," Tandir added. "Why would you name a temple to a dark god after a cow's tits?"

"Udders."

"What?"

"A cow's tits are called udders," Cassandra corrected. "But there was not much to learn aside from what we've already heard. Folk here know of the place well enough, but they don't like to talk about it. There are troops in the area, though—Grimm's, or at least those who followed him before. We might need to stay away from the roads if we are to proceed without being challenged."

The brothers nodded slowly and took long, slow sips of their drinks.

Of course, there was little point in avoiding the roads in the grasslands. Anyone on horseback could be seen for miles, after all. But once they approached the foot of the mountains, there would be some cover for them and a chance to avoid being noticed.

But they would have to prepare themselves for the very real risk of discovery and the violence that would likely ensue. She couldn't put aside the possibility that some of the folk in this little outpost worked as spies for Grimm and now Karthelon, and that was the reason they had been left alive when so many others had been killed or enslaved.

It was probably for the best that they would not remain there for long.

---

This must surely be a dream.

Oddly, that thought fixed itself immediately in her mind as she looked around and tried to determine why she floated above the grasslands and the little outpost where they had stayed for the night. The landscape was drenched by chillingly clear moonlight that cast a soft blue hue over everything and lent it an almost peaceful air.

Her body felt weightless and she shifted to look north along the road they would most likely take once they woke. Time seemed to flash forward and in an instant, the grasslands were gone and replaced by the rocky foot of the mountains to which they would travel. The road split and followed the range toward the west and the east, but a path continued into the mountains.

She focused on this narrow, rocky pass that looked like it was barely wide enough for two horses to travel astride. Most roads like that were abandoned and used only by those desperate for time and with no qualms about risking their lives in such treacherous paths, but this one looked well-repaired and well-traveled besides. It was also the only route that led directly north through the mountains.

A presentiment swept over her, the sense that something important lay ahead, just out of sight. In the next moment, she looked into the Utter-Pit in the wilderness. The old woman had been right about one thing at least—it would be difficult to miss. Like a scar carved into the flesh of the earth, it seemed to make even the mountains dip and tilt around it as if whatever had committed the atrocity still sucked everything else into the depths alongside it.

It was an unpleasant thought, but they had to push closer regardless of the dangers.

In the next moment, she was there and felt a stream of black vapors all over her body. Oddly, she hadn't thought of herself having a body but when she looked down, she realized she was naked from top to bottom. She wanted to press forward but held no weapon in her hand and had no armor, no amulet, and not even clothes to protect her.

With horror, she realized that her body had begun to come apart piece by piece and appeared to be eaten by a drake's acid while she looked on helplessly. A pair of venomous green eyes watched through the shadows. The being mocked her with a low, deep roar that felt like a dragon's yet was deeper and larger and made the ground shake with its vibrations.

It was strange how the pain was recognized rather than felt but when she screamed, the voice she heard was not her own. The voices of the twins were strong and familiar, then Langven, followed by the rest of the Ebon Pack. All flowed through her lips although she had no idea how she could utter a chorus of voices she knew came from the entire community of Draug's Hill.

Darkness descended and the pain left her, although it was apparent that there was not much else left in her to feel pain over. It was all gone. She wasn't sure how that was possible but there was no denying the evidence before her very eyes.

In the darkness, however, she could hear a voice. The whisper felt like it had spoken even while she screamed, but she could only hear it now that she had stopped and listened.

A voice called behind her and she turned slowly, although there was nothing of her to turn. She found no source for the voice but it came in closer, calmer, and quieter and silenced her mind.

"Patience," it whispered. "The Savage One comes with your mantle again. Trust in that."

# CHAPTER EIGHT

Her hand had already closed around the sword she slept beside when she opened her eyes wide and looked around in the darkness. Reflexively, she steadied her hold on her blade but didn't draw it as she waited for something to attack in the blackness.

Cautiously, she sat slowly and willed her heart to slow. Her clothes were soaked in a cold sweat and her whole body trembled, sure indications that all she'd experienced was a dream. She located no sign of the dark-green eyes and heard none of the roaring or anything else to alert her aside from the dull sound of the twins snoring in unison where they were sleeping on the other side of the stall on a fresh pile of hay.

No, she realized, not snoring. They should have been, but both whimpered softly and the small jerking motions they displayed indicated that they were suffering from a nightmare as well. One of them could have been a coincidence but both made that very unlikely. Either there was something in the air that gave them all nightmares while this close to the pit, or something else played a part in the matter.

Cassandra narrowed her eyes, pushed up from her pile of hay, and drew her sword slowly from its scabbard without making so much as a sound. She shuffled forward to touch Bandir's shoulder and shake him gently.

A soft rustle of hay told her he had moved. One as aware of his surroundings as a barbarian would have already been awake the moment he was touched. She stretched over him to shake his brother as well, but all she received in response was another soft whimper like he was in pain and could not pull himself away from the dream no matter how hard he tried. This was not a passive effect of being close to the pit and it certainly wasn't the result of thinking too hard on the matter before they closed their eyes. They were both being kept forcefully in their dream state.

Her amulet was warm against her chest, a sure indication that someone or something had attempted to harm her. While they had been at least partially successful, she had been protected enough to come away from the dream in time to hear soft foot-falls on the stable floor outside the stall that had been prepared for them.

"Very well, then," she whispered and adjusted her grasp on her sword. "If I have to do this on my own, I will."

Whispers from outside warned her of foul intentions, and she pressed close to the door. Shadows were cast by the torches in the open space and she heard a soft creak. Still in the shadows, she lowered herself into the corner out of sight of anyone who stood at the door.

She would give the people involved every chance to prove that they meant them no harm. It might even be intended as a warning that enemies were approaching. That was the only reason she could think of to explain why the innkeeper slipped into the stables this late in the night.

"See?" he said brusquely to the men. "I told you. Sleeping like babes. I told you my mother knew what she was doing. She might not know all the fancy spells those fucking priests like to use, but she knows how to stop unaware folk from waking when she wants to. Come on, get the three of them up and bound."

"Three? Where's the woman? The one who called herself the princess?"

"Maybe she slept in another stall. She paid enough for it and I don't know if I would like to sleep in the same room as the two brutes. A woman like that would want her privacy. Check the other stalls."

"What do we do if they wake while we's binding them?"

"Bind them quick. Mum's spell should hold. The priests want them alive. I have no idea why, but if this is the barbarian princess and her twin barbarians, they'll be more than happy to pay us for our efforts."

Well, that told her all she needed to know about the matter. The bastards had kept themselves alive and in business by selling their visitors to the priests and likely kept the possessions of those they betrayed for themselves as an added reward for their efforts. The old woman she'd spoken to must have possessed some kind of magical power. Oneiromancers were difficult to find, and studies of their abilities were even rarer given that those who had those abilities tended to be the kind of mages who relied on instinct over instruction.

As interesting as it was, Cassandra would not forgive her for the nightmares she kept the twins trapped in. Dream torture was even more terrifying than what was possible while they were awake. All kinds of limits to pain could be exceeded since they were not contained by the rules of nature.

Seething, she gritted her teeth but remained utterly still as two of the men left to find her, while the other six remained and began to manhandle the twins and bind their hands with rope. She needed to wait until the opportune moment and it soon presented itself when a seventh figure stepped into the room. The innkeeper had returned and glanced at the side of the room where she slept and recognized the indent in the hay where she had lain.

It was the clearest sign that she had been in the same stall as the twins and that there was no need to search for her in the other areas of the inn. Before he could open his mouth, she lunged forward, drove her sword through his throat, and opened it cleanly as he turned to call to his companions. He noticed her as her sword came clear of his open throat.

She raised a finger to her lips. It was perhaps a waste of time, especially since he stumbled back and coughed and choked as blood flowed from the wound she had inflicted. Taunting the dying man helped her to feel a little better about the situation he had forced the three of them into, however. She had been lucky to wake or she would have been bound and dispatched to wherever this cult dedicated to Karthelon intended to send them, probably as some kind of sacrifice if they had to be delivered alive.

The other six turned at the noise but she had moved before they could register her presence. Her attacks were deft and lethal. Two of them fell back when their necks and throats were opened like the innkeeper's had been. Cassandra drew the dagger she sheathed at her side, rammed it hard into the chest of the man closest to her, and shoved him out into the path of the three still standing in the small space.

"She's in—"

The shouted warning was cut off when she hammered the hilt of her sword into a young woman's face, crushed her nose, and knocked a few teeth out with the impact as well. She immediately yanked her dagger from the chest of the dead man and punched it into the woman's arm before she forced her back against the wall of the stable.

The flimsy structure was not designed to support the weight of two humans crashing into it. It crumbled in a cloud of dust and enough noise to ensure that any other members of the cult knew someone was offering resistance.

Still, she didn't expect it to be quiet and it was better that they all came to her instead of running away. She wanted a fight and it would be more than annoying if they all scattered like rabbits and she had to hunt them one by one. Their nefarious betrayal had put her in the mood for a fight and the heat of it would keep her on her feet despite her need for rest.

The young woman tried to dislodge her assailant from where she was poised atop her but it was a weak effort, likely as a result of the bones broken in her face and the dagger still driven into her forearm. Cassandra yanked the blade out, plunged it into her adversary's neck, and sliced downward until she felt the spine and pushed through until it came out the other side.

It was a quick way to die. Although she felt the need to inflict pain on the bastards—preferably the same degree of pain she'd felt in her dream—the need to kill quickly and move on was greater. There would be no time to relish any victories. She bounded to her feet, registered the two men who remained in the stall she'd just exited, and noted the sounds of more coming from the larger stable area. She smiled, flicked the blood from her sword, and grasped her dagger in a backhand as the other two rushed at her, while more used the doorway to attack. None of them had weapons, but they attempted to cast nets over her and to bind her with rope and appeared to have no intention of defending themselves as they struggled to contain her.

One man fell almost immediately as she hacked her sword down, split his skull open, and kicked him into the path of his comrade. She shifted immediately, sliced through one net as they threw it at her, and stabbed her dagger through the neck of another assailant. It caught on the bone deep inside and the weapon was wrenched from her hand. She backed away quickly and spun to avoid being tackled as more of them entered the stables. The altercation disturbed the sleeping horses and caused even more of a clatter.

If that didn't wake the twins, nothing would, and she grimaced as she was backed against the wall. The cultists advanced grimly but still showed no attempt to defend themselves. Eventually, sheer numbers would allow them to overwhelm her, however.

Movement in the corner of her eye drew her attention to the oneiromancer, who clutched what appeared to be a magical totem with both hands. Sweat streamed from her face as she continued to recite whatever spell she used to keep the twins trapped in their sleep. She had no doubt come to find out why it took so long to capture the three who were supposed to be sleeping. Maybe she hadn't noticed that one of their victims had woken, but she seemed surprised to see the barbarian princess on her feet while the spell was being cast.

The way she said the words repeatedly meant it likely had to be maintained continuously. Cassandra couldn't tell how long the woman could hold out but knew it was time to attempt something desperate. She needed the twins to help her overcome the overwhelming odds, and that would not happen while she was pinned inside. The only way to the old woman, however, was through the air.

She slashed her sword forward wildly to force her attackers back. Before they could regroup, she hefted the weapon and judged the distance between herself and the older woman. Her target still recited the spell but appeared to realize the danger she was in and began to back away slowly in an attempt to find some way to duck away from her line of sight.

It was time. She had her opening and it would close almost immediately. The barbarian princess readied her sword, felt the weight of it, and took a step forward. She followed the motion with the rest of her body and flung the blade forward with all the power she could manage.

The moment it left her fingers, she knew that it was a good throw. Tossing her sword in a fight was usually frowned upon, especially in a situation when she lacked any other weapons to fall back on, but desperation called for the oddest things to be done to ensure that victory was hers. The sword spun once and as the blade side returned to the front, the old woman raised her hands to try to stop it. What appeared to be a weak wall of fire was raised in her defense, but the weapon cut through it effortlessly and buried itself almost to the hilt in her chest. She was flung off her feet and fell with a wet thud.

Silence fell over the room as all the cultists turned to the woman who lay unmoving. Maybe she was some kind of leader, especially given her magical abilities, but her role was now irrelevant. There was no point in waiting for the fight to continue and while they were distracted, Cassandra leaned forward and pounded her fist into the back of one of their heads. The young man staggered forward for a few steps and finally sank to his knees. She wasn't sure how hard she'd hit him but it was clear that he would need help to regain his feet.

There was no reason to stop, and she twisted her body to drive her elbow into the next man's jaw, kick the knees of the one next to him, and throw her fists into the nose of another. Their surprise did not last long, and her attempt to fight to the door appeared to be doomed to failure as more of them arrived. She estimated fifteen or so and if she'd had her spear on her, it would have been a fair bout, more or less, especially if she had been on horseback.

But on her own two feet with no weapons to speak of and fighting alone, it was a losing battle. It was still one she intended to fight, however, and she smirked with satisfaction at the blood spilled when she cracked her fist over one man's eyes and her elbow landed a solid jab behind the ear of another.

Someone caught her by the hip and began to push her back into the wall before she could resist. She grunted softly and the breath rushed from her lungs with the impact, but she doubled over and hammered her elbow into the back of the young man who had pushed her. A woman tried to catch her wrist but fell back with a broken nose. Another man limped away when his knee cracked under her kick. A rope snagged around her hand

and pulled it away as a hard fist launched into her jaw and drew blood when her teeth cut the inside of her mouth.

Cassandra laughed. "You'll have to try harder than that!"

She spat the blood into the man's face and snapped her head forward. Her forehead crushed his nose but more hands pinned her free hand against the wall and wound ropes around it. She was able to deliver another kick before she was lifted off her feet and thrown onto the stable floor. They worked as a pack to try to restrain her and keep her down while the ropes were tied all over her. It was apparent that they intended to make sure every inch of her was roped and with good reason, given that she would fight with every part of herself that was left unbound.

A young woman who tried to gag her learned the truth of this when the captive latched onto her thumb and bit until she felt the crack of bones as the flesh split. The barbarian princess spat it out and lunged up to bite the woman's cheek when she leaned down and screamed in pain. The heat in her ensured that they would have to kill her if they wanted a compliant prisoner to bring to the priests.

The taste of another's blood was foreign to her, but she ignored it, spat everything out, and tried to find something else to attack while they tried to bind her legs together as well as turn her onto her stomach. The battle was all but over, but she would make them pay for it all. Nothing in her would give in and she laughed as one leg came free. Her knee cracked across the skull of one of the men and he fell, unconscious and bleeding from where she'd split the skin.

A jolt of pain rushed through her body as fists hammered into her ribs to try to stop her from resisting. Their efforts loosened their hold on the rest of her body, however, and more pain came as she managed to arch back and strike someone with the back of her head. She heard a soft cry of pain as they finally managed to bind her hands behind her back.

In that moment, her smile went from bared teeth at the grim

realization of her fate and the knowledge that she would fight it to her last breath, to something a little more genuine. The shouts around her were pierced by very familiar twin war cries. They should have warned her attackers of exactly how fucked they were, although they still attempted to contain her. Steel sliced into flesh and was followed by screams of pain and shouts to retreat as opposed to the earlier calls to attack.

The brothers had woken quickly, and she assumed that the only reason they had taken so long to help her was that they needed to determine what was happening, snap their restraints, and gather their weapons before they rushed in.

The holds on her shoulders, arms, and legs immediately eased and she shook herself to loosen the ropes, turned, and unleashed a kick that hit something, although she wasn't sure what.

Finally, she worked herself free, pushed to her feet, and looked around to assess the situation. The twins had carved a path into the group, killed a dozen of them, and forced the rest to scramble away, although those that remained appeared to be wounded and were overtaken rather quickly.

A soft whimper snapped Cassandra around and her gaze located a young man who crouched in the corner. He seemed terrified and must have realized his mistake in making so much as a sound as his eyes widened to stare at her.

"Please," he whispered, tried to back away, and was stopped by the wall, "have mercy."

"Would you have shown me mercy instead of handing me over to be sacrificed?" she asked, took a step forward, and noticed the ropes he had in his hands. Separate from the mob, he looked like an innocent young lad, barely a man and likely unwed, but when the group had attacked her, he had been eager enough to tie her and leave her helpless.

And he knew it. The boy tried to jump to his feet and make an attempt to run, but she was waiting for it. The moment he was vulnerable, she leaned forward and her foot lashed out to drive her heel into his skull. He was thrown back into the wall with a wet thud and fell, trailing blood down the wall after him.

Cassandra took a step forward and spat on him before she turned to where the twins dealt with the last of the cultists before they focused their attention on her.

"It's about time the two of you woke," she snapped and strode to where her dagger was still buried in one of their attacker's necks and yanked it out. "The bastards almost had me hogtied and sent off to be sacrificed. They would have succeeded if you two had continued with your beauty sleep."

It was a little unfair of her, of course. A spell had kept them asleep and their dreams had likely not been pleasant, but she was angry. Lashing out anywhere she could was the only way she knew to stop the tears from welling. She didn't like the feeling of being powerless and she had been inches from being completely at the mercy of the mob.

"My apologies…" Bandir muttered and pulled her sword out from the old woman's chest. "I don't know why—"

"You don't need to apologize. That bitch there had a spell that kept the two of you asleep and suffering horrifying nightmares too. I felt its effects but I was protected from it somehow. I barely managed to cut her down in time for you to wake, or the two of you would have been bound and sent off to be sacrificed with me."

"Ah." Tandir cleared his throat and nodded. "How do you know—"

"They talked when they came in to take us. I suppose they assumed we would be asleep. From what I could gather, they have avoided the wrath of Karthelon so far by putting those who come here to sleep like they did with us and delivering them to the bastard priests to be sacrificed. It's for the best, perhaps, or they would have simply slit our throats while we slept and not bothered with the dreams or an attempt to capture us."

The twins nodded slowly and looked around at the damage

that had resulted. She breathed deeply as the fire in her belly began to fade slowly, and she was left feeling exhausted and tempted by the need for sleep.

But any delays, even if only for a few hours, would likely cost them dearly. There was no way to know if the cultists had sent word to the priests before they attempted the capture, which meant they might have to deal with more attackers before too long.

"Clean up and gather what you can find," Cassandra ordered before either of them could speak. "Make sure nothing was done to the horses or our supplies."

"You might want to consider cleaning yourself too before we travel," Tandir whispered.

She narrowed her eyes. Something about how they didn't have the time for niceties was on the tip of her tongue before she caught a glimpse of her reflection in the steel of her sword. Her nose looked a little swollen, as did her right eye from where they had struck her. Her sides and ribs felt like they had been trodden on by oxen, but all that fell away given how her whole face was covered in blood—and not necessarily hers either. This was especially the case around her mouth, where she had bitten anything that came close.

"I think you're right."

"There's a well outside."

Cassandra nodded and left the stables as the twins started their work. Maybe it was a little unfair of her to expect them to do everything, but she couldn't bring herself to even consider doing anything at the moment. She had endured the greatest physical beating, after all, and she had to allow herself time to heal if she wanted to be in any condition to travel by the time the sun came up.

And sunrise, she realized morosely, was not too far away. The sky was already turning to a dark shade of pink and a few stretches of light seeped through from the east as she pulled a bucket of water from the well and began to clean not only her face but her entire body. She hissed softly when her fingers touched the worst of her injuries, but it helped her to keep track of where they were. Her teeth gritted, she stripped to make her task easier and took a moment to suck in a deep breath of air.

Even though she was as naked as she had been in her dream, she felt considerably less exposed. It had not been a pure nightmare and as she thought about it, she had no idea what the soft voice had talked about. Who was the Savage One? Why would they bring any garb to her?

It didn't make any sense but she decided to not waste too much time considering it. For the moment, all they needed to worry about was the danger they were currently in. She pulled her clothes on and returned to the stable, where the twins searched through the pockets of the dead and unconscious cultists who had tried to capture them mere moments before.

"There isn't much for us to take," Bandir commented. "I found the coins you paid them for the food and accommodations, and I think they owe us that much. We might need to raid their larders for more food."

"Take what we need. We don't need to overburden the horses but don't know how long it will be before we find our destination."

He nodded and hurried away to do precisely that, although Cassandra assumed he had ulterior motives. Hopefully, it was to find food for breakfast.

"They didn't touch the horses," Tandir told her when he'd finished searching the dead and approached where she had stopped to check their mounts. "Or our supplies. If they intended to hand us alive to the shits who perform the sacrifices, it might be that they intended to keep our possessions for themselves."

"I like to think that would have ended poorly for them."

"How so?"

"It stands to reason that Langven would come to look for us if we did not return. Assuming they kept our items and did not sell them immediately, he would find them in possession of our horses and weapons. It would not take the largest of leaps to assume they had caused us harm, and he would have brought the full might of the Ebon Pack down on the bastards for it."

Tandir chuckled and nodded. "I like the thought of that as well. But I do have...other concerns now given that we have survived."

Cassandra turned to look at him and patted Strider's neck to calm him. He and the other two horses stamped nervously in their stalls, unsettled by the sounds of violence and the smell of blood that filled the stables. It likely meant they would be jittery and on edge all day as a result.

"Well, I'm sure they would have found a way to tell the fucking priests they had us," the barbarian explained. "If they did, we might walk into a trap farther along. Perhaps that the witch you killed could communicate with them and tell them we were here, and the lack of word about their attempt to capture us might cause them to send more troops out on the road. They could merely patrol and watch for us, even if there is no trap."

She nodded slowly and tried not to scowl. There was no doubt that word was out that the Barbarian Princess was on the move, and while that was the intention—it was her way to ensure that Karthelon did not attack Draug's Hill—it would certainly make their journey a little more difficult.

Before she could answer, Bandir reappeared with three bags full of food in one hand and a platter in the other. The latter held enough freshly cooked food to feed the three of them.

"I would say the cooks thought they would celebrate our capture with a feast," he explained. "They bolted as soon as they realized that the fighting hadn't gone in their favor, but the food is still good, I assume. It might be a good idea to fill up before we leave since we might not find the time for food or drink until night falls again."

"You make a good point," she agreed and regarded the brothers speculatively. They tried to maintain the good spirits they had been in before, but she could tell that something weighed on them and she could guess what.

She had not been in the foul dream for as long as they had, and she had woken at the point where she assumed things were progressing to their worst. They had remained in it for considerably longer, and as much as she wanted to convince herself that it was only a dream, she knew better.

"What did the two of you dream about?" she asked as they began to eat.

Tandir looked up, tossed a piece of what looked and smelled like pork into his mouth, and exchanged a glance with his brother. Neither of them ever showed any inclination to discuss anything that made them uncomfortable. Dreams that did not involve copious amounts of killing or fucking were quickly silenced and forgotten. Whatever was in the dreams they had experienced fell into the uncomfortable category.

"You don't need to talk about it if you don't want to," Cassandra assured them and took a bite from the beef the barbarian had likely cut from a larger piece that was still roasting over an open flame, given how warm it still was. "But there are dreams that folk should pay attention to. This is particularly true about the dreams given to you by an oneiromancer, as their instinctive pushes in the dreams tend to drive toward whatever happens to be in their mind."

"Onei…what?" Bandir frowned in confusion

"Dream mages," Tandir explained to his brother. "It was… strange. I dreamed I was being buried alive—at first, at least. Then everything around me was burning and it felt like pieces of me were being carved off as I…cooked."

He looked at the piece of meat he was eating, shrugged, and took another bite.

"I was buried as well, but mine was cold," Bandir whispered

and shook his head. "The cold climbed through my body like something alive and broke bits and pieces off as it went."

They weren't much like hers.

"What about your dream?" Tandir asked.

She grimaced and nodded. It was only fair, after all. They had shared their nightmares and it was her turn to do the same.

"I traveled to the Utter-Pit," she explained. "Something evil was waiting for me there. I had no weapons, no armor, nothing, and the creature took me apart piece by piece. That does seem to be what we all share in our dreams, although…there was a voice in mine. It told me that a Savage One was coming like it was supposed to comfort me."

"No voices in mine." Tandir looked disappointed.

Bandir shook his head. "Nor mine. Only…screaming."

Silence fell and they focused on their meal. It was good to see that the nightmares had no effect on the twins' appetites, nor hers. Being able to separate the horrifying from the mundane was a skill that many soldiers learned, and it made regular folk think of them as monsters when it was merely something they had to do if they were to survive the horrors of war and battle.

It was Theros' voice, she reasoned as she chewed thoughtfully. It had to be. No other gods were prone to send her messages through her dreams. And it was possible that he had protected her as well and maybe even woken her in time to fight the damn cultists. She had no way to know for sure, but it certainly seemed logical.

The food was gone quickly, as was the drink that Bandir had pilfered from their hosts. Without so much as a word, all three gathered their things quickly and started their journey. There was no need for them to wait for more of the bastards to appear, not unless they wanted another fight on their hands.

# CHAPTER NINE

It was annoying how closely her dream held to reality. She had hoped that it had been merely a dream but the more they traveled, the less likely it seemed. Cassandra remembered every second of it—an oddity in and of itself—and the road she had followed in it was identical to the one that they were on now. It circled the cliff face the little outpost had been built on and continued north with only a handful of deviations visible from where they were.

The only real difference was the fact that she could not somehow accelerate to a point leagues farther on the path. Traversing it the slow way had certainly begun to grate on her nerves, especially since the clouds had broken and the heat of the day beat down on them.

Even so, they climbed quickly out of the grasslands. Some brush remained but only whatever was tough enough to grow on the increasingly rocky terrain they now moved over.

Any number of different points along the road gave a commanding view of any who might travel on it, but they saw no sign of any patrols or scouts in position who could send word of their approach. Although they studied the terrain warily, no camps were visible, not even those that might have been abandoned hastily if the travelers had been seen and those on watch immediately chose to leave to notify their superiors.

It was annoying. While silence had hung over their group for long hours after they'd left the outpost, she expected some presence to indicate that they were being watched. Surely there must be something to show that they had caught the attention of their adversary.

"This isn't right," Bandir said belligerently, the first words spoken since they'd left the stables.

"What isn't?" Cassandra asked, looked at him, and followed his pointing finger to the cliffs ahead of them.

"If there was a military presence in this area, they would have someone stationed there." Tandir had an odd habit of completing his brother's thoughts, and the worst part of it was that neither of them realized what they were doing. She did not want to bring it up with them, especially not when they were discussing something far more important. "It's the perfect position for an outpost. The outcroppings would make it difficult to be seen, even in the dead of night when they need to light fires. It would give a view of any approaching armies, and it would allow them to defend that location on the road almost indefinitely if they needed to."

She agreed with that. "There are no spotters, scouts, or outposts in this area because they've never needed one. Legends of the Utter-Pit have been spread far and wide, likely by the cultists we killed as much as any survivors who managed to escape. There is nothing of value here—nothing that would not be more easily obtained by traveling into the mountains. An army could not be fed or maintained here without considerable cost. And besides, while a god might prefer that there be underlings to do his dirty work, he can still watch over the lands he holds dominion over. He knows we are here. He merely...does not care."

"How do you know that?"

Cassandra raised an eyebrow and both twins watched her carefully. "I don't. I'm making assumptions. It's better than letting the thoughts fester in my head like an open wound."

"I know the feeling." Bandir scowled at the cliff face.

Tandir grinned. "Except in your case, your words are open wounds and we all might benefit if you keep them to yourself."

"I'll give you an open wound, let it fester, and watch you die while I steal all your trophies."

She chuckled when she realized it was the first time that rough humor had been bandied between them since they started their journey that morning. It was a good reason to have the twins around. Like the drakes they hunted, they were thick of skin and nothing would keep their spirits down for long. Not nightmares, not gods, and certainly not cultists.

"Well, if they have no presence in the area," Tandir muttered as they continued to ascend the path that now wound higher into the mountains, "it would be the right place for us to camp for the night. It looks like there are a couple of trees for us to get wood from if we want to cook the food we took."

They still had some of the perishables Bandir had collected from the kitchens on their way out, and if there was ever a time to cook proper food, it would be this night. Aside from their evening meal, they would also need to find a way to turn the perishable foods like the potatoes and carrots they'd taken into food that would last a little longer. If they managed to mash them into stew, it was the type of fare that would last for about a week if stored properly in the skins they had. While it wasn't quite as palatable when cold, almost anything would be a relief from a bland affair of dried meat and waybread.

Tandir was right about the location being a good site for them to set up a small camp, for most of the same reasons that it would be a decent position for a scouting base. It gave them a decent view of the area around them, was easily defensible, and was almost invisible to anyone on the lower plains they had journeyed through earlier.

Cassandra realized she had a hard time looking at the mountains to their north, where the road would split and leave them a narrow path to follow into the mountain.

"How do you think these people would be able to live so close to such a cursed place?" she asked and shook her head as she turned to help the twins cut a couple of the smaller, tougher trees around them.

"What do you mean?" Bandir handed her a hatchet and she began to hack into some of the bushes and take the light, dry wood to where Tandir worked to set their camp up.

"Well, they might have some kind of arrangement with the priests to send visitors and maybe some of the nomads to be sacrificed, but there is always the possibility that these priests might decide that not enough people are brought to them. If so, the locals might find themselves in the belly of the beast they've been feeding. Why would they remain?"

"There might be more to the arrangement than we know about," he suggested as he helped her to pile the wood they had collected.

They did not even have to discuss the option before the decision was made to have a fire burning for the whole night. None of them wanted to be left in the darkness this close to the Utter-Pit.

"How close are we to it anyway?" Tandir asked once the fire was burning and the sun began to disappear on the horizon.

"None of the maps seem particularly clear about it," Cassandra answered, scratched her chin, and watched the barbarians prepare the meal now that the fire was going. "But...if I remember correctly, that ridge over there—where you see the paths splitting—should be the last obstacle that prevents us from seeing the damn thing. It's less than two days' travel from the fucking outpost. There isn't enough coin in the world for someone to pay me to live two days ride away from a place like that."

"And yet you have no issues with living four days away in Draug's Hill?"

"Well, I would have had more issues with it if I'd known we were so close to the Utter-Pit, and I would likely have suggested somewhere a little farther away. Still, four days is better than two."

Both chuckled softly at her words, but she realized they were seated with their backs to the mountains as well. At least knowing that they were as unsettled by it as she was brought some comfort, little though it was.

---

Cassandra stiffened under her cloak and reached for her sword. Her fingers curled around the hilt and squeezed it a little tighter than was necessary before she dared to open her eyes. The soft crackle of the fire nearby was enough to tell her that she was in their little campsite. The dreams had continued, and despite how tired she had been after a long day of travel, there was no reason for her to return to her dreams tonight—and not only because she was meant to wake in about an hour anyway to take the watch for the rest of the night.

It had been a repetition of the dream from the night before, and the words spoken into her ear still echoed within as she pushed from the ground. A few blankets had been spread to ensure that she wasn't directly on the ground, but it was still not the most comfortable sleeping conditions she'd ever enjoyed. It was far from the least comfortable, of course, and hard rocks were much better than soggy marshlands.

"It's not your watch for another hour," Tandir whispered and she looked to where he was propped but still wrapped in his blankets. He looked exhausted.

"I can't sleep."

"Are the drakes keeping you up?"

She shook her head, although it had been one of the reasons why it was difficult to fall asleep what felt like days earlier. The howling and screeching from above them made all three imagine that they would be attacked at any moment, but for some reason, the creatures held back. Perhaps they had camped a little farther out than the beasts were comfortable hunting from. Or Karthelon did not want them to be attacked immediately. It seemed like he wanted them steeped in fear before they even laid eyes on the damn pit, although she couldn't help but think there was no way that the Utter-Pit could live up to how it was being built up in their heads.

"Bad dreams," she admitted.

"Do you want to share them with us?"

"Not particularly."

"But we were so close before while sharing our dreams. I thought we could discuss our hopes next. Maybe while braiding each other's hair."

"Your hair could use a good braiding. I'm not sure what you attempted to do with it, but all I can see is a messy tangle that barely does the job of keeping it out of your eyes in battle."

Tandir grinned at her as she moved closer to sit next to him.

"It was the same dream—for the most part. I don't remember much of it, but there was the overall feeling of dread, death, and destruction, while something whispered in the back of my head that some savage is bringing me my garb."

"Do you think it means Langven? Maybe Theros is trying to remind you of some piece of your armor that is missing and he'll follow us to deliver it to you?"

"Possibly, but I doubt it." Cassandra shook her head. "You can sleep if you like. I won't rest now so I might as well keep watch."

"It's appreciated."

He didn't appear to have any difficulty sleeping and she

couldn't help but feel a little jealous when he snored softly within minutes. Maybe they didn't care much about the screeching and howling of drakes in the mountains above them. They hunted drakes, not the other way around.

Her mind still insisted that she had heard Theros' voice in the dream, but it felt like he was playing games with her. He always had and always would. She could imagine why, of course. If she lived hundreds and thousands of years in a world that had little to offer by way of threats to her existence, she would soon be bored with how everything went and would find ways to entertain herself. Maybe by playing games with people fighting for their lives, the gods managed to stop themselves from going completely and utterly mad.

She still didn't appreciate it. Given that she was one of those people whose lives depended on the help of the gods to prevent other gods from ripping the continent apart, her patience with the games they played was significantly reduced.

The screeches from above slowed and finally stopped altogether, and she fought to stay awake as the stars faded slowly from the sky. There was no sign of any impending attack as the sun began to illuminate the area for them, and she finally stood from her comfortable seated position and nudged the twins awake.

"A few more minutes," Tandir muttered under his breath and tried to pull his cloak over himself again.

"Extend it by a lifetime," Cassandra answered, "and I'll simply leave you behind."

He opened an eye to stare angrily at her as she tossed the last bit of wood they had collected onto the fire and brought their pots closer to the flame. They could at least enjoy one more warm meal before they pushed farther into the mountains, where there would likely not be enough wood to collect. None of them wanted to put in the effort of carrying firewood for them to use.

It would simply be a waste of effort.

Warm food was a luxury they could indulge in for the moment. It seemed worthwhile but they couldn't tarry there for the whole day. She could feel eyes on them as they gathered their camp and mounted for the day's journey.

Despite the heat that she had expected would reach unpleasant levels, a slight chill had already touched the air in the morning as they proceeded cautiously toward where the road split into three.

"We're traveling up that?" Bandir whispered as they looked at the narrow road they had to follow. "Who would have gone through the trouble of carving a path on the side of the mountain if they didn't bother to make it safe to use?"

"It looks safe enough," Cassandra answered and tilted her head to study it carefully. "It's narrow but I see no sign of any rock outcroppings that would cause an avalanche and block the road."

"It's too narrow for my taste." Tandir agreed with his brother. "One wrong step and you'll fall hundreds of feet to your death. Assuming a drake does not swoop in to catch you."

"Why do they do that?" she asked and nudged Strider forward first. The twins followed her in single file. "I've always heard of drakes plunging in to catch rams and humans as they fall, but it seems like it would be easier to simply let their prey hit the ground, die, and collect the remains."

"The way our father explained it, there are a handful of reasons," Bandir stated from directly behind her. "Firstly, your prey would be dashed on the rocks and probably into many pieces. The beasts prefer to have their food a little easier to transport. Another reason is that other predators wait for the prey to drop—even other drakes. Catching those that fall in the air ensures that they can enjoy the meal without having to fight others off. Drakes and even the larger birds find a way to drag their prey off—"

She twisted to look at the man, who peered into the sky as if to catch sight of anything that might be coming down for them.

"Drag their prey off of precarious perches." She completed the thought for him. Maybe it was not the best decision to follow this path.

"Lastly," Tandir continued after the silence continued a little longer than she liked, "they like to bring live prey to their nests. Not always, of course, but nesting mothers want to bring something living and able to fight back. It's how they train their young to hunt before the little beasties can fly."

"Little is...one word for it," Bandir muttered humorlessly. "DrakeHunters would go on nest raids from time to time, and they would find monsters almost the size of wolves waiting for them while the parents were away. It's never something you want to battle in a precarious position, but our grandfather had a trick of kicking them out of the nests. Teaching the bastards how to fly was how he liked to describe it."

Cassandra wasn't sure if she liked that, but it was an integral part of the name. Nest hunts, as they had described them to her, were only held when the drakes bred a little too much and made their nests too close to population centers. Sometimes, the DrakeHunters worked of their own volition and at other times, they were hired to eliminate the beasts. The easiest way to do it was to clear the nests. Once those were gone, the drakes would find somewhere else to nest, usually away from the humans. It was an interesting balancing act that did necessitate them to kill the young drakes.

It seemed like the monsters that had the twins on edge had no interest in attacking. There was no sign of the beasts coming from above or below, although she caught a glimpse here or there of movement at the tops of the mountains, closer to the snow line. It appeared that Karthelon had no inclination to attack them yet. Or the drakes did not like to fight in the heat.

"I suppose I would describe that as a scar on the earth," Bandir whispered.

Startled, she lowered her gaze, confused about what the barbarian meant. She frowned when she realized that they were already on the approach to the pit. It seemed impossible that she'd missed it, and neither twin appeared to question the path they were taking. None of the maps had shown clear routes this far into the mountains, and the path they were taking had not been marked. They merely followed the road she had seen in her dream without so much as questioning whether they were being led into some kind of trap.

Nevertheless, Bandir was right. With only the description of the Utter-Pit to work from, the area ahead of them was rather difficult to miss. The scraggly edges made it look like a massive sword had been drawn across the surface of the earth to force it into the ground to the point where even the mountains around it appeared to lean into the hole that was created.

The narrow path they were on continued into a small canyon that cut between the mountains and opened the area directly into the pit, where a dull green mist still seeped from within.

There was no telling what the mist was or where it came from, but something about it made her want to turn away. Of course, any attempt to turn on the narrow road they were on was more difficult than it might have seemed.

At least it did not appear that they would have to spend the night on the ledge. That was another way to avoid sleep—not only the fear of the drakes coming to take them or their horses but also the fact that one bad roll would end with them falling over the cliff.

It didn't help that it became colder the higher they climbed into the mountains, and from the looks of it, the temple spanned between the mountains and opened into a smooth entrance that likely led into the scar. The warning in the pit of her stomach was enough to tell her that nothing was right about the place as they approached. And the lack of bickering between the brothers was a sure sign that they likely felt the same way.

Cassandra realized that she had snaked her hand to where her spear was held and she curled her fingers around the haft and lifted it slowly from its little notch. She could see that the twins reached for their weapons as well, but their gazes were directed upward, away from the mists and at the rocks above them.

Dozens of nests were spread over any nook and crevice in the rock face that would hold them, and movement came from above as well. Drakes, possibly in their hundreds, hissed and growled at the three who approached the entrance to the temple.

She didn't like how they held back from attacking for the moment. It felt like they should have already swooped at them but they made no attempt to do so and restricted themselves to more hisses and growls.

These did not look quite like those that had attacked Draug's Hill, she noticed. For one thing, they seemed perfectly comfortable in the colder clime—too comfortable for creatures that were supposed to be cold-blooded. They had darker scales and appeared to be a little more streamlined with a longer wingspan as well. She assumed this meant they were smoother fliers than those they'd fought already.

They reached the canyon, which opened into a clear path to the entrance to the temple. The most disquieting feature was that there were no priests, no guards, and nothing standing in place to hold off any intrepid adventurers who could pose a threat to whatever waited inside.

Even worse, the mist encompassed them now as well. She had expected it to be hot on the skin like water steaming from something that heated it deep below like a sauna. But instead, it was cold and chilled her increasingly as they approached the doorway leading inside.

"I don't like this," Tandir whispered.

"Me neither," Cassandra responded, hefted her spear, and held it a little closer as she scrutinized the area around them. They were there for a reason, and she knew they would face some kind of threat, but it worried her that everything seemed to guide them in a little too easily.

As much as she wanted to press in and prove herself to be better than anything or anyone that would attempt to do her harm—or do harm to the people she cared about—she knew reason needed to win over bravado. There was no point in springing this trap unless they had a damn army with them.

She raised her fist to stop the two coming in behind her and motioned for them to turn.

"This is not where we make our stand," she decided aloud. "There is no point in pitching ourselves into the fucking pit."

The twins both nodded and she couldn't tell if they were merely following her orders without question or if the lack of questions was simply because they hadn't wanted to commit to this fight either.

Cassandra nudged Strider around, still holding her spear, and let the twins take the lead since they were in that position as they began to return to the shelf road that would lead them away from this cursed place.

She scowled when she realized that the barbarians had stopped and her mount tried to circle their horses.

"What's the matter?" she asked.

Tandir raised his mace and pointed it at the cliff face that towered above them, and she immediately realized the mistake they had made. The drakes had followed their movements along the canyon and now waited for them to return to the road. They practically licked their chops in anticipation. She cursed inwardly and acknowledged that they weren't walking into a trap. They were already inside the jaws and nothing they could do would stop it from snapping shut to kill all three of them.

The drakes could attack any time they wanted to. They had urged the humans into the canyon and pushed them toward whatever waited inside, but if they decided to retreat, they would attack. Even worse, given their numbers, it would be only too easy for the beasts to simply drag them over the edge and they would plummet to their deaths. It would be a violent and somewhat ignoble end to the Barbarian Princess and the twin Drake-Hunters who followed her.

There was no escape and nothing for them to do but move forward, so Cassandra pulled her horse around.

"There is no way out of this." Somehow stating the obvious out loud made it feel a little more final, but it would allow them to enter the fight with no impossible assumptions. "So best we at least make an attempt to finish our mission before we're killed."

The twins nodded.

"I'd rather die fighting than being flung off a cliff," Tandir stated and grasped his weapon a little tighter.

His brother agreed but she remained silent as she stared at the opening into the temple. It was only five or six hundred paces away but she had a feeling it might as well have been three leagues underwater for how accessible it would be in the next few moments.

She heeled Strider forward and gave him full control of the reins as she released her spear and picked her bow up. The gelding surged into a gallop across the open space while she selected three arrows from the quiver. She could hear movement from above, shrieks from the beasts as they called their challenges, and a moment later, their wings beating when they decided that the time for watching and waiting was over.

It was time to attack and none of them wanted to be left out. Cassandra gripped Strider with her thighs to maintain her balance as she twisted and raised her bow. She held two of the arrows in her bow hand and pressed the third to the bowstring as she looked for any sign of the beasts.

Her blood ran cold when she focused on the groups of monsters that swooped into the attack, but she steeled herself, chose one of the creatures, followed its movement, and launched an arrow.

It was quite possibly the best she'd ever loosed and it cut through the mist and punched into the mouth of the beast that was closing on her.

It fell suddenly and a blast of blue light erupted from around its mouth and engulfed the rest of the head as it crashed on the rocks below.

"Fire drakes," Cassandra whispered and shook her head. "We should have known."

They were less common than the acid drakes but considerably more dangerous—almost as dangerous as proper dragons. She nocked another arrow to her bowstring and released it as well. It was considerably less precise than the first, although it still struck her target and buried into the tough scales on its skull.

The third flew truer, but the drake she had aimed at had already begun to drift earthward with one of the twins' javelins in its neck. It picked up speed and careened down as fire started to billow out of the wound.

She realized that she was approaching the temple entrance and reached out to grasp the reins but in that moment, Strider panicked underneath her. A shudder and a wild neigh were all the warning she had before he reared and tried to fight off something in front of her. As useful as he was in battle, it was still enough to unseat her from her perch on the saddle.

*Foolish. Idiotic. Imbecile.* She should have paid attention and at least kept her balance at all times. Her trainer would have been so disappointed.

Her shoulder ached as she found her feet. Strider had been effective against the drake that had dropped in front of him and crushed its skull with his hooves before he veered away and moved to where the twins rushed to join her. It seemed the gelding had not realized that she was no longer on his back.

"Go!" Tandir shouted and launched another javelin to bring

yet another one of the beasts down. "We'll hold them off for as long as we can!"

There was no telling how long that would be, but it was all she could hope for and it was much better than heading into the temple while having to fight the drakes that attacked her from behind. She drew her sword, thankfully carried at her hip instead of on the saddle where the rest of her weapons were, and immediately rushed toward the entrance.

The darkness inside fought her. Not physically, of course, but it pushed at her mind and jolted the instincts that would have made her run from this place, screaming the whole way. It was deceptive how wise those instincts sounded at the moment.

Cassandra almost didn't realize she was moving before it happened and she dove to the right as she was about to push herself across the threshold. A gentle gust of air pressed against her, evidence of how close whatever had swung at her was.

Her gaze settled on another drake, although this one looked larger than the others. A crown of horns protruded from its head to indicate some kind of prominence over the rest of the creatures. Hell, it almost looked like the most painful way to declare itself king—or queen. There was no telling if it was a male or female without closer inspection.

She scrambled to her feet again, grasped her sword, and wished she'd had the presence of mind to snatch her spear before she was dislodged from the saddle. Still, a sword in hand was better than fighting with her bare hands. She steeled herself and looked into the creature's eyes as it sauntered to where she stood. It exhaled a blistering tongue of flame that forced her back, away from it and the temple and toward the edge of the cliff not so far from where she stood.

If it thought she would simply fall over, it would be disappointed. The beast would have to work much harder at it.

"Come on then, you glorified wyrm," she snapped and twirled her sword in her hand.

It appeared to take offense at that and snorted some of the blue flame from its nostrils as it rushed toward her. The wings spread to give it a little more speed and height as it attacked.

Against everything in her that said that it was time to run, she held her ground and stared at the beast as it advanced. She drew a deep breath and waited for the right moment when it swept up and looked down at her with its massive jaws hanging open.

Bright blue light seared from inside and was immediately flooded by some kind of liquid it spat out and ignited with blistering heat.

Cassandra jerked forward, dove over her shoulder, and felt a snap of pain as it met the stones, but the heat of the flames was more than enough to drive her forward. She landed on her feet as the beast lunged toward her.

She was there waiting for it and screamed as she thrust the sword forward with as much power as she could muster, a surge of strength that powered from her toes through her hips and into her arms as the tip sliced through the tough scale armor the beast wore as skin. The blade sank deeper until she could feel the heat of the flames inside it touch the weapon's steel.

It was a successful strike, but one she hadn't quite planned all the way through. The creature continued its momentum, barreled into her, and hurled her out of the way as it continued to tumble, now unable to stop itself. All she could do was stay clear as her sword was wrenched from her hands. She followed the beast as it scrabbled through the flames of its own making, but with blood and fire pouring from the wound she'd inflicted, there was nothing it could do other than fall over the cliff and out of sight.

Stunned, she waited and expected the creature to return, still alive and willing to fight. The seconds ticked past and all she heard was a dull thud when it finally reached the rocks, taking her sword with it.

"Son of a whore," she whispered as she turned away. The

twins were still fighting and she directed her attention to the temple and pushed into a sprint toward it.

Her boots skidded across the rocks when she forced herself to stop and her heart hammered in her chest as something moved inside. Bright green eyes stared through the darkness emanating from within. Her mouth went dry and she tried to convince herself that there was no danger in there that she would have to fight.

The dream, however, flashed vibrant images through her mind—the beast waiting inside, knives made of shadow, and her standing with no weapons and nothing to fight it with as it appeared to invite her into its lair.

In that moment, a shadow slipped away from the entrance and moved actively and independently against the light around her. The ground shook as the all-too-familiar roar struck her directly in the chest. She stared in horror as the black vapor began to pour from the recesses of the darkened temple like black tendrils reaching out for her.

Her mind raced to consider her options but there was nothing she could do. She had no weapons and no armor and might as well have been as naked as she remembered herself being in the dream. Courage meant nothing when it earned her nothing, and she saw no reason to be brave. All she could hope to do was survive and live to fight another day.

And run like her life and the lives of all her loved ones depended on it.

# CHAPTER TEN

There was no need to attempt research, as much as she wanted to study what was happening in the area. It would help to have a better understanding of what they faced and how she could battle it in the future but she couldn't take the time to do it. Ironically, enough academics out in the world would ensure that she never wanted for anything for the rest of her life if she studied what they stood against.

But Cassandra knew when to put her curiosity aside. Someone else was welcome to have the opportunity to study what the black vapor was, preferably without her as a test subject. It began to spread across the canyon and tendrils groped to where she stood. This was not the time for her to be a paladin but to listen to those instincts that told her she needed to run as fast as she could.

She needed no additional confirmation when she noticed that the drakes now climbed up and away from the vapor as well and even went so far as to stop attacking her if it meant they could avoid coming close to the substance. They might be controlled by Karthelon, but even that couldn't protect them from whatever attacked from the cave. It was very evident that they intended to allow the monster inside to have its due while they turned their attention to the twins.

Her only weapon was the dagger at her hip, and she doubted that she could do much with it aside from something desperate while her death was already in progress. She needed to return to the horses.

It was not that difficult to find them. The twins had been separated from the three mounts, who were being harassed and attacked by the smaller drakes. These were likely the young who weren't able to breathe fire yet and weren't able to outright overpower the horses, especially since they fought back. The mares the twins had elected to ride followed Strider as something of a leader and bit or rose on their hind legs to beat back any attacks that came too close.

They wouldn't last long, however, and she rushed to where they fought valiantly and dove under one of the drakes that swooped in to try to stop her. She found her feet, snatched the spear she had left on Strider's saddle, and thrust it smoothly through the chest of one of the creatures that attempted to attack from the horses' flanks.

It screeched and fell back and the other beasts turned their attention to the true threat, especially as she drove the spear through the jaw of another.

"Nice work there, Strider," she whispered and swung smoothly into the saddle. "What say you we leave this cursed place behind, hmm?"

There was no question now if he understood her or not. He turned and immediately trotted to where the larger beasts had gathered around the twins, who continued to fight fiercely. She hefted her spear and tightened her grasp in preparation to enter the fray. She'd lost her bow when the gelding threw her and knew it was now engulfed by the vapors she tried desperately to escape. Still, the spear was better than no weapon—hells, it was better than most weapons, even in their current situation.

While she hadn't looked back, she knew the twins' horses were following her and Strider. She made a mental note of how she might have unconsciously intended to leave them behind since she hadn't even thought about taking their reins to lead them with her. Skharr would have scolded her for that and she felt like she'd betrayed them, even if they followed of their own accord.

Cassandra heeled her mount into a full gallop, lowered her spear, and thrust it through the back of one of the larger creatures that appeared to try to fly low for a smoother attack on the twins. The barbarians had been forced toward the road on the shelf of the mountain. It wasn't the best position and none of them wanted to be there with drakes approaching, which was likely why the twins made no effort to run.

Another of the beasts turned and tried to strike her but she shifted in the saddle and caught it across the eye with the haft of the spear before she switched the weapon to her left hand and buried the blade in its throat.

This one was old enough to breathe fire but it didn't use the flames to attack the twins, even though her strike brought fire out like it had with the others. She had a feeling they wanted to avoid the twins being burned to a crisp. Maybe they would be more edible that way. When the larger drake burst into flames, it was enough to drive the others back. While their insides appeared immune to the fire, their scales were not and it bought the team a few precious seconds as she slid from the saddle.

Tandir was the only one standing, his mace as coated in blood as the rest of him. A score of injuries were visible across his arms and shoulders, but nothing needed her immediate attention. Bandir was another story. That much was immediately apparent.

"Is it done?" Tandir shouted as she drew the horses in closer.

All she could do was shake her head. Speaking it out loud felt like it would be too physically painful. Even so, the young barbarian appeared to understand when he realized she was wounded and without her sword. Still, now was not the time to consider that she had abandoned the reason for their coming this far. There was nothing for them to do but retreat and hopefully regroup where they could find a solution to the problem. Assuming they survived, of course.

She approached Bandir where the young man had propped himself against a rock and tried to reach for his weapon.

"I can fight," he whispered. "It's nothing but a cat's scratch."

"It must have been a rather big cat," Cassandra answered and moved his hand away from his weapon. While it was difficult to tell the true nature of his wounds under the armor and blood, there was enough of the latter to tell her he was already fighting for his life. Blood trickled from his mouth, bright red instead of dark-brown that told her at least one of the three massive claw marks across his chest and stomach had nicked his lungs. He coughed up more as the organs started to flood with it.

"Tandir!" she called as she moved Bandir's armor carefully from his wound. "Keep the fuckers away while I work to heal him!"

He nodded without a word but as much as the twins enjoyed facing the beasts they were named for, she knew him well enough to see there was more to it than merely the glory of the battle. He swung his mace with an almost manic effort at the first creatures that managed to rush through the flames and she knew he was genuinely concerned for his brother's safety.

She hadn't experienced it but could understand that it would be the stuff of nightmares to watch someone he had likely been close to from the moment they both pushed out of their mother's womb struggling to breathe the way that Bandir was now and not be able to do anything about it.

At least he could draw a certain benefit from having a vast

number of drakes ranged against them on which he could take his frustrations out.

Cassandra forced her focus away from the airborne monsters around them. She had to trust that Tandir would be able to hold the beasts off as she placed her hands on Bandir's chest, careful to not make the wounds worse as she reached in with her mind, and began to heal him. At this point, all she could do was stem the bleeding that had already weakened him and push the body to heal itself at a much faster rate than it had been.

Although she could do any number of other things to make it better, she knew that if she let the barbarian bleed any more, he would die despite any healing she could administer. Of course, she could always force the issue to make it go faster, but it would likely take too much energy. She might collapse before the healing was complete and even if she didn't, she would most certainly be unable to run, much less fight to aid their escape.

Bandir's heart beat rapidly, desperate to keep the body it was maintaining alive. If it possessed the ability to think, it would likely be thankful for the help to sustain him. She couldn't replace all the blood he had lost but she could make his body produce more. He would feel the effects of that in the coming days and would need to drink considerable water and eat red meat to replenish all that was used, but he would survive until then.

"It is always fascinating to watch you work," he muttered once she had finished and offered him a hand to help him to his feet. They weren't quite as steady as either of them would want, but the fire of battle would be enough to keep them both alive and fighting for the moment.

"Welcome back." Cassandra paused to check the wounds, which had closed to leave pink and likely sensitive skin beneath, clearly marked by the lack of any hair on the scars on his chest or stomach, but he would survive. "There's no time for us to talk. We need to leave this place. Now!"

"If we leave across the shelf road, we'll be killed!" Tandir shouted as they both lunged forward to kill the beast he'd managed to force to earth. "Traveling that road would be suicide!"

It was true enough, but something more terrifying was on its way.

"Remaining here would be suicidal as well," she answered and pulled the horses away from where they could be struck. "Whatever is coming out of that fucking temple will kill us with much more certainty than anything the drakes could do us."

The twins didn't like the idea of turning and running into certain death, but they couldn't deny the vapors that spread from the temple more aggressively now. Even worse, none of the three could argue its power once it had engulfed one of the smaller drakes that attempted to escape. The beast had been injured by Strider when the horses had fought on their own and was too slow for the insidious mist. All they heard were a few shrieks before the sound cut off and nothing remained, not even a body.

"We'll take our chances on the road," Tandir decided immediately and helped his brother into the saddle.

Bandir did not like the idea that he had to be helped, but he was weaker now and likely would be for the next few days. Still, it was better than having three gaping wounds across his chest, and he was still able to swing his ax to lop the legs off one of the drakes as it swooped in to try to attack them from above.

They no longer questioned the need to leave and Cassandra heeled Strider into motion but immediately let the twins take the lead so Bandir was between her and his brother. He was protected as much as they could as they began to run, both from the drakes and from the temple monster.

She would return, she promised herself. If she survived, she would return to deal death and vengeance to the creature in there for all the lives it would claim and all the lives she would prevent it from claiming in the future.

"Come on!" she yelled.

Strider needed no more urging and broke into a full gallop.

They pulled away from the drakes that still tried to kill them and for a moment, they had a reprieve. It would not last, of course. The beasts would find a way to ensure they did not escape and already alternated between flight and climbing the mountain in their efforts to find the right angle to simply knock their prey off the mountain while they were on the precarious road.

Her mind argued briefly about which she dreaded more—waiting for the vapors to reach them or their vulnerability on the shelf road. The decision was likely to kill them either way but somehow, death by drake seemed preferable to being killed by whatever pursued them from the temple.

The first of the beasts finally found the perfect position to attack them from, but Tandir was already waiting for it. The barbarian fixed his gaze upward and let the horse navigate the narrow road now that they were on it. He paused and tossed the javelin up as it began its descent. Already committed, all it could do was flare its wings in an attempt to shift its trajectory before the weapon drove into its wing. It wasn't a killing blow but was enough to spin it into the mountain on the opposite side of the canyon.

Although a fine shot, it was likely that they would not be able to maintain their defenses for long. She didn't have her bow and he was already out of javelins. All they could do now was wait for the beasts to descend and hope they were lucky enough to avoid being struck. Even if they did manage to land a blow on the drakes, the force of the impact would likely be hard enough to knock them from their horses and send them plummeting to the depths below.

Three of the creatures launched a combined assault this time, and Cassandra heeled Strider to go a little faster. The twins did the same with their horses, although there was little doubt that the beasts could adjust their dives in time to reach them. She gritted her teeth, grasped her spear a little tighter, and focused her gaze on their attackers. They had aimed their trajectory a little ahead in anticipation of the humans' movement along the road.

The song of bowstrings startled her from her narrow-eyed concentration, and the air above them was suddenly filled with arrows. Cassandra shook her head in confusion and wondered for a moment if she merely imagined whatever was happening. She tensed and tried to determine the likely source of the projectiles.

Perhaps it was only the damn priests coming to finish them off if the drakes couldn't. It made sense that Karthelon would leave nothing to chance. No matter what happened, he would see his prey dead in the trap he had planned for them.

But the arrows were aimed a little too high to hit them. If that was deliberate—and she could see no logic in that—they would sail well over their heads and clatter into the mountainside. Instead, they were very clearly intended for the drakes that attempted to attack them. As if to prove the point, the three airborne monsters were cut down and they powered into the rocks and finally plunged into the darkness below.

She squinted to see where the arrows were coming from and was unable to contain a burst of laughter when her gaze settled on a group of men in armor and in formation who positioned themselves against the mountain and beckoned for her group to hurry.

Even better, they all wore the fang of the Ebon Pack. She wasn't sure how it was possible but could see no reason for it to be some kind of trick, not at this juncture.

"What the hell are you doing here?" Cassandra shouted once they reached their rescuers and had to slow their horses so they didn't run the group over on the narrow road.

"We've come to save you all," the officer in charge answered with a grin. "Provided that's all right with you?"

She turned and smirked at the confusion among the drakes as they attempted to find a way to attack the newcomers where they were positioned. Before they could, men of the pack moved forward and managed to maintain a formation of four men abreast while still leaving what appeared to be about a pace between themselves and the edge as they raised crossbows and fired into where the beasts attempted to regroup.

Large, powerful crossbows with steel limbs launched the bolts faster than she could see and immediately decimated the large massed group of flying monsters and forced them back again.

A squad of about twenty waited for them there, and she had no idea how they had managed to follow her and the twins without being seen.

Then again, their focus had been on what was waiting for them rather than on looking back.

"How—"

"Langven decided he would not trust the gods with your fate. Once you were out of sight, he sent us to follow closely and to come to your aid if you were attacked by overwhelming odds."

She reined Strider in to allow the twins to pass. "How did you know we needed your help?"

"We were being harassed by the drakes and suddenly, they began to flock here. We could only assume they were being driven to attack you, so we made all haste to come to your aid. Come on!"

It still seemed like a lost cause. While the drakes were out of sorts and caught off-guard, hundreds of them continued to assemble in the nests above. It would not be long before they decided they would not let a few bows and crossbows stop them from finishing the troop off.

"We need to move!" she shouted and gestured for the men who were reloading their crossbows to join the group. They mounted their horses quickly and started their retreat.

One of them turned and handed Cassandra a bow so she was able to continue shooting arrows at the drakes to stop them from attacking without their group sustaining losses as they hurried along the narrow path.

It was tenuous but better now that they were able to prevent them from launching at them from above. Still, it wouldn't last and the beasts had already begun to climb into the mountains. They seemed to judge the range of their bows and remained out of reach as they continued to try to encircle the group from above.

The road led them rapidly to flat ground and another volley of crossbow bolts caught her eye. These climbed higher than the bows could manage and felled a group of the drakes where they attempted to position themselves for an attack.

More of the pack waited for them where the land turned flat and immediately began to reload their crossbows as the group on horseback moved past them two by two.

"Best of luck!" the officer called to the dozen or so fighters who remained in formation, waited for the troop to pass, and took their shots at those creatures that dared to approach.

"Mount up!" Cassandra told the group sharply and looked back to where the drakes began to surge forward despite the bolts and arrows flying at them. "You won't be able to hold this position long!"

"No, ma'am," one of the men snapped in response. "But we can hold them off for long enough."

"No man dies here," she said and shook her head. "Not if I have any say on the matter."

"Apologies, but you do not, ma'am," he answered with a stiff nod. "We have our orders and all have our part to play—to make sure that what happened here this day has meaning."

She knew she wouldn't change their minds, certainly not in the short time they had before the drakes launched a concerted assault from the sky.

"I will kill Langven when I see him," she whispered. It had no doubt been his orders to ensure that she was dragged out kicking and screaming if need be, and he'd instilled something like honor in the thieves and blackguards who were part of the pack.

As hard as it was, there was nothing she could do. She heeled Strider into a gallop to catch up with the rest of the troop and refused to look back as the sounds of screeches and howls from the drakes were joined with battle cries, pained screams, and eventually, silence.

# CHAPTER ELEVEN

The riders made no effort to camp even as night fell. The drakes would likely not stop for long, and if the group remained near the mountains for any longer, it would be an invitation for the beasts to attack their camp.

It wasn't until the moon was high in the sky and the mountains were well behind them that the troop came to a halt. They immediately set defenses up and established a rolling watch to ensure there were always at least ten men to keep their crossbows aimed at the sky and ready for an attack.

Cassandra felt the fatigue fight for control of her body but even so, she refused to rest before she had ensured that Bandir was given water and food and he settled beside his brother. That done, she sat with the night guard to watch for any sign of the rearguard they'd left behind.

She had little expectation that they would have been able to escape at all and could only hope that their honor and duty kept them in their position for only about as long as it would have taken the rest of the group to make their escape.

Once that point was reached, they would have been able to find a reprieve from the assault and start their retreat. The drakes would be at a significant disadvantage the farther they traveled across flat ground, especially the larger, heavier ones that appeared to prefer climbing the rocks to flying.

Their weight would have made a flight over long distances a chore unless there was enough wind to carry them aloft.

But when the rest of the group began to turn in for the night, there was still no sign of their return. She searched the moonlight but saw no horses or even any sign of the drakes circling above their prey, trying to pick them off.

Cassandra steeled herself as her body fought to surrender to the weight of what she'd put it through during the day but she refused to sleep, not if she could help the men who had been willing to die so she could live.

Still, a little koffe would not have gone amiss.

"They died well."

She turned to look at the officer as he sat next to her and wrapped himself in a cloak.

"What?"

"The rearguard. They were under orders to ensure that you got out of that place alive at all costs. If they had thought they could make a retreat of their own, they would have reached us by now. They were brave men, all of them, but they weren't stupid."

"You don't know that."

"True enough. Maybe a few of them were a little duller than most. I blame the lack of schooling that runs rampant in these parts."

She turned to look at him again and made sure that he knew she did not appreciate his attempt at levity. It was a decent enough joke but a rawness within swallowed any semblance of humor.

He nodded and cleared his throat. "You know the kinds of men who joined Langven's Pack, yes? They aren't...uh, all the most honorable of soldiers. Some of them might have chosen to be bandits and reavers because they were shit characters to begin with, but I feel I can speak for most of us when I say we were... well, desperate. Nothing drives an honest man to crime faster than children with empty stomachs. And for many of us, we thought that life would be our fate until we died. Sooner rather than later, by the looks of it."

"I assume you have a point to this?"

He nodded slowly. "Aye. Not long ago, we were given the option to fight for something more than a little coin to drop on a few vices we used to pass the time between battles. Langven is a good enough leader, but I wager that even he would have had difficulty convincing bandits and killers to join and battle the army under the Herald's command—and again against the army led by Grimm. There might not have been much of an option for us before but you gave us the ability to fight for something greater than what we were. You help folk and let them live their lives. I've committed more than my fair share of foul acts before."

"If this is your way to repay me, I would rather you merely buy me a drink when next we are in Torsburch."

She turned when he placed a hand on her shoulder.

"This is my way of telling you that this is not only about you. Fangs of the Pack will bite down on whatever they need to from time to time, but you've proved yourself to be more—a symbol of peace and stability in this region. If you were to die, all you and Langven fought for would soon be lost and the men knew that. Which is why, when our captain called for volunteers to come and fight alongside you, each man you see before you and dozens more you don't raised their hands."

Cassandra wondered how long he had planned that speech. Or maybe Langven had given it to him to tell her like he thought it would help her feel better about leaving men behind to die at the claws and fangs of monsters.

"I appreciate what you're saying," she whispered and drew a deep breath. "What...what is your name?"

"Mavros."

"Well, Mavros, I think you're all a group of idiots, but I'll watch and wait for the rearguard to join us all the same."

"Aye. I think I'll do the same."

She could respect that, at least. Whatever he had said in hopes that she would feel a little better about what they were doing was all well and good, but he still worried about the fate of the men under his command.

The truth was that she could understand the dream now. It was a warning from Theros, an assurance that he would send help to her before too long. But if he had thought she would simply sit around while people died all around her, he was wrong.

A god who had lived as long as he had must know about her temperament. He had to know of the threats they were facing. Why hadn't he sent help before if he intended to at all?

It wasn't until she was in the saddle and they were riding to Draug's Hill that she realized Theros wasn't who she was angry at.

Maybe it was the lack of sleep, she reasoned dully. She caught herself almost falling off her saddle a few times as they continued through the day and acknowledged that she was in desperate need of rest.

But even weariness was merely an excuse. She was angry with herself for ignoring all the warnings to the contrary. Her decision that she had to be the one to solve things had been supremely arrogant and it had resulted in the deaths of twelve men and had almost killed the twins as well.

They might have thought they made the choice to join her, but they must surely have questioned her decision as it drove them into the jaws of the beasts and almost resulted in all three of them dying.

What would she have done then?

It was a long trip to Draug's Hill and she still struggled to sleep at night, even when it became apparent that the drakes would not give chase. The result was that she found it difficult to stay awake in the saddle.

At least Bandir appeared to be recovering well enough. His vigor returned quickly and the brothers began to pester each other by the second day of their ride back.

Still, some spirit was missing from them when they finally came into view of the keep. It was like they forced their previous habits to the surface and tried to act like what they had seen in that temple had not affected them.

The feeling seemed to permeate the rest of the group as the gates to the keep were drawn open for them to ride through.

A few youths came out immediately to tend to their horses. Cassandra struggled to swing her leg over so she could dismount. Perhaps she could simply ride Strider into his stable and drop into the hay there for a rest.

It wouldn't be the most dignified of returns, but maybe that was for the best. She needed to hide from the world for a while and if it meant sleeping in the same stall as Strider, maybe that was where she was meant to be.

Hell, she couldn't even complain about the horse's foul smell since she probably reeked as badly and didn't even have the excuse of having to carry the full weight of a human on her back.

With gritted teeth and more effort than it should have required, she managed to dismount but had to breathe deeply and struggle to stay on her feet as someone else took Strider's reins. The cobbles looked like a perfect place to curl and sleep for a few hours until she'd regained her strength.

Her knees wobbled and she almost sagged but for a pair of hands that caught her before she could land on the street.

"You look like shit."

The familiar voice and familiar hands made her frown in bewilderment and she tried to decide if she had fallen asleep and wasn't merely dreaming. She forced herself to focus on the head of bright red hair, a thick beard of the same color, and eyes the shade of the winter sky as her rescuer settled her on her feet.

Cassandra continued to stare as she straightened to her full height. She was no slight woman and easily matched the height of most men.

Very few barbarians were this large.

"Skharr," she whispered, shook her head, and uttered a soft, bitter laugh. "The Savage One. I should have known."

"Either you've been struck by the sun or you're happy to see me. I've known a few who grow weak in the knees when they see me but I never thought you were the type."

"Eat shit, you big bastard," she answered and rubbed her eyes. It was most certainly not a dream. There he was, the size of a fucking tree, his hand still on her shoulder to make sure she didn't fall over while he talked to her.

"It is not my preferred meal after a long journey."

She shook her head. "He brought you here, didn't he?"

"If you're referring to Theros…well, yes, although that might imply that he was in any way helpful in bringing me here."

"I guess he didn't bother to transport you across the continent to help?"

"He mumbled something about how gods could not involve themselves in the matters of men or some bollocks like that. Horse and I had to see to our transportation."

He began to direct her into a slow walk to the main hall of the keep but helped to hold her upright as they moved.

"That fucking cheap deified bastard."

"Indeed. The least he could have done was pay for the transportation of all your gifts. I feel like even couriers can expect some kind of gratuity for their service."

Cassandra paused to look at him. "What gifts?"

"Maybe calling them gifts is a little inaccurate since they technically belong to you."

"I've never known you to speak in riddles, barbarian, and it's immediately apparent that it was for a reason. What are you talking about?"

He grinned. "That can wait a while, I think. For the moment, you need to get inside, eat something, and rest before we start that kind of talk. Besides, a little man inside has been worried sick about your return from the moment I arrived."

"Little man?"

# CHAPTER TWELVE

Langven was not a small man by any means, but Skharr towered over most humans, elves, dwarves, and likely more than a few orcs on top of those. This no doubt gave him a reason to single the Ebon Pack captain out as small over all others.

Cassandra liked to think there might have been some jealousy involved, playful though it was. From what she'd heard, Skharr was happily married and expecting a child, although she wasn't sure if they were still expecting or the child was already born.

It seemed to her that he would not leave Sera to bear the little one on her own and likely would not leave her to care for the child while he went riding across the continent—or walking, rather.

She would put her mind to remembering how long it had been since she'd seen him when she'd regained some control over it. Somehow, knowing he was there settled her somewhat and she slept like the dead after eating a bowl of hot soup and a few thick slices of dark bread.

The sun had been up for a few hours already when her eyes opened and she looked out of the window to where troops were going about their business in the keep. They had likely been busy for hours.

There was no telling if there was a reason why folk hadn't woken her as soon as the sun was up, but it appeared that they were waiting for her inside the hall when she arrived.

"Welcome back to the land of the living," Langven called, unable to restrain a grin as he approached her and extended his hand. "We thought you lost to the afterlife."

She could tell there was more meaning to that than simply the joke he tried to make and she ignored the hand and immediately dragged him into a warm embrace.

"I'm sorry," she whispered and buried her face in his shoulder.

"What for?"

"For everything—not listening to you, for…for the men you lost trying to save me. I'm only—"

He pulled away, placed both hands on her shoulders, and smiled. It looked like he hadn't slept well while she had been gone either.

"You did what you thought was right for…for everyone here. I know that. We all do. No apologies are needed."

"Like hell." She realized she was fighting tears back and she looked around the hall and narrowed her eyes. "Where are the twins? Are they all right?"

"They are being tended to by a few of the local physicians, as are the rest of our wounded. From what I heard, you brought Bandir back from almost certain death, but he needs a few days of rest and they say he is nutrient deprived. Tandir had a few wounds become infected on the way back as well, but he is on the road to recovery. They will be fine."

She nodded. Of course Tandir wouldn't have thought to clean his wounds while they were riding, as concerned as he had been for his brother. She knew she should have thought of that before but at least someone had realized her mistake and was tending to them.

"Come," Langven invited her. "We've gathered for a morning meal and you can tell us what you saw."

Cassandra was famished and the smell of food already made her mouth water. It wasn't quite a feast but the smell of sausage, bacon, and eggs being prepared was something that would leave any man, woman, or child of any race with a dull ache in their belly.

Except perhaps high elves. She'd heard they only ate plants, never the products of other living creatures.

She was handed a platter stacked heartily with the food, as well as a few slices of bread that had been fried in the grease left by the cooked meats and made all the better for it. It made her wonder if they used stale bread for the toast, but it did not detract from the meal.

Three-quarters of the way through the platter, she finally realized there were others in the hall when she paused to take a sip of the koffe that was offered to her.

She assumed Skharr was responsible for supplying them with that particular treat since they'd had none of it when she left and it didn't look like any other merchant caravans had made an appearance.

Karvahal and Sifeas had joined Langven and Skharr at the round table. They ate their morning meals and talked quietly between themselves and with aides and soldiers who filed in and out.

It seemed Bandir was not the only one who lacked proper nourishment after their ordeal, although she assumed he'd suffered the worst of it.

"My apologies," she whispered and wiped her mouth carefully with a napkin before she cleared her throat. "I suppose you all have questions about what happened out there."

"Only what you feel you need to tell us," Karvahal answered with a smile. "I think I speak for all of us when I say we are happy to see you alive and recovering your strength."

"I appreciate that," Cassandra answered and took another bite of the sausage. "Our first warning came when we reached a small outpost that appeared to cater to the needs of the local nomads. We spent the night there, which was a mistake as they proved to be in league with the priests of the temple."

"The Ebon Pack reported that they came upon the place," Langven answered. "They mentioned that bodies were found like a massacre had taken place. We assumed it was the work of Karthelon."

"You assumed wrong. They used an oneiromancer to keep us trapped in dreams while they attempted to capture us. We were able to wake before they succeeded, and…well, the whole outpost attacked us. What you saw was the result of us defending ourselves."

They all nodded and she continued with her tale.

"While we were trapped in the dreams, I was sent a…a vision from Theros. He warned me about what was waiting for us and told me that 'the Savage One' was coming to meet us. I now think he meant Skharr but it didn't occur to me at the time and we pressed on. I suppose we should have turned back at that point."

"Vision is always improved when looking into the past, my da always told me," Sifeas muttered.

"Maybe. Anyway, we reached the temple after a couple of days of traveling, and hundreds of drakes were waiting for us. Your men likely told you about the narrow path we took to reach it. I thought of retreating then but it was clear that the drakes were waiting for that, so I pressed on…"

Her voice trailed off and Cassandra tried to stay calm. Her sleep had been thankfully devoid of dreams, but even the memory of the eyes, teeth, and the black vapor reaching out to her was enough to make her wish she had her hand on her spear again.

"There was something inside the temple. Like the woman said, a beast that cut like knives in the shadows. I was barely able to escape, and we were caught between the darkness inside the temple pressing out and making for the narrow path. We chose the latter."

"Where my men found you." Langven nodded. "They told me of the drakes but they never came within sight of the temple. The area was too heavily guarded."

"Hundreds of drakes nested there. We were only allowed to get so close to the temple because whatever controlled them wanted us to die at the hands of what waited inside."

"That seems logical." Langven scratched his jaw.

"If I had listened to the warnings from Theros, we could have avoided losing your men like that," she muttered and rubbed her temples. "I only… It's…I don't know how we could have prepared to fight something like that. An army would have had difficulties reaching the temple. It was folly to even try, but I thought I could."

"You must not dwell on that." Skharr moved to sit next to her. "Like the dwarf said, we can all look back and judge the mistakes we made in the past. What matters is that we acknowledge them and move forward. If nothing else, we now at least have some idea of what we'll face from this point."

Langven's eyes narrowed when he saw Skharr rest his hand on her shoulder, and he looked like he wanted to stand and approach them as well. He placed his hands on the arms of his chair like he would push up but quickly thought better of it and sat again, cleared his throat, and looked away.

"Still," Cassandra answered. "Theros gave me all the warnings I needed to direct me to turn back."

"And from the sound of it, he even failed to get that right, the bastard." The barbarian grinned. "He might have simply appeared in your dreams, told you everything, and walked away. No, he plays his games. I'm not saying you're not a bull-headed barbarian, but that's what's brought you through the impossible odds you've faced thus far, from what the litt—what

Langven's told me of what you have done here since you arrived."

Hearing Skharr almost call him small again seemed like enough to spur Langven into action. He stood and moved around the table to sit next to her on the other side from the barbarian.

"If you hadn't gone and the drakes had come and made another attack, there is a good chance that some of my men would have died anyway," the captain told her with a small smile. "Likely a few of the townsfolk as well."

"So what are you saying? That we're doomed either way?"

"I think..." Skharr started, paused, and cleared his throat before he continued. "I think what he's trying to point out is that if you are looking for something to blame yourself for, you'll always find it when you put yourself in your position. If you hadn't gone, you would have blamed yourself for the lives lost that you might have been able to save if you'd attempted to kill Karthelon when you could. There will always be a cost in defeating the evils of this world."

"But this cost was suffered because I made the wrong decision. Hells, the gods themselves tried to warn me."

"Maybe, but that doesn't mean you should stop making decisions. Hells, it doesn't mean that you can, either."

"How can you say that when my decisions are what has not only ended with people dying but also injured my friends and put this whole community at risk?"

Skharr looked like he was a little confused by what she had said. Langven had likely told him about the glowing battle feats she'd accomplished without going into the details of the consequences of what she'd done while fighting Grimm's attacks.

"Because without you making decisions, none of this would have been possible in the first place," the mercenary captain explained and came to the barbarian's rescue. "All these people would be dead or living as slaves under Grimm's fist if you hadn't stepped between him and them. That is the point. Whether we choose to act or not, there will be consequences. You've always been the one to make a stand, make a decision, and act when no others will."

Skharr nodded. "Sometimes, inaction is its own decision."

"That's...I just said that." Langven frowned

"I agreed with you."

There was some tension between the two men and while Cassandra wondered if there had been some contention between the two before she arrived, she could appreciate that they were attempting to put their need to measure dicks aside for her benefit. Still, she wasn't necessarily sure what they tried to accomplish.

It wasn't like they told her what she didn't already know. Maybe they thought reminding her of all the good she'd managed to accomplish would somehow offset the bad.

She took the last mouthful of toasted bread with some egg still on it before she scowled at the two of them. It looked like they made the effort to bring her mind back to the matter at hand and relieve her of the guilt that had wracked her during the ride to Draug's Hill, and she could appreciate it in an odd kind of way. She almost felt like she was outside her body for a moment, looking down on it and somehow able to consider the matter clearly while the rest of her languished in the grip of guilt and the knowledge that folk had died because of her.

In that manner, she could appreciate what they were doing, but the rest of her was not quite ready to release the responsibility for what happened to them. It was a matter for her to deal with on her own and it was not the first time she had felt this way. Of course, the last time she'd felt it, she had chosen to no longer be a paladin and had gone off with a barbarian to fight a damn dragon. At least this time, she knew what she was looking at and even better, she knew how to get through it— kill every damn thing that stood in her path until she felt better.

For now, she needed to wallow. Soon, that would turn to rage she could use as a weapon.

"I made a mistake," she said finally and hated the tremor in her voice.

"That might be true," Skharr replied. "But you can choose to learn from it or let it cripple your ability to make choices in the future. Either way, you cannot change the fact that folk are looking to you and waiting for you to lead them."

That was a painful realization and maybe it was fate that he was there to pick her up when she was low again. Fighters surrounded her, men and women who waited for her to stand and lead them into the dark. Skharr and Langven were right, of course. The officer Mavros, who had led the men who had saved her and the twins, was right as well. This was not about her. It had never been about her.

And she could not give in to despair like she had before.

Cassandra could hear the town in action below and even saw the smoke rise from the blacksmith and the others who needed fire during the day. It wasn't enough to signify that they were under attack, of course, and there were others inside the keep as well. All were people who knew that decisions like the one she had made would have consequences.

But it didn't mean she needed to stop making the choices. Like Skharr said, she had to learn from it and push forward.

"Right, then." The barbarian saw a change in her overall demeanor and slapped her on the back. It was likely meant as an affectionate gesture but the giant of a man hadn't held his strength back and left a dull ache across her shoulder and back where he had struck to remind her of where it had happened. "I suppose now would be as good a time as any to deliver what I was sent with. Theros wanted to ensure that you were properly armed and armored for the battle ahead, and as...interesting as your choice in armor might be, he assumed you had need of something a little more familiar."

She turned to look at him and made sure he was not watching her when she rubbed her shoulder where he had no doubt caused a bruise.

"What are you talking about?"

Skharr did not explain and instead, lifted a package from what appeared to be a saddlebag. Horse had likely been the one to carry it all the way, which meant she owed the beast more thanks for delivering it than the warrior. Still, it looked heavy, even though he held it with one hand. The other held another package carefully wrapped in leather that was meant to protect whatever was inside from the elements.

She tilted her head as he placed both on the table and turned away, probably to collect something else that he had to deliver to her. Cassandra leaned closer and started to peel away the tanned hide from the smaller package first. A single touch immediately told her what it was before it was even uncovered. It stirred the feeling of meeting with an old friend, speaking to them, and exchanging stories about what had happened since the last time that they were together.

The helmet was familiar enough. The barbute design had been perfectly fitted to her head and it was light enough but provided her with all the protection she might have needed in a battle. Of course, many dangers could penetrate the plate steel, but as much as she trusted the amulet to keep her protected, there were limits to it, the kind proper armor would not have.

She did not need to look into the other package to know what was within. Her paladin armor was difficult to miss and was designed to be as imposing as it was useful in a fight. The breast-plate was made to be as protective as it could be without impeding her movement and fitted perfectly into her shoulder pauldrons and the placart. Each one moved over the other like a fish's scales. The vambraces were there as well, and beneath it all, as added protection, a hauberk of steel rings was intended to cover her to where her greaves rose to her knees.

It wasn't light by any means, but she knew better than to think that plate armor was too heavy for a trained fighter to move around in easily. With training, it had little effect on one's stamina during a long battle.

Better still, the armor was charmed. Each piece, large or small, had been touched by spells to make them stronger and lighter, to prevent them from being deformed under strikes, and to maintain their usefulness without the need to be attended to like other suits of armor demanded.

Cassandra ran her fingers lightly over the metalwork. Even before Theros put his hands on it, a certain care and skill in the crafting of it made her assume that whoever had designed it genuinely cared about the quality of their work.

"It is truly magnificent," Sifeas whispered and approached the armor once it was exposed on the table for all to see. "If I may?"

She gestured for him to feel free to do as he pleased and allowed the dwarf to pick the helmet up.

"Let me guess," she said as he inspected the work. "Fine quality for human hands?"

"I daresay even dwarf hands should be proud to produce armor of this quality." He replaced the helmet, lifted the hauberk, and held it close so he could inspect the rings. "My specialty falls in the crafting of stone, but I have many members of my family who would like to study this. They would be able to tell me if there are any flaws but I cannot find one. It is truly exquisite."

"I'll take your word for it," she replied. "It survived dragon fire at one point and has been repaired since."

"I would wager that the same hands that crafted it were those that repaired it, in that case. I cannot even see where it might have been damaged."

Cassandra leaned forward and tapped a place on the breast-plate where the silver assumed a blueish hue. "It was marked with the dragon fire there and had warped to press against my chest and directly transfer the heat of the flames. The healers at the temple of Theros needed a blacksmith to help to remove it from me."

Skharr winced visibly at the description. He knew what she was talking about better than most, probably. She had been lucky, of course. The other paladins who had been with her when the dragon attacked had worn armor similar to hers and they had died screaming.

"If you think the armor is impressive," the barbarian announced as he approached with what she assumed was the last package intended for her, "wait until you see this beauty."

The protective leathers were pulled aside and he handed the sword to her. She knew what it was and a sense of excited anticipation thrilled as she took it in her hands and drew it smoothly from its sheath.

Her gaze studied the pale silver steel that glinted coldly in the dim light of the hall. The hilt was crafted in ivory and carved to fit her hands perfectly with ridges to make sure she had a solid grasp on it even when blood and sweat covered her hand. The crossguard was bronze and steel intertwined in a thick braid that ended in a smooth diamond shape. This led directly to the long, leaf-shaped, double-edged blade, marked only with the runes that were required to maintain the spells that ran almost the full length of the steel.

The blade itself was forty inches long, matched with a seven-inch hilt. She had measured it on the night she spent in the temple with nothing else to do but sit. Of course, she had been supposed to pray and supplicate Theros for his help, but she had gone through all the prayers and supplications she knew twice in as many hours, which allowed her the time to inspect the weapons and armor she would wear for the next decade or so.

It was lighter than it looked and could be handled with one or both hands, although Cassandra knew she was more skilled when she used it with both. There was once a time when she was quite proud of the skill with which she wielded the weapon.

"I almost didn't bring either," Skharr admitted as he sat again as if to leave her to reacquaint herself with it. "I was half-sure you wouldn't want them but I didn't want to have to deal with the smug old bastard condemning me with his 'I told you so.'"

She narrowed her eyes at him and directed the point of her sword slowly toward him. "So the fact that I might or might not need them never played into your calculations. You merely did not want to be proven wrong by a god."

He shrugged. "We all have our ways to reach the right sum."

Cassandra lifted her blade again and paused before she rested it delicately over her fingers in the way she had many times over the years to ensure that the balance was perfect. Of course, it always was. "I'm not sure if that is the way arithmetic is calculated. Then again, I am not a bearded academic who's spent so much time reading old books that he's started to look like one. I shan't complain."

Skharr grinned but a commotion at the entrance of the hall interrupted before he could answer. Guards entered quickly behind a young man in the Ebon Pack's garb who looked like he had ridden a long way with little rest and almost no food as he approached the table.

"Captain!" he shouted but paused when he realized the presence of a large group. His gaze lingered a little longer on Skharr, likely the only one at the table he had not met, but he turned his attention immediately to Langven. "I have urgent news from Torsburch. A group of raiders threaten to occupy the city in sufficient numbers to pose a risk. The town elders have requested aid in the form of fighters to fend them off. It is...they bear the mark of Grimm and carry his banner as well."

"There's nothing better than having new armor while fighting a group of raiders," Skharr told Cassandra. "You might want to position yourself at the front of that skirmish to let some of that rage I see building inside you out."

"Don't pretend you aren't coming as well, barbarian," she

responded and a smile curled her lips upward as she sheathed her sword smoothly again. "Tandir and Bandir will be crestfallen that they cannot join us. I know they would be honored to fight alongside the most famous DeathEater."

"For now," he muttered and shook his head. "I'd heard you'd fallen in with DrakeHunters, the poor bastards."

"Be nice. They have fought alongside me for a while. I trust them, and they are my friends."

He nodded. "Aye. That is what makes them unfortunate."

"Fuck you."

The giant laughed. "Well, I have a feeling they will have the opportunity to fight before too long."

# CHAPTER THIRTEEN

"I suppose there's no reason to try to talk you into increasing your pace?" Cassandra asked.

Skharr looked at her and raised an eyebrow. "I see no point in pushing too hard. It would take an army a few days to fight through the walls at Torsburch with more than enough time for us to intervene. The town is less than two days from Draug's Hill if we are on a leisurely stroll. It took that scout less than a day to reach us. I would imagine we are somewhere in the middle, and there's no reason to push ourselves to the point of exhaustion. What good will that do to the good citizens of Torsburch?"

"And here I thought you merely didn't approve of the kind of town it is."

He smirked. "I have all kinds of respect for towns like that. I spent more time than I would care to admit in some exactly like it."

"How closely did those towns resemble Torsburch, precisely?"

"What are you asking?"

"I am asking," she clarified with mocking patience, "if there are tales of a giant of a beast who refused to ride his horse and who terrorized the area when you saw little point in following any kind of morality."

"Memories in towns like this don't last very long. If there are such tales, I would imagine the people who remembered them have long since moved on, either as better opportunities presented themselves, or...well, let's be honest, they likely died before they could spread the stories."

Cassandra looked at the group of Ebon Pack warriors Langven had sent with them to help shore up the defenses of Torsburch. "I guess there might not be much for us to do other than step in and fight the bastards. We both know you're worth a small army in your own right."

"Not if I have to rush there. At least, not without a moment's rest. There was a time when I could charge across half the continent and still be ready and willing to fight any I encountered. I find myself...uh, not quite the man that I used to be."

That made sense. It would happen to all of them at some point, but she still had no idea how old he was. It was said that barbarians had some elf blood in them that allowed them to live longer than most humans, but she believed that to be largely rubbish. Still, there was no real explanation for the phenomenon. It wasn't as though they put in the effort to extend their lives like many others did. Too many of them ended up dead in some battle or another but those who survived, like him, inevitably fought battle after battle for decade after decade.

If there was some elf blood in him, she would have to be the one to inform him of it. Cassandra wanted to see his face when she revealed it.

"You and Langven, then?"

She coughed and almost fell from the saddle before she turned to look at Skharr, who appeared to hold his laughter back. There was no real reason why he would show restraint at this point.

"What?"

"I've watched the good captain. He's a little possessive of you, I noticed, and not quite familiar with the feeling. I wager he doesn't like it and probably makes an effort to make himself look and sound as removed from the possibility as he can. And still… well, I noticed it first when he described his adventures with you. The way he worried about your well-being was also telling. And again, it showed when he noticed me close to you and tried to approach as well."

"I don't know what you're suggesting."

"Sure you do. You look at him the same way too, although you're a little better at hiding it. I wager it's all that paladin training."

Cassandra tried to laugh but it was apparent that he wanted to keep the conversation as serious as he could, which was likely why he didn't laugh when she almost fell off her horse.

"I'll admit to certain…well, affections there. And I've noticed that he feels the same way about me."

"Have you told him that you and I fucked?"

"The matter never arose. Why? Do you feel jealous?"

She didn't like how he smirked at her when she said that.

"I've never been the type to feel possessive of other people. Maybe I will be someday. No, I merely wasn't sure why he felt like he needed to be there when I was with you. I assumed it was because you told him we'd fucked, but I guess he might have come to the conclusion on his own. He wouldn't ask, of course. Once a knight, always a knight, especially when they're that type, but he'll feel threatened. I think I might have brought about a change in his perception of you and he might profess his feelings to you shortly if only to ensure that he doesn't lose you for want of opportunity."

"What the hell are you talking about?"

"He might have felt like it was not something either of you would be interested in—love, romance, that kind of thing. I suppose he could have assumed that something might happen between you two if you were both drunk and the opportunity arose, but he did not want to force it otherwise. As things stand now, however, he might fear that you will fall back into bed with me and any opportunity he might have in the future would be lost. So, with that in mind, he might make a grand gesture to ensure that the chance to romance you is not lost forever."

"Oh." Cassandra scowled as she considered this. "I don't like that."

"I thought you did entertain the possibility?"

"Well, yes, I did, but I've seen knightly grand gestures. They are cloying, annoying, and expect a response immediately or hearts are broken. That wouldn't do at all."

"In that case, might I suggest that you make the gesture first? You do want to and it would ensure that it is under your control."

She turned her scowl on him. "You see a little too much but… I'll think about it. Thank you for bringing it to my attention."

"A man as old as I am learns a little too much. The difficult way, too."

"And how old are you, precisely?"

"Honestly? I've lost count."

She snorted and shook her head since she didn't believe that for a second.

---

It would, he reasoned morosely, likely be his luck forever. Others had always told him that his luck in games of chance meant he would have none of it in the realm of love, and Langven had scoffed at the notion, but his time around the barbarian princess had begun to sway his opinion on the matter. It was an uncomfortable realization but when he considered it, the more the idea of a life alongside Cassandra appealed to him.

He wouldn't deny that it had been years since he'd considered the possibility of romance, but something existed between them —chemistry, he'd heard it called.

Now that he had sent her off with a man she clearly cared for and appeared to have some physical connection to, he knew there was no chance that the massive barbarian would not try to find his way back into her breeches. He'd seen the way Skharr looked at her. Lust was obvious in his eyes, but the captain promised himself that he would never be that type. She was not the kind to ascribe physical intimacy to anything more than what it was and he'd thought he felt the same way.

"Fucking hell," he whispered. "I should have gone with them."

Karvahal could have taken control of the defenses in his absence and they would have returned in a matter of days.

"You're being an idiot. Stop acting like this."

He didn't like it. Jealousy was an ugly feeling and he'd always thought himself immune to it, yet it twisted in his stomach and all but tore a hole in it. Langven hated that he felt a very physical pain over it, but he could think of no solution other than trying to find some way to show her how he felt and hope she felt the same way. He would respect her decision either way, but while she likely knew how he felt about her, he suspected she was waiting for some kind of clear signal from him.

Logic dictated that this was what he needed to do—provided she and the barbarian weren't together by the time they returned, and maybe even then. He had no high moral ideals that might dissuade him.

The sun had begun to set and the mercenary captain realized that it was his job to find the patrols that returned at the end of the day and ensure that those who kept watch during the night had the right orders for it. Instead, he was sitting around and pining after a woman.

He needed to find a way to ensure that he was focused from here on out. While he had been worried about her survival for most of the time after she had left to kill the god, he could not afford to have folk think she was the sole focus of his attentions.

"Nothing to report on the rounds, captain," one of his pack snapped when she saw him stride to where the patrols were coming in. "Still, there was...something."

Langven paused in his step and turned to face the young woman. "Something?"

"It was only a feeling, sir. I'm not sure how to explain it. I would not mention it but the other men felt it too—a general sense of unease while we were heading back. I don't know how to describe it, but you ordered us to return with all the information we could gather and it seemed pertinent."

A feeling. He knew better than to disregard the instincts of his soldiers but at the same time, if he issued orders based on feelings, folk would start to question his fitness as their captain.

"I'll keep that in mind, Lieutenant."

"You must think I'm mad."

"Well, yes, but that is a separate issue. I encourage you all to listen to your instincts on this. We are fighting an enemy who will find all kinds of ways to attack us, and I don't want any warnings to be disregarded on the basis that you think I don't want to hear it."

She smiled and nodded. "That's appreciated, sir."

"Get something to eat and rest. You'll be on patrol early tomorrow."

She saluted and moved to where they had set up an improvised barracks for both his soldiers and those who were under Karvahal's banner to call home while they were inside the walls.

Langven narrowed his eyes when he saw the twins seated in the courtyard in front of the gate, chatting to a handful of the scouts before they headed out. Both jumped to their feet when they saw him, which likely meant they had been waiting for him to make an appearance. He had a feeling he knew what they wanted.

"Langven," Bandir said and appeared a little more recovered than he had been the day before. "We would like to have word with you."

"I don't have any say in what Cassandra and Skharr do, aside from sending them with an escort. It was her decision to leave and let the two of you recover. Besides, it is a simple matter of raiders—one that likely needed to be addressed but will not be the focus of our efforts here."

"She rides off with another barbarian." Tandir shook his head. "Do you think we're being replaced, my brother and I?"

He didn't want to say it but Langven couldn't help but relate.

"She'll be back," Bandir answered. "Last I heard, Skharr has taken lordship of some territory or another, thanks to being friends with the emperor. He has himself a wife and a child on the way from what she told us when she last met him. He'll leave again and she won't join him. It's too cushy a life for someone like her."

The mercenary captain had not heard that himself and he decided that it could be good news. Skharr was not a permanent addition, although from what he knew of lords and ladies, there was little to their marriage vows, especially if the marriage happened to be one of convenience.

Perhaps he wanted to convince Cassandra to join him and be his mistress. It would be an offer that she would likely turn down if he knew her at all.

"You two wished to speak to me?" Langven asked and raised an eyebrow now that he was more or less settled about the matter that had been on his mind before.

"Well, assuming Cassandra and Skharr are delayed, we would not want to be stuck in the keep with naught to do but twiddle our thumbs in the meantime," Tandir answered with a firm nod. "All play and no work is set to turn us mad if you understand. We might need to find work to do among your men if you need two pairs of hands for it."

MICHAEL ANDERLE

He could understand that too. The two barbarians lived a life of eternal movement for a reason, after all.

"I'll see what I can do to get the two of you on the roster while she's gone," he promised and placed a hand on both their shoulders. "But in the meantime, you are still recovering from horrendous injuries. You'll not want to rush into battle before you're fully recovered."

"If we're honest…" Bandir paused, cleared his throat, and looked around before he leaned a little closer. "I think we would be less inclined to physical exertion if we were to join your men on patrols than if we remained here."

The captain narrowed his eyes. "Explain."

"Word has spread among the local womenfolk about the… well, stamina of barbarians, and they have come looking for a taste even while we are in the infirmary."

"You know you can simply send them on their way, right?"

"Of course. But it's a challenge no barbarian would back down from unless he or she were on the brink of death."

Langven paused, shook his head, and tried to not think too hard about what that could possibly mean. Barbarians were famously promiscuous, but he'd always been under the impression that the attraction only went one way until he heard stories about Skharr the Barbarian and how even high-born ladies wanted a taste of him.

Perhaps he had reason to be worried about Cassandra riding into the sunset with the barbarian who refused to ride his horse named Horse.

Still, he couldn't help but laugh at the problems the twins reported.

"Well, I'll see what I can do to help. Until then, get your rest. Or…lack of rest, as it were."

Both twins turned toward the infirmary, and the mercenary grinned and fought his laughter back as he ascended the steps of the wall. He counted at least three patrol groups that still hadn't made an appearance, and he waited for them to arrive. If too many of them went missing, he needed to make the assumption that they were being killed and hadn't simply headed off to Torsburch to spend their coin, only to return and report that they hadn't seen anything.

It was a growing problem but one he allowed at the moment since it meant more men patrolling the road between the towns.

A few of the troops had returned, although they appeared to have paused in the town below before they came to give their reports. The sun was already setting and since there appeared to be no hurry in their steps, he could assume they had no news of concern. While it was good to know, he couldn't help feeling that everything was a little too easy. A trap had been set for Cassandra, and nothing had come of it aside from the death of a few of his men. While that certainly carried weight, he doubted that Karthelon cared much about it. He wanted the Barbarian Princess.

Unfortunately, there was no sign of what he might do next to try to find her.

The sun finally set and left the moon and stars to emerge. It was a full moon, which meant the whole of the grasslands around them were easy to watch over. Even the cloud cover that had marked the arrival of the drakes was gone, which meant that if something attacked them from the skies, it would be seen from miles away.

Which begged the question of why he felt so uneasy. Maybe it was from the patroller's conversation about something being wrong. That seemed reasonable enough. If they spoke to him about being uneasy, he would no doubt feel the same way, but his instincts sensed something more to it.

Langven rested his hand on his sword as he looked into the moon-washed darkness and tried to discern what the internal warning could be about. Part of him wondered if this was merely another sign of his distraction over Cassandra. If so, he had to return to being the type of person capable of leading the Ebon Pack.

His gaze flicked to the moon and he narrowed his eyes and tried to decide whether he was merely being paranoid for no reason. Still, he could have sworn he saw something move in the blackness above, even though nothing appeared in his immediate range of vision.

The sunlight was completely gone, of course, but the stars were still in place and as he leaned in a little closer, a handful of them appeared to go out at a time but reappeared quickly. Something was moving in the sky. It wasn't particularly small by the looks of it, but it seemed to be too far away for it to be any kind of threat. Still, caution dug itself into the back of his mind and he continued to watch the shadow's approach.

It grew ever larger, although it was still miles away. When it flickered across the moon again, he knew what it was. Very few creatures looked like real dragons when in flight. Drakes always came close but it was easy to identify them since their bodies looked a little more like bats and they tended to be smaller. Whatever this was must be considerably larger. He watched it arc in its flight and climb a little before it slowly righted itself and settled into a direct trajectory toward the keep.

"Oh, fuck," Langven whispered. "Raise the alarm! Alarm! We're under attack!"

He waved frantically to the two men who kept watch in the tower close to where he stood, and they looked around quickly and tried to identify something that advanced along the ground. Finally, they realized where he was pointing and noticed the massive shadow that closed the distance with impressive speed as it soared toward them.

One man snatched the horn up and blew into it to make sure the alarm was relayed across the fortress. It was echoed immediately by the rest of the watchtowers, although the mercenary captain wasn't sure if it was because they'd seen the dragon or if they merely made sure that an alarm was raised without checking.

It didn't matter. He already had his sword out, although he wasn't sure precisely what it could do against a beast of that size. In all honesty, he had no idea if they could do anything against one that size. All the stories of battling dragons told of finding the creature in its lair after it had attacked the landscape. Unlike drakes, they were reported to have armor that unenchanted weapons had no chance against and breathed anything from fire to ice to deadly effect. This creature appeared to dwarf even those he'd heard about.

He was already scrambling down from the walls when something pounded him on the back like a hurricane and hurled him from the steps to the courtyard below and he heard a thunderous crash. By some miracle, he barely managed to catch himself, landed on his feet, and rolled over the cobbles while he protected his face as he had been taught so many years before as the correct way to fall from a horse. The drop was significantly higher, however, and his shoulders, arms, and legs ached from the impact.

Still, he'd survived and now realized that the dragon had managed to slow itself in time to avoid a collision with the fortress but created a wind that was powerful enough to fling him from the steps like a piece of straw.

A moment later, Langven registered the fact that the dragon had crashed into the first tower to raise the alarm. It had likely only slowed to prevent injury to itself, but the monster had managed to somehow demolish the whole tower with the impact. The pieces of the structure plummeted into the keep and killed the two men who had been inside, although he couldn't see if more were dead in the courtyard. Somehow, the darkness had grown considerably heavier and he struggled to see anything.

Screams and shouts to locate friends and family came from all around him. Fires began to spread and folk rushed out to try to discover where the attack had come from. Others had already stepped forward to help the injured.

The eyes drew his attention. He wasn't sure how he'd missed them at first. Bright green, they gleamed in the darkness that appeared to radiate from it. The beast was still perched atop the tower it had destroyed almost effortlessly and traced its gaze across the earth like it was looking for something. The way the lights from the fires, moon, or stars failed to illuminate it unsettled him the most. It was almost like a black cloud of vapors looked at them and simply watched and waited for something to attack it.

Langven studied it for a long moment and decided it was looking for something. It scanned the grounds and waited for its target to appear.

Given the black vapors that seeped from its skin like a cloud —enough to remind him of the beast Cassandra had described seeing inside Karthelon's temple—he could only assume it was the same creature and it was there to finish the work the drakes near the temple had failed in. It begged the question of why it had waited so long, of course, or why it had not surged from the temple when she was there, but he would ask the fucking thing when he had its head mounted in the hall of the keep.

"Oy!" the captain shouted, drew the attention of his men, and directed them to the beast as he picked up a spear that lay across the street, likely dislodged from where it had been stored under the tower. He reversed it quickly in his grasp and took a step forward to launch it with all the power he could put into it. The weapon flew true, arced smoothly, and streaked into the beast at the center of the cloud of vapor.

He stared as the spear splintered on impact, but it told him that something large and armored was at the center of the cloud. They weren't dealing with a creature that was merely vapors.

Its attention turned to him almost immediately, but a handful of archers had already launched their projectiles at it. They did not appear to have any better luck than his spear had, and a dull roar issued from the beast. He wasn't sure how he could feel it more than hear it and it rattled the ground like an earthquake. His bones ached and his ears screamed in pain but all he could honestly claim to hear was a low wail.

Still, the beast had announced its presence as it elevated from the tower with heavy wingbeats that spread the vapors across the keep. Whatever it was comprised of began to seep into his skin. He was filled with the same sense of dread the rest of his patrollers had reported feeling during the day but amplified beyond anything he'd ever experienced. His knees felt weak and his stomach roiled uneasily as he reached for the sword he'd dropped when he was flung from the walls.

For a moment, he saw the creature in all its glory. It might have been a dragon once but dark magic had seeped into it to the point where he had no idea what they faced at all. His every instinct as the creature swept onto the keep was to run—much like Cassandra had felt when she had faced it, he assumed.

While a part of him somehow still managed to think clearly, the purely reflexive part of him reacted before he realized it was happening and he was already running as the beast settled into the keep. It did not appear to breathe fire but claws and fangs lashed out from within the darkness and claimed anyone who happened to be standing in front of it.

Langven came to a halt outside the workshop the dwarves used and forced himself inside instead of simply rushing past it and as far away from the monster as he could get.

Inside, a group of the dwarves clutched their weapons but they appeared to be in no position to use them as they cowered in the corner. Whatever was in the vapors affected them as well and seeing them afraid was enough for him to drag himself from the terror that seeped through his every limb.

"Sifeas!" he whispered when he realized the beast was just outside. No, that was a delusion from the vapor. It was nowhere close to where they stood. "Come on out, you bearded shit. I need your help!"

"What…what do you need?"

"Your supplies. I know you use chemicals to blast the rocks out from under the keep. I think that will be enough for us to at least put up a fight against the beast."

"Wha…" The dwarf needed a moment to gather his senses. He looked at the door where more screams could be heard and the oddly unheard roar made the ground shake whenever it was uttered. "We cannot fight that. We need to…to hide and wait for it to move on."

"Take hold of yourself!" Langven snapped and caught the dwarf by the shoulders. "Can you hear what you're saying? We will fight and we will win, but you need to fucking help me. Now, where is that blasting powder?"

The dwarf still looked like he was a hairsbreadth away from his courage deserting him completely. His hands shook and his teeth chattered, but he turned, looked through the shelves, and pulled out a heavy metal container that he placed carefully on a table nearby.

"It'll blast with an impact," Sifeas explained. "We usually use a blasting hammer to keep us far enough away, but…but…"

"But what?" The mercenary captain tried to curb the impatience in his voice.

"Well, we have these pods." He pulled out a group of small copper balls that were hollowed out and he began to pour the powder carefully into one before he sealed it. "Throw them at the fucker and they should blast. I don't know if they'll do any good but they will likely grab its attention."

"Good enough." Langven waited for the dwarf to finish two of the pods and took them warily. From the way the mason handled them, he could only assume there was every chance that the powder inside would rip his hands apart if he jerked them around too hard. He inched toward the door, nudged it open with his boot, and peered out to determine where the beast was.

He could feel the steps it took and the roars. Hells, he could practically hear it breathing in his ear, and it was all he could do to not snap around, convinced that he would find those eyes looking at him.

It took tremendous effort to stop his body from shaking as he forced himself to walk toward the source of the black vapor instead of away from it. Finally, the claws lashed out at a member of his pack a short distance away from where he stopped. He recognized the young woman, the scout he'd spoken to who had told him about the bad feeling she couldn't shake.

The claws caught her around her midsection and in a second, she was split in two. Her legs fell, and most of her torso suddenly tumbled across the ground, followed by sprays of viscera.

Somehow, that made him angrier than anything else. The beast didn't merely kill his people but slaughtered them as a means to an end and didn't even bother to eat the dead. With ghastly disinterest, it left the bodies strewn across the cobbles as it continued to move. It could have flown over them to reach what it was looking for but instead, it strolled across the courtyard at a leisurely pace and cut down any who were caught in its path. Others of the Pack, of Karvahal's men, and even the locals who had nothing to do with the fight were felled when they were left unable to fight as the vapors appeared to overcome them.

They dropped their weapons, sank to their knees, and tried to shield themselves. Whatever black magic was in the fucking mist, it addled their minds and left them defenseless while the dragon savaged them without a thought.

There was no mystery as to why that made him angry. The only question in his mind was why it had taken him so long to reach that point. He screamed defiance, took a step forward, and hurled the first of the pods across the courtyard. It exploded as it made impact with the beast's back and showered sparks in a wide radius. The blast was strong enough that he felt it at fifteen paces away and for a moment, it appeared that it had driven the vapor away and allowed him to see the creature for what it was. It looked gaunt and emaciated like what it was doing drained the very life from it.

The eyes turned to him. The air filled with blackness again but there was something different. It was like a spell had been broken in him and the rest of the fortress. The fear was gone and more of the men began to shout, throw spears, and launch arrows at the beast. Langven felt the change. While he'd been crushed by overwhelming dread before, all he could feel now was rage and something like bloodthirsty anticipation. Fighting the beast was all he had to do. He needed to fight for his people and with his people.

With slow menace, it turned to face him, its fury immediately apparent as it moved across the ground at a terrifying speed to reach him. The mercenary captain was waiting and ready. He took another step forward and threw the second of the pods directly into the creature's face. Although he had been able to stop it from destroying his hand long enough, the blast was stronger than anticipated and especially this close. Bits and pieces of the copper of the casing sliced his right cheek, but the beast took the most damage. Once the smoke had cleared, he could only see one eye but felt the roar it uttered that was enough to make his chest ache.

He could hear it as well, an animal in pain, but he was far from capable of feeling remorse for the injury he'd inflicted. Its wings lashed out and knocked back those who were a little too close to it, including Langven. He was thrown off his feet and into a small cart that held cabbages, tomatoes, and other vegetables that thankfully cushioned his fall. The beast was on the move. It was no longer leisurely and clearly felt threatened, but it did not run away. The wings flapped, carried it up, and moved it to the other side of the keep, looking for something.

Its tail swished downward to catch a few more of his men as it flew low and directly toward the infirmary.

What could it be looking for there?

This was not the time for curiosity. He pushed himself out, tossed aside a few squashed tomatoes that clung to him by the stems, and sprinted to where it had pounded through the walls of the building and undone weeks of work by the dwarves in less than a second.

"Attack it!" Langven shouted and waved his men forward. Sifeas handed out more of the pods and shouted at the men and women carrying them to be careful as they could blow up at the wrong time and kill them all.

The fear that had tormented the whole keep was suddenly replaced by anger and rage, and his men hurled spears and rocks at the creature as it attacked something inside the infirmary.

Their reactions were a reflection, he realized in a sudden moment of clarity. The vapors were used to project something into those who were under its influence but as the beast was injured, it had less control. Its rage was what now stirred the rest of the keep into a fury to attack it.

Perhaps it was madness to even think this, but it was the only thing that could explain the change that had come over the defenders. He grasped his sword firmly and opened himself willingly to the fury that drove him to kill the beast before it could take more of his men.

In that moment, the dragon jerked away from the building and destroyed a few more walls on its way out. It appeared to have received more injuries to its wings, chest, and limbs. The mercenary captain only needed a moment to realize how that was possible.

"Come along, then, you big pile of shit! Come see what a DrakeHunter does against dragons!"

"Aye, you bit off a bit more than you could chew with us, now didn't ya?"

The twins rushed out of the infirmary, their weapons coated in the creature's blood. They had been wounded as well but did not appear to let it give them pause as they pursued the beast. It might not have been the wisest choice but if there was ever a time to attack, it was now when its vapors didn't have their intended effect and it was wounded.

Its wings whipped again, caught the twins across the chest, and catapulted them into the infirmary before it spun to face the humans who tried to encircle it. Another roar issued from it, but this one was more powerful. Langven could feel it press into him and his mind in an attempt to close him off from his senses. In the next moment, he felt the dread again, the unspeakable, unknowable fear that made him want to curl into himself and never rise again.

He could tell that his men felt it as well. All of them fell back, screamed, and covered their ears as the beast tore through them. Fangs like daggers and claws like swords, ripped them to pieces as it finally allowed itself to indulge its need for violence.

Thankfully, enough of his anger remained to drive him forward. He screamed almost as much in fear as anything else as he drew his second sword, lashed out, and sliced the beast's wings away from him, then ducked as its claws reached for him. The vapors in his body fought his every movement and weakened him from the inside, but he refused to be drawn into it. He knew now that creature had come there for Cassandra. Her scent had been on the twins, but she was not there.

The beast hated them all for it. It felt cheated and it wanted them to know what came from cheating it of its prey.

Langven had no idea how he knew that or how his mind had suddenly melded with the creature's. It had felt it too and immediately latched onto him and pounced before he could get out of the way. Fangs, dripping with black venom, sank into his shoulder and he screamed in pain as he was lifted off his feet. The massive beats of the monster's wings carried them high. There was no reason for it to not kill him immediately, except that maybe it had something more painful in mind for him.

He wouldn't let it win. While he couldn't move the arm that was trapped in the creature's jaws, one hand was free. He twisted his body, gasped as his flesh was torn by the fangs, and thrust hard to drive his sword into its eye.

The attempt failed. It blinked in time and his blade bounced off the armored scales. Perhaps it was painful but not enough. He groaned, twisted, and realized that they were still close enough to the ground. If he could force it to drop him, he was reasonably sure he would survive.

His gaze moved to the other eye that he'd managed to strike with one of the dwarf's pods. The scales were still mostly in place, but a few had been knocked loose and blood seeped from the wound. It wasn't much but would be enough.

Screams dragged from his throat and he almost changed his mind. His teeth gritted, Langven stretched his free hand up to grasp the monster and drag himself higher and, with all the power he could summon, he drove his sword through the wound.

Dragon shrieks now joined his. He heard them rumble from deep inside the creature's chest and its jaw moved again and dropped open. The ground approached him rapidly and he braced himself as he landed hard on the cobbles. Something was broken—perhaps many somethings—but the fight wasn't over. Arrows were loosed and the beast pounded through the gate-house and damaged the stonework that remained there before it began to climb again. Wingbeats snapped their force like thunderclaps as it climbed out of the range of the arrows, away from the spears, and higher into the sky before it banked away.

Langven watched to ensure that it didn't decide to circle to attack the town below, but it continued away from the town and from them all and finally disappeared into the night sky.

"We...we need to go after it," he yelled and looked at the rest of the men. "We cannot let it escape."

"It's already escaped, Captain. You—are you all right?"

He paused and looked around him. Given the beast's size, he was surprised it hadn't simply torn him to pieces like the others. Instead, he had been lifted carefully and the almost delicate touch was still enough to tear through most of his shoulder. But things were worse than that. His wound dripped with the same black venom he'd seen on its teeth and it began to show in his veins that spidered under his skin.

"Captain?"

The stones hadn't been that close before. He was practically kissing them so must have fallen. But he couldn't sleep now, as much as he wanted to. He needed to warn Cassandra.

"Got...to warn...her..."

# CHAPTER FOURTEEN

"This wasn't the kind of troop one might think was capable of taking a town like Torsburch." Skharr sounded scornful.

Cassandra shrugged. "I don't know. Folk around here don't see many real armies, and it isn't like Torsburch is that well-defended either. The stockades are more of a deterrent against the smaller groups of bandits who might think they could tear through, but I would wager that the three hundred or so we found marching on it would have been able to take the town if they had been left unchallenged. It was as close to an organized army as they might have ever faced. If we hadn't arrived, Torsburch would likely have been lost to us."

He chuckled softly as they continued. She glanced at the fighters they still had with them. The barbarian might have been right to show some derision. As skirmishes went, it had been over rather quickly. The deserters had the advantage of numbers but he had called on the members of the Ebon Pack to join them in raiding their camp as the sun was rising. They'd made the mistake of camping a little too close to the town, no doubt confident of their numerical advantage, and had failed to establish scouts or any kind of watch.

They'd attacked while most of the group were still sleeping and it soon became a rout. Of the three hundred who started among them, she calculated that about half had been killed in the battle. A few dozen had managed to escape, and the rest had immediately surrendered. They'd left the Ebon Pack to collect what loot had been left by the enemies as payment for their efforts. She had retrieved a couple of purses to pay the twins with since they would have wanted to join her in this fight as well.

It would be a peace offering so they would know that even though she fought alongside another barbarian, she had not forgotten them.

She had been surprised that Skharr hadn't taken anything for himself. From their past experiences together, she knew for a fact that he was never one to fight for free, but he appeared to have more than even he'd expected since he'd assumed the lordship of whatever lands the emperor had given him. His clothes were overall of higher quality than what she had seen him wear before and his armor was better as well. Instead of relying on whatever gambeson he'd found that fit him with a little work, he wore dwarf-made armor that she remembered him carrying before.

He didn't have the DeathEater ax to fight with but his sword was certainly one hell of a replacement and he had grown more skilled with it. She would have mentioned that he was even a little graceful in handling the weapon, but there was no point in saying it out loud. He would have laughed at her for even thinking that about him.

"Still, it was a nice fight," Skharr said and nodded firmly. "It's a good way to warm the muscles for a real fight to come. I would say you have one of those in mind for us a little further down the line, yes?"

"Of course. I still mean to put Karthelon on his back foot. If he is a god, I would imagine that we cannot kill him unless your lover, the goddess of thieves, was to make an appearance."

"I don't think she's allowed to do that now. And...she's not my lover."

"Truly?"

"Not anymore."

Cassandra grinned and leaned forward to pat Strider on the neck. "Of course, you are sworn to one woman now and with a child on the way too. How is that treating you?"

"It's not quite what I thought would be in store for Skharr DeathEater but not an unpleasant change. Sera knows me well enough to know that I need some freedom, and I've headed into the nearby lands to deal with problems that need a strong hand. I've not looked for mistresses, though, so if you lust after this barbarian, you'll have to look elsewhere."

"Believe me, I have more than enough barbarians to deal with as things stand."

"Ah yes, the twins." Skharr looked at her. "You and they have not...you three wouldn't..."

"Have I bedded them? No. I doubt there is any interest."

"Honestly, when I remember what I was like at their age, I doubt many knowledgeable, educated women would be interested, although they are considerably more mature now than I was then. I suppose they have you to thank for that."

"I can only imagine the kind of mad monster you were when you were barely out of your teens."

He grinned and shook his head. "It feels like centuries ago. I am genuinely embarrassed by what I did then, and I can thank the gods that not many remember. Or, at least, they don't associate me with the giant shit who tried to steal a horse from a nearby army that had been confiscating horses in the area."

"You didn't."

"I did." Skharr nodded grimly. "I caused a stampede that destroyed half their camp before I was caught."

"They didn't kill you for that kind of thing?"

"Well, they tried. The lord leading the army ordered that I be executed in trial by combat. I was naked and unarmed against three of their finest fighters."

"I take it that did not end well for them."

"Indeed not. Three more died after the first three and finally, the lordling decided that since he'd lost six of his best men, it was in his best interests to bring along the dumb shit who managed to kill them all, and thus the legend of Skharr DeathEater was born."

Cassandra laughed and shook her head. "I think I would have wanted to meet you back then."

"I am not sure you would have been born at the time."

"Which means you are at least older than forty."

He extended his arms with a smirk. "And still looking good, eh?"

"Not too bad."

"Oh, and Sera already had the baby."

"She has?"

"Aye. The baby girl will be a month old in a few days and looks every inch the barbarian her father is."

"Well, congratulations." She laughed. "What does Sera think of you rushing halfway across the continent to deliver my armor to me?"

"It's not that far away. Less than a week walking and less than half that for a good rider with a strong horse. And…well, she understands that when Theros calls, there is little one can do but answer."

"But she's on her own caring for the child."

"Please. She's the emperor's sister. She was surrounded by helpers and maids from the day we moved into the castle."

"A castle now, is it?" She smirked.

"Well, I think that is the word for it."

"I see." She found her smile starting to disappear slowly. "What do you think she'll do if you're killed in this fight?"

"What?"

"It is a possibility. You might think of yourself as immortal but you are the same flesh and blood as I am. You must have thought about it before leaving."

"I did," he admitted after a moment's consideration. "And I spoke of it to Sera as well before I left. She did not like the idea but she understood. There is no safety for a DeathEater in this world and I would not be contained inside the walls of a castle like some…prisoner. It is better to die doing something of import than be stabbed in the back by a political rival or another, I think."

"She agreed to this?"

"Aye. And she said that you can expect her to come along and kill you all if I die, so… Well, you had best protect me."

That drew a hearty laugh from Cassandra, although it died quickly as they came over the last of the hills that blocked Draug's Hill from view and she saw the damage to the wall. One of the towers had been destroyed, that much was immediately clear, and she could see that the gatehouse had been practically knocked over by something large. It didn't look like they had fought off the kind of army that would have been required to deliver that kind of damage.

"Skharr…"

"Go on ahead. I'll be right behind you."

If there was ever a time to convince him that he needed to jump on Horse's back, it was now. He remained steadfastly against it but he began to run forward and the stallion trotted behind him. She shook her head and promised herself to address his stubbornness later. First, she needed to find out what the hell had happened to Draug's Hill.

She pushed ahead of the troop and held Strider at a strong pace as she closed the distance and continued past the town at the base of the hill. Members of the Ebon Pack were there, digging what appeared to be graves for the fallen, and they looked up and recognized her but seemed to know that she was needed at the top. She wanted to ask them what had happened but there was no time to spare and Langven would likely be able to give her a better overview of events.

Instead, she followed the winding path that led to the gatehouse that was in the process of being repaired. More groups of the Pack carried the dead on stretchers covered by sheets. Still, there was enough blood to tell her that whatever had happened had resulted in heavy casualties.

Men dug through the rubble of the fallen tower, and claw marks across the insides of the walls and the buildings around displayed all the signs of some kind of monster having made an appearance. She frowned, at a loss as to what was large enough to cause this degree of damage.

"Cassandra!"

The twins approached and rushed to where she dismounted quickly from Strider. Both appeared to have sustained new wounds but were already on the mend and had been deep into the work of rebuilding and constructing what looked like additional defenses.

"What the hell happened?" she asked, examined them hastily, and checked their wounds, which thankfully appeared to be superficial. "Are you all right?"

"We're fine," Tandir answered and pulled her into a warm embrace. "We thought for a while that the beast had left us to go find you when it was finished here."

She pressed herself into their arms, closed her eyes, and silently thanked any gods who happened to be listening to find them still alive. Despite their wounds, she knew they would have involved themselves in any fight there was to be had and likely would have been killed in the process.

"What beast?" Cassandra asked and finally drew back from them.

"I'm not quite sure," Bandir answered.

His twin scowled. "Well...not much in the world can emit black vapors like that."

"Black vapors? It was the monster from the temple?"

"Aye." Tandir nodded. "It looks like a dragon but is filled with black magic. I'm not sure if something like that is still a fucking dragon but I guess in the absence of anything else to call it, the name fits."

He shrugged to finish his thought and she looked around.

"I would have thought it would have done more damage if it attacked."

"It did more than enough damage as it is," Bandir muttered and rubbed his chin. "We were in the infirmary for most of the fight, but the folk who saw it said that it looked like it was looking for something—or someone—and it flew away when it didn't find what it was looking for. Or...uh, who it was looking for."

"It came here looking for me?"

"Well, it might have been looking for us given the way that it barreled into the fucking infirmary. We punished it for rushing into a fight with two DrakeHunters, though."

They were distracted from the conversation and turned as Skharr stepped through the gates as well. He looked like he had maintained a decent pace, although the rest of the Ebon Pack traveling with them had arrived before he did.

Tandir waved the man to where they were standing. "It's best to speak about that later. Langven will want to see you."

Of course. How had she forgotten about him?

"Where is he?"

Bandir nodded, his expression oddly blank. "See for yourself."

They moved to the hall, where it appeared that most of the repair work was being organized. A handful of the men and women raised their hands when they saw her and Skharr, but the grim mood that had settled over the place was unshakeable and she couldn't blame them for it.

Still, the fact that she hadn't seen Langven at the front lines of the repair effort was enough to explain why the Ebon Pack was in low spirits. She stepped into the hall and paused as the Pack's healer rushed out. She stopped when she saw her.

"Cassandra," she said and looked like she hadn't had much sleep over the past few days. "It's good to see you alive and well. We feared…well, we feared the beast had gone to find you when it didn't do so here."

She gripped the woman's wrist and smiled as much as she was able to. "Thank you. How is Langven?"

"Come."

That was about all the answer she would get from anyone, which meant that whatever had happened to him, it was bad. At least it indicated that he was still alive. It brought some comfort to her as she was guided into one of the rooms that had been set up for the injured after the infirmary had been destroyed.

The smell struck her immediately, although Cassandra had certainly smelled worse. A strong, putrid, and yet almost sickly-sweet scent was mixed with at least a dozen herbs that had likely been used to treat the wound. Langven had been settled on a small cot, his shirt cut away and his left arm in a sling and covered in bandages. They looked like they had been freshly applied, but something dark seeped from the wounds beneath.

Still, he was conscious and grinned when he saw her approach, although it faded somewhat when he saw Skharr there as well.

"It's nice of the two of you to join us," he said and his voice emerged in a thick, harsh rasp. "How are matters at Torsburch? I swear the elders there would be frightened by an army of chickens."

"Never mind them," she whispered and lowered herself into the chair next to his cot. "What the hells happened to you?"

"It's funny you should mention the hells because I'm fairly certain the beast came from one of them. Some kind of dragon came here looking for you, and when it couldn't find you, I think it tried to fly away with me as a consolation, or maybe a snack. Either way, I made it pay for it. I put my sword in its fucking eye for the trouble, and it flapped away to lick its wounds."

"The other wounds are healing well," the physician explained. "But those caused by the creature's teeth refuse to seal and I am reluctant to close them with the poison still inside. It… Well, I've treated it every way I know how but I fear this is beyond my skill to heal."

Cassandra leaned forward, touched his bare skin, and closed her eyes as she reached out into the poison that flowed slowly through his body.

She snapped her hand away quickly and felt like she'd been stung. "It's beyond my skill as well. I've seen this kind of poison before. It is—at least in part—divine and needs a divine touch to heal it."

"How long do you think I have left?" Langven asked and sounded a little too comfortable with his impending doom for comfort.

"It's moving slowly but attacks your body everywhere it goes. I would say your liver will likely be the first to fail in a week and…well, days after that."

He nodded and shifted on the cot.

"How do you feel?" Skharr asked and approached slowly.

"Well, the herbs the good healer here gave me help to dull the pain and let me sleep, but…I feel like my body has been drained of energy."

"We need to return to the Utter-Pit," Cassandra stated quietly. She had known it was inevitable, but this soon after their first attempt felt like picking at a raw wound.

"What?" Langven snapped, tried to sit up, winced, and subsided.

"We have to take the venom from the source and use it to craft an antidote," Skharr muttered. "That sounds about right."

"Karthelon would want his dragon's venom to be slow but

inexorable. He would want his victims to suffer as much as possible before death."

"Lucky me," Langven whispered.

"With Mira's efforts, we might be able to help him survive for longer. And by then... Well, we'll have something to help heal him. Do you think you can do that, Mira?"

The physician nodded. "A combination of yarrow and honey applied to the bandages and given to him in tisanes appear to have slowed the effects of the venom but not stopped them, I'm afraid. I'll do what I can."

"You know I'll come with you," Skharr told her.

"I...appreciate it," Langven said, although she wondered if he would say it was not necessary. "A big bastard like you should be able to draw the beast's attention away from Cassandra."

"Aye, that is what I'm best known for. I assume it'll be what gets me killed one day, but it's my nature to push my luck."

The mercenary captain chuckled at that, although it quickly became a harsh cough. Cassandra could see black in what came up, which told her it had already begun to ooze into his lungs.

"We'll join you as well," Tandir declared and took a step forward. "I imagine four barbarians should be enough to defeat the beast. It's only ever fought one or two of us at a time, but Bandir and I managed to do some damage to it. Now, if we're joined by the mighty Skharr DeathEater, I think we have a fighter's chance."

"A fighter's chance is all we need," Skharr responded, drew a deep breath, and patted the wounded man gently on his uninjured shoulder. "Stay alive, little man. We need to find out which of us sings of the Seven Little Wenches and their Orc Companion better. We'll have to think of a wager, but I'll have you beat. I learned the dancing steps from the bard himself."

Langven scowled at her. "You...fucking told him?"

"Of course I did. He was very interested to find out everything about you."

"I wouldn't say very interested," the barbarian muttered.

"I would." Her tone indicated that she would brook no disagreement. "We'll need to leave as soon as possible. Skharr, take the twins and gather all the supplies we might need. I'll check our weapons and the horses and have them prepared for the journey."

He nodded, and the twins joined him as he strode to the door of the hall.

Cassandra leaned forward and pressed her lips to Langven's cheek. She closed her eyes at the touch before she finally drew back.

"You had better fucking survive until I get back," she whispered and pressed her fingers over where her lips had left their mark.

"A kiss from the Barbarian Princess should keep me alive at least until then," he answered with a smile.

# CHAPTER FIFTEEN

"So…" Skharr didn't look at her as he broke the silence

"What?"

"No, nothing."

"Skharr, you've never been one to shut your mouth before so why would you start now? Spit it out." Cassandra curbed her impatience, knowing it was more a reaction to the stress of the task ahead than anything else

The giant barbarian nodded slowly but still appeared to need a moment to reword what he had in mind to ask.

"Well, you could remind me why in the hell you called yourself the barbarian princess."

"We already talked about this," she replied.

"Did we? I confess, I don't rightly remember."

The truth was that she couldn't remember either. She'd discussed it with enough people that she couldn't remember if she and Skharr had talked about it at length. Besides, she wasn't in the mood for cheerful bantering, at least not with Langven's life still hanging by a thread.

"I'm not an actual, proper barbarian, so if I were to make a claim to be one—something no one has ever seen—I would need to claim to be something they've never seen as well. Given that there has never been a barbarian princess, it is guaranteed that they have never seen the likes of me."

She rushed through it and had to breathe through the last few words as she ran out of air. Skharr nodded and scratched his chin.

"I suppose that makes sense. It sounded a little rehearsed, though. Have you given this speech often?"

Tandir laughed. "You have no idea."

She wished she could join them in their mirth. Barbarians appeared to have a more pragmatic and accepting attitude toward death in general, so she tried to not take it as them being unconcerned about whether Langven survived or not. Nothing seemed to soothe her irritation, however. They had to make good time to the Utter-Pit, face the beast with their finest attempt to not die while they gathered what could be used for a cure, and rush back to save the bastard's life.

As simple as the plan was, she couldn't shake the feeling that the execution of it would prove to be the real challenge. After all, their first attempt had come from an even simpler plan and that had gone straight to shit.

Skharr paused and shielded his eyes with his hand as he peered in the direction they were traveling toward like he was trying to locate something.

"Those shapes in the sky are a little too big to be vultures, right?" he asked finally and pointed skyward.

It was farther than Cassandra generally paid attention to, but as she leaned forward and focused, she identified at least a dozen or so flying shapes that circled and dove over something on the ground.

"Drakes," Bandir confirmed and heeled his horse forward. "They likely need fresh meat for all the new young that are hatching to replace those we managed to kill."

"We'd best hurry," Skharr muttered and gestured them

forward. "If they're attacking along the road, the chances are they have found some hapless travelers to kill."

He was probably right. The local animals, even the predators, were shy creatures that avoided humans on the road as much as possible and melted easily into the tall grass to avoid being seen by anything attacking from above.

"Fucking hells," Cassandra whispered and took her bow out of its saddlebag along with a couple of arrows as they broke into a gallop to where the beasts continued their swooped attacks.

The figures on the road were clearly human, or at least half of them were. An older man and his donkey attempted to fend the creatures off. He raised his staff and waved it from side to side to keep them away.

She had begun to learn a little about how drakes liked to attack, and it became more apparent that the smaller creatures were the females who usually hunted to find food for their young. Given that they were smaller and lighter, they didn't need to put as much effort into flying the longer distances. The males, as the larger beasts, were a little too heavy to comfortably fly the longer distances and probably remained with the nests to protect their eggs from other predators. Those were doubtless as likely to be other male drakes that would want to cleanse the area of any competition.

This meant they didn't have the larger drakes to deal with and she raised her bow, nocked one of her arrows to the string, drew it back, and let it fly.

Her skill had improved with practice and the first of the beasts screeched when its wing was pierced, and as it spiraled down, the others realized they were being attacked. They turned their attention immediately to the group that advanced on them from the south.

Cassandra already had the second arrow nocked and loosed before any of them could wing down to attack. The second one spun away although the arrow didn't bite deeply enough to ground it.

As the others launched their airborne assaults, the twins bellowed their battle cries and flung their javelins to kill two of the beasts. This sent the rest into a fury and they plunged in a concerted attempt to swarm the new arrivals before they could continue their assault.

With no more time to retrieve any arrows, she immediately stowed her bow, snatched her spear up, and thrust it high to catch the one she'd managed to wound before. She twisted it out of the air and flung it hard into the dirt.

She began to turn again when she heard the twang of a bowstring. For a moment, she thought that maybe the old man on the road had been a little better armed than they'd thought.

Before she could blink, one of the larger drakes was suddenly punched out of its dive and drawn into the path of another by an arrow about the size of the twins' javelins. Both creatures were impaled and plummeted. Only one archer she knew of was capable of launching arrows that large, but she still looked to where Skharr had settled on one knee and was already fitting another arrow to his massive bow.

Another twang pushed only one drake away from its attack with an arrow in its chest. The three or four that remained decided this was not the easy prey they had thought they would find on the road, immediately gained altitude away from the foursome below, and turned north to their nests.

Cassandra brought Strider to a gentle stop on the road to watch their retreat and make sure there was no possibility that this was a feint by the creatures, who could return with rein-forcements to attack them.

It did not appear to be the case, however. She scowled, lowered her spear, and flicked the blood from the head before she slid it into its slot on her saddle and looked around for the old man they had saved.

She found no sign of him on the road, but the smell of smoke immediately drew her attention to a small clearing in the grass not far from where they stood.

He and his donkey both appeared to be alive and well, and in the time it had taken for them to drive the drakes away, he had managed to set up a small camp with a crackling fire, some stew steaming over it, and seating places all around—one for him and four more for the new arrivals.

"How the fuck..." Bandir whispered.

"He must have had the camp ready," Tandir explained and shook his head. "He was setting it up when the drakes came along to pester him. That's the only possible explanation."

It wasn't the only one as she well knew. She looked to where Skharr collected their arrows from the felled drakes and he nodded slowly. They had seen this kind of trickery before, which likely meant that their intervention had not been necessary at all.

Still, it seemed like Theros had something he wanted to discuss with them, and as much as she hated it when he tried to fool folk into joining him, she needed to have a word with him too.

Besides, the smell of the koffe brewing was a little too difficult to resist.

"Well met, Skharr, Cassandra, Tandir, and Bandir," Theros called and beckoned them to join. "Come, have a little food and drink with an old man."

Skharr nodded but looked as cautious in approaching the camp as Cassandra felt, although the twins didn't appear to realize who their host was. They guided their horses to a nearby tree, secured them, and settled on the seats provided for them.

"It's mighty kind of you, old'un," Bandir commented with a polite smile.

"Truly," Tandir agreed.

"Of course, I could have blasted the beasts on my own," Theros answered. "But your help is appreciated."

"Like hell," Bandir muttered in disbelief.

"Bandir, Tandir," Cassandra said quickly before they did or said anything that would require the deity to make a show of revealing himself to the humans. "Allow me to introduce you to the Lord High God Theros, and…his donkey."

"Yern is the old beast's name," the god offered helpfully.

"It's rich of you to call anything else in the world old," Skharr told him as he dropped onto one of the seats.

"Well…one could say that I'm not quite as old as the hills. Most hills, anyway."

She was the last one to sit and she noticed that the old man's gaze was focused on her.

The twins now appeared to be a little too awestruck to say anything, but at least they had the good sense to keep their mouths shut instead of voicing their doubt again.

"I went through a fair amount of trouble to see to it that you had the proper armor for this fight," Theros pointed out once they'd all been furnished with a tin cup of the koffe.

"You don't wear armor while traveling."

"Your armor would be comfortable enough, wouldn't you think? Besides, I would want my paladin to show to any and all who might see that she is present."

"I'm sure the lions and gazelles would be most impressed," Skharr quipped.

"Most of the folk who would appreciate the armor were killed during our first trip through," Cassandra told him. "Have no fear, I do intend to wear it and wield the sword when we are properly engaged in battle."

Theros raised an eyebrow and shook his head. "And here I was thinking you two would be a little less belligerent once you'd worked the violence out of your collective systems."

"You'll need more than a pack of drakes for that," Skharr stated. "For future reference."

"Please don't appear with a fucking army on your heels next

time," she added quickly before the barbarian could put any bad ideas in the god's mind.

"I'll try not to." Theros cleared his throat and sipped his koffe before he spoke again. "Now, I suppose I should speak to the four of you about more pressing matters."

"If you're here to warn us away from the Utter-Pit again, I'm afraid we cannot be dissuaded," Cassandra answered.

"Again?" Tandir almost coughed up the mouthful he'd swallowed.

"Never fear. As it turns out, your efforts are quite necessary, but you'll need a little knowledge if you are to defeat Karthelon."

"It doesn't seem that complex to kill the dragon," Bandir muttered with a low snort. "Especially if it's still wounded from our first encounter with it."

"The dragon will be child's play compared to he who controls it," the god answered with a small smile. "Even if you do destroy the dragon and the temple, it will not be enough to undo the dark god's power. You will have to force Karthelon into manifesting himself and attacking you. In doing so, he will violate the rules decided on at the beginning."

"At which point, you will appear as an avenging god to smite the bastard with your almighty smiter." Skharr completed the thought for him.

"The idea is that I intercede before any avenging is required," Theros corrected. "Once it is done, the world will be a better place without Karthelon's influence, although he is likely to rear his ugly head to cause trouble in a few hundred years or so. Well, that bridge will be crossed when it is reached."

Cassandra narrowed her eyes. Of course, it would all come down to a test of faith for them and for her especially. If Karthelon did make an appearance, the chances were that even with Skharr to fight with them, they would not stand a chance against a real god. Instead, they would be immolated and Theros would no longer need to pay such close attention to his two most troublesome followers.

Or he could simply choose to not appear at all. A god was likely busy with issues across the continent.

"I suppose there is no other way, is there?" She tried to voice it as a rhetorical question, but there was some genuine hope that there would be another way for them to perform their task.

"Nothing comes to mind," the god answered and looked like he wished there was another way for them.

She scowled and finished her koffe as it had begun to go cold. "Shit."

"Look, I don't make the rules..." He paused, looked at the four who had joined him in the camp, and winced visibly. "Well, I might have had a hand in forming the rules when the world was young, but you have to trust me when I say that they help you a great deal more than they hurt. You wouldn't want the gods to simply rush about and commit whatever acts of madness they happen to be in the mood for. Occasionally, it does mean that they have to employ minions to do their bidding."

"That would be us," Skharr explained for the benefit of the twins.

"And Grimm. And that fucking dragon." Theros shook his head. "Can you imagine the kind of damage Karthelon could do if he attacked instead of sending his minions to cause you all trouble?"

The four paused and exchanged glances before Skharr sighed.

"He makes a good point," the DeathEater admitted.

"Maybe," Cassandra agreed. "But it does not change the fact that this is a shit deal."

"I won't let you down," the god assured her.

"Well, I suppose if you do, I won't be around long enough to talk your ear off over it."

# CHAPTER SIXTEEN

"Do you honestly think he'll be there to help us?" Tandir sounded skeptical.

Cassandra could understand why the twins would ask the questions now as they approached the narrow road they had barely survived not that long before.

If there was ever a time to consider the possibility of a god stepping in to intercede on their behalf, it was now. She had a feeling they would all be a little too busy fighting for their lives once they approached the temple.

Skharr didn't look like he appreciated the situation either and patted Horse gently on the shoulder. "I'll admit you were right. We should have stayed home."

"We never said you should have stayed home," Tandir noted.

"He's not talking to us," Cassandra explained.

"How did the three of you survive across this fucking shelf of a road the first time?" the DeathEater asked as he began to take his weapons off Horse's saddle.

"A squad of Langven's Ebon Pack were here to cover our retreat," she explained. "They had a group waiting here and another went in to try to find us. Archers and crossbowmen were enough to stop the drakes from swarming us on the road, and they left a small team behind to cover our retreat."

"Ah. The team that did not survive the return journey."

She nodded and dismounted carefully from Strider's back. Despite her words to Theros about not wearing her armor while riding, when they broke camp in the morning, she had strapped it on. It was logical to anticipate that she would not have the time to do so when the fight started.

It was light, comfortable, and perfectly fitted to her body. Aside from the occasional clatter when the plates slapped against each other while they were riding, it was about as easy to wear as her clothes were.

Perhaps she had merely been a little reluctant to put it on. Now that she consciously thought about it, she had felt like she would officially return to her post as a paladin once she did, and she wanted a few more days of freedom before she was forced into that decision.

It felt a little stupid now that she was wearing it. If the truth be told, she didn't feel different at all.

She left her bow and quiver on the saddle. Her sword was sheathed at her hip and she had the spear in her hand. She felt ready for battle, almost in the same way she felt when she wore the attire she'd made famous as the barbarian princess.

Maybe she'd never stopped being a paladin and changing the scale-mail undergarments for a suit of plate armor didn't do much to change that either.

"Are you not taking your bow?" Skharr asked. "You have acquired some skill with it."

"It doesn't quite go with the armor," she admitted and noticed that the twins were doing the same. They had their weapons and looped their bags of javelins over their shoulders in case they were needed.

All four were properly armored, armed, and about as ready for battle as they could be. None of them wanted to bring their horses into that charnel house, however. They had no intention to beat a hasty retreat this time, and they didn't want their mounts to be killed in the fight. None of them wanted to walk back.

She could appreciate the fact that they were already planning for success, but even with Skharr at their side this time, she wasn't sure what chance they had against a dragon infused with the power of a dark god. Regular dragons were as dangerous wounded as they were at full health, and Karthelon would put in all the effort needed to stop them this time.

"Well, nothing will be done if we stand around," she whispered and hefted her spear. "Let's finish this."

The twins laughed and adjusted their grasp on their weapons to hold them relaxed but also ready. Skharr only grinned. It was odd to see him in real armor that was designed for someone his size. It would have made more sense for him to fight in nothing but his undergarments with an amulet that protected him like armor, given how difficult it must be to find anything that fitted him.

But after his misadventures with the emperor, it was about time that he was issued with something that would work to keep him alive in battle.

"You're staring at me," he told her. "Is everything all right?"

"I'm merely wondering why you would come into this battle with me," she lied smoothly. "There isn't reason for you to as a general principle and even less since you have a wife and child waiting for you in your castle."

He grinned. "If you're that concerned for my safety, you should insist that I return lest Sera come along and kill you all for it. You know that she is a blademaster? She was trained by some of the greatest swordsmen and women in the world and she proves to be among them as well."

"She's the one teaching you to swing that sword around like it is not an ax?"

"Yes, as a matter of fact."

"Well, my wager is that if you find yourself dead by the end of this, so will I and the twins. That probably also means that Langven will be dead, so your wife will not kill anyone I happen to care about."

"You are a dark one," Skharr muttered. "But at least you admit it."

"Admit what?"

"That you genuinely care for Langven. You might want to tell him when next you see him—in this life or whatever waits for us afterward."

"I think I will."

She smirked and rested her spear against her shoulder as they began their advance along the road. The DeathEater kept his sword sheathed for the moment and held his bow ready as he kept watch on what they knew would come from above. Cassandra had a feeling that there would be no standoff to allow them to slip inside to meet a trap. They all knew what they would battle from this point forward, and the only real surprise would be if the beasts decided to ignore them for some unaccountable reason.

After everything they had been through, she hoped Karthelon would feel the same way. If she had to provide the little song and dance he seemed inclined to demand, she would comply, but it would be simpler for them all if there was merely a direct confrontation.

"Drakes above," Tandir warned and pointed toward the mountain.

She'd thought those were merely outcroppings, but she had learned to trust the word of the barbarians. They had keener eyesight than hers and she pointed the closest one out to Skharr.

"Let's see to it that they know we're here," she told him roughly.

Skharr nodded, drew the arrow back, and loosed it in a smooth motion.

The drakes failed to realize they were being attacked until the arrow had already struck its target. He had no need to aim for the wings, and she had a feeling there wasn't much in the world that could fully stop the arrows he fired. She could have sworn that his bow was broken when last they met, but that didn't mean he couldn't have obtained another that was as powerful as the last one.

His skill and the efficiency of his weapon were impressive. The first of the creatures died almost immediately when the arrow cut effortlessly through its chest and out the other side. She expected him to have already drawn the second arrow and be ready to fire it, but he waited and watched for the other beasts to move and begin their flight above them. He judged their movement as they jumped away from the mountain they were nesting on and pulled the bowstring back. The twins had each selected a javelin and stood ready for the drakes to come into range.

Cassandra wished for a moment that she could have brought her bow with her, but as she waited for them to dive in close enough for her to catch them with her spear, she realized that they had already begun to pull back, likely returning to their nests. She assumed they would regroup to attack again.

It likely meant they were still hurting from the losses they had sustained during their last encounter, and despite Karthelon's influence, they appeared to be a little more willing to defend themselves rather than throwing themselves directly into the fate that waited for them if they simply went on a rampage.

Of course, if they attacked with sufficient numbers, they could always swarm the barbarians who waited for them, but it also promised more than a few deaths. They appeared to be willing to give another the honor of dying at the hands of the humans.

She lowered her spear with a deep breath.

"I wouldn't relax yet," Skharr muttered. "It looks like they have nests up there, and even if they weren't being whipped into a frenzy by Karthelon, they always offer stiffer resistance when attackers approach where they raise their young. Still, the Drake-Hunters appear to have earned their name already."

"Honestly?" Cassandra asked and glanced to where the twins looked away to hide what she assumed were faces flushed both pleasure and embarrassment.

"Aye. They are fine javelin throwers. I always preferred to fight flying beasts with my bow, but the idea of throwing javelins at the fuckers has become a little more appealing."

"I've seen you throw javelins before—or spears, at least. Oh, and the odd ax too."

"Of course, but never quite as well as that. Tracking something moving through the air and striking it from that kind of distance… I don't think an old dog like me could ever learn such tricks."

She tried not to grin at the twins but realized they were now a little more anxious to plunge deeper into a fight after overhearing his compliments. Of course, a DrakeHunter would never want to seem pleased that a DeathEater had complimented them, but she imagined it went a little deeper than that, especially since she knew of the twins' borderline idolization of him.

Still, teasing them over it would cause more trouble than they needed at the moment, and she needed them focused for the fight ahead.

"They are circling," she alerted them and gestured with her spear to where the larger creatures—again, she assumed these were the males—began to advance on them. Instead of flying directly at them, however, they climbed across the treacherous rocks with the kind of precision that could only come from familiarity and considerable practice. If these were the kinds of creatures that fought over mates and dominance, that was probably how they managed it since fighting each other in the air would have ended with many dead drakes.

Skharr already had another arrow nocked and ready. He studied the way the drakes moved toward them and launched it deftly. It traveled at least a hundred paces before it struck its target, an impossible shot for almost anyone else on the continent. She assumed the power provided to him by the bow allowed for better accuracy over longer distances, but it gave the twins a clear view of what had made the legend of Skharr something even they had heard of.

That he was mad and an incredible fighter was true enough, but he appeared to know how to shift the odds of any fight in his favor, and she drew a deep breath and felt a little more secure. They would face stiff opposition, but there were few out there she would have preferred to face their enemies with other than those she stood alongside.

"We need to move," Cassandra shouted and gestured for them to continue along the shelf road and deeper into the canyon between the two mountains where it descended to where she knew the temple was. The pathway twisted and turned and followed the natural curvature of the mountain, but it wasn't long before they could see the mist rising from the Utter-Pit. Mere moments later, the entrance to the temple loomed ahead.

The DeathEater paused when he saw it and studied it for a moment like they had when they had arrived the first time. She took that to mean he'd never seen the Utter-Pit before either, but he recovered from the view almost immediately, drew three arrows from the quiver at his hip, and pointed them toward where the monsters began to gather near their nests again.

"I have a feeling the real fun is about to begin."

# CHAPTER SEVENTEEN

The drakes would undoubtedly not make the approach easy. Even though Skharr and the twins managed to prevent them from swarming the path, it wouldn't last. She knew that if they did not push forward immediately, things would go badly for all four of them.

"I'll push forward," Cassandra called, "and draw their attention to me. Follow when you can."

All three nodded as she forged ahead, alert for any of the drakes that would have the opportunity to swing down and drag her over the edge. One did manage to avoid being picked off by remaining close to the mountain, but it moved a little too slowly. She watched as it elevated, flapped its wings, and tried to force her to fall off the road. When that failed, its head finally snapped down. She ducked under the bite, drove her spear through its chest, and dragged it from where it still grasped the side of the mountain to the ground beside her.

She still had no fucking clue if these were the males or the females, but of most animals she knew, the males were the larger ones that fought over territory. Especially when it came to lions, it was the smaller, lither females that did all the hunting.

This was not the time to think about that, she scolded herself. She vaulted smoothly over the felled drake and immediately noticed two more that decided to attack her now that she was isolated from the rest of the group. Of course, this was the whole idea of rushing ahead on her own.

Three of the beasts began to climb toward her and ignored the arrows and javelins launched at them. One was knocked from the rocks and shrieked as it plummeted past her, while the other two overshot the distance when they tried to attack but landed on the road between her and the canyon leading to the temple entrance.

Cassandra breathed in slowly and made no effort to slow her pace. She had no intention to give the shits an easy shot at her, though, and she rolled away from a stream of fire that was spat at her and used her spear to push to her feet. A scream of defiance escaped as she drove the spear upward through the closest drake's jaw, snapped it shut, and spread the fire across itself as she shoved it hard into the path of the monster directly behind it.

Her spear was lodged in place, and with no possibility to draw it out in time, she reached instead to her hip with her left hand, grasped her sword's hilt in a backhand, and drew it in a smooth motion. She flicked the sword into a sweeping motion and brought it into a proper grip before she twisted the spear to push the drake she'd already impaled on it to where it would fall over the edge. At the same time, she closed the distance between herself and the drake that backed away from the swinging blade. There was no telling how long she would be able to continue to pressure it before it took flight so she shoved harder and stabbed the sword directly into its chest.

The first monster dropped off of the shelf and she all but charged through the second one, drove into it with her shoulder, and rolled over the body to emerge with both her weapons free. She wasn't sure where the inspiration for that came from, but as she found her feet, an odd sense of accomplishment rushed through her and a smile touched her lips. Buoyed by the moment, she finally raced free of the narrow road and sprinted to where the ground flattened and gave them a little more space.

Without thinking, she tossed the spear up far enough for her to reverse her grasp on it before she twisted her body forward and launched the weapon. She did not have to throw far as one of the largest drakes had begun to swoop toward her. It was still a damn decent throw, though, and buried the blade deep into the creature's abdomen with enough power to make it fall heavily before it was able to reach her.

"That looks like a fucking barbarian to me," Skharr shouted from behind her, and his bowstring sang a moment before another of the creatures dropped to the dirt in front of her. "Although I'm not sure it would be a princess' work."

"You've never seen a barbarian princess working." Cassandra shifted the sword to her right hand, held it firmly, and twirled it in a smooth figure-eight as she accustomed herself to the weight and balance of it again. It was the perfect sword and fitted to her hands almost seamlessly. "Therefore, anything you see me doing is a barbarian princess' work."

"I've seen some rather unprincess-like things that you've done."

"And yet they were still what a barbarian princess would do."

He grinned and turned to make sure the twins moved away from the road to join them. It was a danger for them to be on it, but she had a feeling it was far from the most dangerous part of their mission. At least at this point, they could move forward on an even footing against whatever came forward without needing to worry overmuch about being flung over the edge.

"Come on, then!" Cassandra shouted and looked for any sign of the beast that had attacked Draug's Hill. For the moment, all she could see were the drakes that still tried to gather and swarm the humans waiting for them at the bottom of the path.

It seemed none of them were willing to risk themselves yet,

though. As more of them were killed or wounded, those at the top became increasingly angry. Eventually, they would reach their peak of berserker rage and simply swarm with no fear of death or injury. She'd seen it happen in animals that weren't driven by a dark god's impulses and could only imagine how much worse it might be. It wouldn't be long either.

She imagined there was only one thing that stopped them from rushing down. A few spat flames and streamed them to the canyon below, but these fell well short of the humans. She drew a deep breath, settled her focus, and turned her attention to where she knew the real threat would come from.

The vapors had already begun to seep from inside the temple, and as she approached the columned doorway, Cassandra knew the beast would not be far behind. It had not made an appearance yet but she knew it was in there. Few creatures in the world gave off that kind of mist, and she steadied herself and stood not ten paces away from the entrance when it appeared that the vapors made no effort to reach out for them yet.

"Come on, then!" she shouted and stood her ground. "If you wanted to hide from me, you shouldn't have attacked my friends. You came looking for me and now, I'm here!"

A low, thunderous rumble made the ground shake, and she noticed that it appeared to make the drakes retreat to their nests. They didn't quite cower but they still seemed to fear the beast as much as any of the people who were brought to be sacrificed to it. She felt a distant tremble of the same voice that had warned her there were better ways to die than to be consumed by the creature, but she refused to run from it a second time.

Perhaps a little vanity reared its head, but there was also the knowledge that she could stand her ground against it. She could fight it and she could win because she had something that had been denied her the last time—or, rather, something she had denied herself.

A presence moved inside the shadows, shifted them slowly,

and made it look like the beast had been sleeping or resting and somehow, she had managed to disturb its slumber. It was not difficult to feel no sympathy for it, especially when she remembered the condition it had left Langven in.

Finally, the activity inside the cavern increased and the creature moved closer to the entrance. She could practically feel the anger radiating from it as it came into view and barely fitted through the doorway while the vapors began to spread more aggressively. Where she had once seen two eyes gleaming at her out of the shadows, there was only one now but it held enough hatred for two.

"I guess Karthelon never bothered to heal the wounds you suffered once it was obvious that you'd failed in your mission," Cassandra whispered and ignored the small voice that told her to run again as the beast moved from inside the temple and walked slowly to where she waited for it.

With a soft snort, it shook its body and stared at her. The deep, low growl sounded almost like an answer, although it was spoken in a language she could not understand and had no interest in learning. She was well aware that dragons were sentient, powerful beings, and either it had been forced into its servitude by Karthelon, or it had chosen the position. Either way, she had no elvish potions that would let her speak to or understand it.

Instead, Cassandra took a step forward, kept her gaze focused on the beast, and raised her sword in response when the vapors extended toward her like tentacles that wanted to curl around her. The twins had mentioned the effects they had on those who were touched by them, but there was more to merely feeling weakness and fear of the creature. Magic was in them, something that allowed the being to control whatever came within the realm of its power. The twins had told her there was a sudden change in the effects that practically pushed the whole keep into attacking it.

A connection existed there somewhere, but she couldn't quite put her finger on it. Still, there was no need to worry about what the vapors were capable of if she had never felt the effects.

She raised her sword and pointed it at the beast where it stood in front of her. "I'm here now, bitch. And I have more in store for you besides that little scratch that chased you off."

It certainly understood that and this time, it took a step forward through the shadows and uttered a roar that she felt more than heard. The odd but powerful nature of it made it difficult to focus on anything else but she stood firm and drew a deep breath when it almost knocked her back.

"Come on!"

Heavy wingbeats drifted the vapors toward her at a faster rate, but Cassandra extended the blade, held it in her right hand, and reached her awareness into the steel. It responded immediately and empowered her as she launched a blast of blue light from inside. She wasn't sure where the inspiration for the magical blast came from but it seemed to work through her armor and provide her with what she needed to beat the vapors back.

As the blue light touched them, the black tendrils were driven away and immediately set alight. They burned with the same blue flame and combusted like paper snakes to spew flashes of orange here and there as they were turned into harmless black ash that settled on the ground.

"It looks a bit like a dragon," Skharr muttered as he approached and flicked his sword from side to side. "Something's twisted it, though."

He wasn't wrong about that. She'd not caught a decent look at the creature the last time, and while it did look like a dragon, there was something else to it that was unsettling. It had all the familiar features but it was emaciated like the darkness sucked its life from the inside and turned it into a shadow of itself. She could see its ribs and spine pressing into its scales but not in the way that would make it look like it was merely underfed. Instead, it looked even more dangerous now, a beast that was eternally hungry, and while it needed to feast, she had a feeling that the flesh of its victims was not what it consumed.

Life stealing had a particularly pungent smell to it and it was likely what gave the dragon its power.

Another bone-shattering roar was uttered as it moved toward her and beat its wings to lift itself from the ground.

"What are the chances that you and I fight a dragon together for a second time?" Skharr asked. "Most folk wouldn't see a real dragon in their whole lives and here we are fighting another."

"And it's not even the second dragon you've fought," she added.

"That," Tandir muttered and pointed his mace at the beast, "is not a dragon."

Maybe he was right. But given that it had likely been once and since there was no other name for whatever it now was, Cassandra was content to simply call it that and let academics who heard of their battle with it fight over the technicalities.

Assuming they survived, of course.

The twins rushed forward to engage it, and she gestured for Skharr to join them in the fight as she circled to the flank. She noticed that its eye was still focused on her as she shifted to the left.

"Show me what you can do," she challenged, jumped forward, rested her sword on her shoulder, and grasped it with both hands while she waited for the beast to make its move. It was less patient than she was and lunged forward and snapped its fangs outward like a snake's as it tried to bite her. It hovered in place and its wings held it up while the long neck reached down. She jerked back and leaned as far away from the fangs as she could, remembering precisely how dangerous the venom they carried was. It dripped from the fangs and spread across the dagger-sized teeth that waited deeper inside the jaw.

As she swept her blade out, its head snapped away and she nicked the side of its jaw but failed to go deep enough to cut into the scales.

Still, it elevated sharply away from her as if it had been stung. After a moment, she realized that it hadn't attempted to avoid her but rather the barbarians, who had managed to attack its flank. A few fresh wounds were visible on its hind legs thanks to them striking at the same time.

It shifted sharply and she was a little too late to call a warning before the tail swung at the barbarians. The twins managed to jump clear, but Skharr was struck hard in the chest and sprawled with a grunt as the impact knocked the wind from him.

Cassandra cursed, twisted, and sprinted to the drake she had felled with her spear. She yanked the weapon out from where it was still buried and turned to face the beast. While she had made a decent throw of it the first time, there was no need to press her luck. All she needed was to distract it while the giant of a barbarian recovered. She couldn't tell if he had become a little slower or if something about the strike had made more of an impact, but he pushed to his feet without his usual dexterity while the dragon prepared to attack him.

She screamed, threw the spear with all the strength she could muster, and scowled when it sailed just to the left of where she had aimed. Maybe hoping to down the beast with a spear throw was a little ambitious, but the weapon appeared to be caught in the gusts caused by the massive wings and twisted toward one of those.

The creature caught sight of the weapon in time, ducked its head, and jerked its wing to push the spear away, but the head still cut into its shoulder and sank through the scales of its wings. She winced as another roar tore through her, but it was about what she could expect and she had the beast's attention again, which enabled Skharr to stagger away and regain his composure.

He favored his left leg, but that was something she could question him about at another time.

Her adversary descended to where she stood, landed on its hind legs, and swiped at her with the claws of its forelimbs. Even with the claws about the length of swords, the swing still came well short of reaching her by two or three paces at least.

That was possibly the result of missing one eye and being unable to properly judge how far away she was, and she applied her mind to making sure the chance was not wasted, especially since the wings swept around to reach for her as well. The crests of its wings also had claws, and those appeared to be aimed a little closer to where she stood.

Cassandra feinted to the right and jumped to the left instead before she dodged a series of strikes aimed at her. The claws dug directly into the rock, which meant there was probably some magic to them as well—or maybe some kind of venom allowed them to eat into rocks.

No, that didn't make any sense. She dove to the right as the tail swept toward her, and the beast began to rise from where it tried to attack her when the twins flung javelins to distract it. She appreciated their efforts, but it was always dangerous to attract the attention of a dragon, and this one in particular. One strike would be enough to kill or stun them. Of course, she couldn't battle it on her own, but bringing her friends to fight it with her began to feel like it could prove to be a distraction.

Where was Skharr?

She paused and looked around for the giant barbarian. Something that large should have been easy to locate, but it took her more than a moment to see that he was climbing up the columns of the temple to find a position to attack it from above.

"Oy!" he roared at the creature and its long, agile neck whipped toward him as he drew an arrow back on his bow and launched it smoothly. It was an accurate shot, but even his arrow would likely not be able to cut into the armored scales.

To her shock, it did. She stared, confused by the success of the arrow as it sank into the creature's eye until she remembered that was more or less where Langven had managed to stab the beast. It was impressive given how quickly its head moved.

Then again, maybe she needed to simply take moments like these and press their advantage. The twins looked like they were throwing javelins at its legs but both javelins had some kind of rope attached between them.

Once they were buried in deep where it appeared the scales were not quite as armored, Cassandra's eyebrows raised when Tandir lifted Bandir to grasp the rope hanging between the beast's two hind legs while it was busy trying to deal with Skharr. Of course, they had to know a handful of different tactics they could use to keep a dragon engaged, and once Bandir was able to bring it down far enough, his brother caught the rope too and both began to pull the dragon down.

She rushed forward and snatched her spear up from where it had fallen beneath the beast. Skharr still endeavored to prevent it from catching him on the rocks and managed the outcroppings almost as well as the drakes had done. Of course, she should have remembered that DeathEaters were about as comfortable climbing rocks as they were walking on the ground.

She couldn't help the grin that slid over her features at the sight of the massive barbarian bounding from rock to rock with the nimble grace of a dark elf in the forest but reminded herself that he kept the monster occupied.

They needed to attack while it was distracted. She approached the dragon and thrust her spear into its underbelly. It failed to cut deep but was enough to finally drag its gaze from the DeathEater. The twins were successful in their efforts to drag it out of the air but it tried desperately to take flight again. This wasn't because it needed to or even because it couldn't kill them while grounded but simply because they were trying to force it into something and it resisted instinctively.

Its efforts kept the wings extended and Skharr immediately took advantage. He bounded away from the stone wall he'd been climbing and pushed to where his sword and dagger could attack the beast's wing. Both weapons penetrated almost effortlessly and sliced through the thinner and lighter scales that weren't quite as armored as the rest of it.

The wounds were deep and long and by the time he reached the ground again—having moved only slightly slower than if he had not cut methodically through the appendage—the beast was no longer able to fly. One side worked efficiently, but the wing he had attacked flapped uselessly like a sail with a massive hole in it.

He had effectively grounded the dragon and it was now forced to engage them with nowhere to go.

Still, being trapped made the creature no less dangerous. She could all but feel the pain seeping from it. It crept over her and made it difficult to focus on anything else and she tried reflexively to reach her back, distracted by the feeling that she had been sliced open by the DeathEater's attack.

Cassandra paused, frowned as she looked around, and realized that while they had fought the creature, the vapors had begun to drift from its skin again. They washed over her and appeared to ooze through her armor to leave a chilling, ghostly impression wherever her skin came in contact with it.

This was a mental bridge that connected the beast to its victims and instilled them with fear, anger, anguish, and almost anything it wanted them to feel. She had never encountered anything quite like it but decided it was not much different than what she remembered a handful of druids had used to keep wolves away from their sheep. They had infused the mist with a sensation that the marauders were being tracked by a much larger predator.

Of course, this was far more powerful. She assumed that while the creature had a great deal of practice against the sacrifices who were brought to it, it wasn't as accustomed to using the vapors while it was under attack. As a result, the bridge created merely showed her everything and anything it happened to feel at any given moment.

This wasn't quite as powerful as the sense of dread she remembered from the first time but it was still a distraction they could not afford. A glance at her companions confirmed that it had begun to affect the twins as well, although Skharr inched away from the vapors. He looked like he was not sure what to do but was curious enough to see what it was like to simply let himself be touched by it.

"Typical barbarians." She snorted and tried to decide whether that was her feeling or something that transferred from the beast. Either way, she would not allow it to have the advantage, not only because they could not afford to have their minds on anything other than the battle but also because she knew that bridges like this tended to work both ways. As she felt what the dragon felt, it would be in touch with what she felt as well.

And it undoubtedly had a great deal more experience. Letting something like this creature delve into her mind was not something she was interested in exploring the possibilities of.

Cassandra reached out again and her power pooled into the sword in her hand. She closed her eyes and traced all the familiar pathways that had led to her attack the last time but added to them and built the power steadily. Focused, she pushed as much as she could stand into the sword and finally released it like a stone from a catapult.

Although painful, it was a relief as well. When she opened her eyes, she realized that the entire sword flickered with the same blue fire she'd seen before but burned with enough intensity that she could feel it begin to sear her hand.

It was a good kind of pain, though, and she endured it as the flames poured from the blade and consumed the vapors everywhere they went. They followed each strand and tendril and burned it to the point where it vanished completely and left no ash behind. The magic now began to push forward into the dragon to dig deep and find where the vapors came from under its skin. She could feel the burning and the connection was still there, but all it did was enrage her and drive her to push harder until she found each and every source of the mist and burned it.

Of course, she would not be able to kill it that way. They were born from fire, after all, but it would still prevent it from being able to reach out to them.

On top of that, she knew it hurt like all hells.

The roar was enough to shake boulders and rocks from the mountains all around them. Its wings could no longer provide flight, but they were still functional limbs with claws. She gestured for the twins to back away and Skharr rushed to her side.

"What did you do?" he asked as he studied the beast speculatively.

"I'm not sure but I think I stopped it from being able to produce those vapors. Now we need to kill it."

The DeathEater nodded and glanced at his sword. "I can draw its attention. You'll find the opening but you'll probably only have one attempt, though."

"I'll make it count."

He broke into a sprint toward the twins, who flung the last of their javelins at the creature as its tail whipped faster than they could blink. This time, Tandir was caught by its lash. Cassandra winced at a loud crack from the DrakeHunter's knee and he screamed and fell. Skharr lunged forward, swung his sword into the tail, and sliced a few gashes into it, which the two younger barbarians could sink their blades into. They all but pinned the tail down as they drove their weapons deep and almost to the other side, where they were stopped by the armored scales.

Skharr ducked as one of the wings swung over his head and almost severed it with a single swipe before the tail began to move again. Bandir managed to sink his ax into it before it pulled free and he shouted as it dragged him about fifteen feet before he was finally forced to let it go and leave his weapon buried inside.

"Oy!" he shouted and scrambled to his feet again. "Give that back! It don't belong to you!"

Despite his indignation, the beast merely roared in response, turned, and attempted to snatch the barbarians as they scattered. The DeathEater lifted Tandir and carried him on his shoulder as he began to run. The claws lashed out and again, it appeared as though it had difficulty judging the distance of its targets. It had likely meant to cut him in half but instead, the claws barely grazed the backs of his legs.

Still, a graze from claws as large as those was more than enough to make him stumble and fall, which elicited a groan of pain from the barbarian he had tried to carry to safety. The dragon turned to face them and roared again as it snapped its enormous head forward with fangs extended to kill them both.

That was Cassandra's opening. Skharr had been right when he'd said she probably wouldn't have another one, but she would be damned if she would allow it to claim their lives. She screamed in fury, threw the spear for the third time, and grimaced at an ache in her back from the pressure she had put it under. The throw was a good one and she couldn't help but grin when the enchanted spearhead powered cleanly through the armored scales, into the beast's throat, and finally emerged on the other side.

"That was my finest throw of the day," she whispered and grasped her sword with both hands when the attack made the beast stumble forward. It landed hard on its stomach and sprawled, all but incapacitated. For a moment, she had it where she needed it to be.

She rushed forward to where it tried to turn its head to face her.

"You were looking for me when Langven took your eye." Rage

bubbled through her body as she stamped her boot on the creature's jaw to keep it still. "I'm here to claim the other."

It did not appear to fear her. For the first time, however, through all the rage, anger, and sadism she could feel through the rapidly diminishing connection, it felt tired. Its remaining eye closed a moment before she drove her sword through the lid, and she continued to push until the beast shuddered and twitched violently but finally went still.

Perhaps it had been forced by Karthelon to do his bidding but that did not mean she could leave it alive. Still, she couldn't help but feel a pang of guilt as she realized that she'd now claimed two of a species that was rapidly disappearing from the world.

Cassandra drew her sword from the creature's skull and it twitched a final time.

Skharr pushed slowly to his feet and took a moment to confirm that his armor had taken the brunt of the damage to his legs.

"Thanks for nothing, you big oaf," Tandir muttered as he struggled into a seated position.

"It is interesting that you think saving your life is worth nothing," the older barbarian responded with a grin and settled on his haunches next to the twin. "How does that leg feel?"

"It'll be fine with a healing draught."

"Save the potions for when we need them," she told him as the beast's blood was cleaned from her sword before she sheathed it. "We have time here so might as well conserve resources."

"Including your strength," Bandir replied as he pulled his ax from the dead creature's tail. "Healing me in our first attack almost killed you."

"That was from gaping wounds to your chest that would have killed you in minutes," she pointed out and placed her hands on Tandir's knee. "I've mended more broken legs in my lifetime than I'll ever remember."

Her exploration revealed that it wasn't quite broken. The

knee was a little dislocated and a few tendons were torn and blood vessels had ruptured. A first-year student at any academy of healing could make it better with little effort, and it was not long before Tandir was helped to his feet and twisted his leg to check for any more pain.

"It's like it never happened," he whispered and grinned. "Right, then. What's the plan now?"

"Now?" Cassandra looked at the temple entrance and tilted her head in thought. "We have to anger a god enough to make him manifest in a corporeal form."

"I seem to have a talent for that," Skharr quipped with a grin.

# CHAPTER EIGHTEEN

There was less time to plan than she'd thought. In all the excitement of fighting the dragon, it had slipped her mind that the beast's presence stopped the rest of the creatures in the area from attacking them.

At first, it didn't seem like the drakes believed that it was dead. Cassandra almost missed a couple of them that descended from their nests. They were smaller creatures, no doubt younger ones that were a little braver and dumber than the older beasts that remained where they were and watched the events from above.

They approached the body warily as if they weren't quite sure it wouldn't simply spring up and kill them for so much as looking at it. The closer they came, however, the bolder they became. It wasn't long before one of them leaned in and bit one of the beast's hind legs. She doubted it would make a fine meal given that it was nothing more than scales and bones with very little meat that she assumed was stringy and fouled by dark magic.

Still, there was no longer any doubt in their minds that it was no threat to them. One of the small creatures looked up and uttered a screeching cry to those that were still in their nests and watched and waited for any sign of danger down below.

"You know," Bandir whispered and flicked the beast's blood from his ax, "I think we should go now."

"Where can we go?" Tandir asked and looked around warily.

"We cannot go back," she pointed out. This would expose them to the very real danger of the drakes attacking them on the narrow road again. More importantly, however, they had come this far already and there was no point in a retreat now. "Forward is therefore our only option."

Of course, the threat of the dragon was dealt with for the moment, but there was no assurance that Karthelon couldn't bring it back to life or failing that, could simply present another beast to be a problem for them. It was always possible and a new one might even be more powerful and more dangerous now that he knew what kind of threat she posed to him.

Skharr raised his sword and pointed at the temple and for a moment, Cassandra thought he was directing them to where they needed to go until she noticed movement inside. Figures in dark robes stepped out. They carried thick elderwood staves and gems at the top indicated with certainty that magic flowed through them. Their hoods were up, which made it difficult to tell what kinds of mages they were. Given that they were comfortable sharing the temple with the now-dead dragon, she could imagine that their magic had something to do with transforming it into the creature they had faced.

Two of them raised their staves and pointed the gems at the nests overhead. Blasts of orange flame were directed upward, not to strike the drakes but to force them from their complacency and into the fight. It seemed Karthelon's control over them was not quite absolute, and while they were more than willing to attack her and her companions, she wondered if there was a way to turn them to attack the priests as well.

She realized that the barbarians would not wait for any plots or plans to develop. Skharr already had his bow in hand and drew three arrows from his quiver. Instead of directing his attack at any of the monsters that had begun to descend, it seemed he intended to make sure that the mages would be forced back into the temple.

His first arrow was loosed without having been pulled to the full draw of the bow, but it still launched smoothly, punched through the chest of one of the mages, and elicited a scream as the target stumbled back. The priest's hood fell to reveal what she could only imagine had once been human but like the dragon, had been twisted and warped by the dark magic they embraced.

Black veins were visible up his shoulders and neck and had begun to trace through his jawline. The whites of his eyes were replaced with a dark blue and the irises gleamed with green light —the same green she'd seen in the eyes of the beast but not quite as brilliant.

It made sense. The light came from the innate magic inside the creature and few humans in history, if any, could match the kind of magic dragons had in them from birth.

Still, it seemed they had absorbed the same magic from the dragon and it had begun to affect them in a similar manner. A few hundred years more—assuming they survived—would render them emaciated, undead creatures that were nothing like what they'd started as.

Killing them early on in the process felt like it was a mercy.

Skharr already had another arrow nocked to his bowstring. The mages—or priests, since that's what they were—began to back away and tried to launch an attack at the man before he could inflict further injury or death. Even so, before they could duck into the temple, another of them fell with an arrow protruding from his throat. The next stumbled with an arrow in his leg, and while there was the opportunity for a handful of his friends to help him into the protection of the temple, they didn't so much as make an effort to rescue him.

"There is no love lost between them, I see," Cassandra muttered, sheathed her sword, and dragged her spear out of the dead dragon's throat as their small group moved forward to cut the mages off from their planned escape.

Of course, the barbarians had already done a better job of it than she had. The DeathEater made sure that the two who attempted to pass through the entrance first did not survive, and with only one arrow between them too. It appeared that the bastards did not have any real armor beneath their robes, but it was still an impressive shot that had drilled through the first man's neck and hammered into the back of the one in front of him.

"Go!" Skharr shouted to the other three and waved them forward as he took more arrows from his quiver. He approached the dead dragon, thrust his hand into its mouth, and with a single tug, removed one of the venom-filled fangs. "I'll draw them all out and away from you."

"What?"

He grinned and gestured for her to move forward. "I have a knack for pissing folk off. Priests especially!"

It appeared that he did much more than merely piss the priests off, as the drakes guarding the temple were also felled easily in flight by his arrows.

There was no disputing the fact that he possessed a particular skill, and while she didn't like the idea of leaving him in a fight for his life like that, he had his bow, sword, and dagger, as well as the dragon's fang. It was no great leap to assume that he had some kind of plan in mind already and they had seconds before the drakes launched an assault in full numbers.

If there was ever a time to act, it was now and while she didn't like it, Cassandra rushed a little closer to the entrance of the temple, leapt to cover the last distance between her and her quarry, and thrust her spear through the chest of one of the priests who attempted to stop them from escaping the drakes.

The others realized that they were not in any position to prevent the intruders from entering and began to retreat while they fired blasts of power at the barbarians.

She realized that they had flung a few attacks at her as well, but they rebounded in different directions every time they came within five feet of where she stood. Her armor was intended to provide some kind of defense against magical attacks as well as the physical ones, but she'd never noticed the wards acting quite as obviously as they did when attacked by Karthelon's priests.

Ignoring the enemy for the moment, she paused, looked at where the dragon still lay, and hacked into its neck. Her sword bit deep, but she needed a second and a third strike before the head rolled free.

The twins noticed something protecting her and immediately stepped closer to her. It was no surprise that the attacks directed at them were deflected into the mountains around them as well as the drakes swooped into their attack. The barbarians grasped the beast's head once it was fully removed from the body and with her help, they began to move toward the temple.

Skharr rushed away. It appeared there was no longer any control over the beasts and two of the larger ones pounced immediately on a priest, crushed him under their weight, and began to bite and tear into him. The others in the mage ranks now directed their attacks at the creatures rather than the outsiders.

Perhaps they realized they needed something a little more powerful if they wanted to overcome the armor she wore.

All three invaders reached the temple safely, and Cassandra paused when she saw that the twins had skidded to a halt just inside the doors. They still carried the beast's head between them.

"We'll hold anything that tries to come in off," Tandir told her. "You'll have enough difficulty trying to piss a god off without anything nipping at your heels."

"We'll have the advantage against anything that attacks in here anyway," Bandir agreed.

Folk seemed to make it a habit to put themselves in danger based on their belief that she would know what to do and how to do it. They even assumed she was as willing as they were to sacrifice their lives to see their goals achieved.

In the end, she had no idea what she could do to draw Karthelon out to where they could deal with him. She didn't quite have Skharr's ability to anger the gods.

"Well," she retorted, "either it will work and all will turn out well, or we'll all be dead soon enough and it won't matter. Stay close behind me, though. I might need some help deeper inside."

"Naturally."

A glance behind her revealed more of the priests approaching via the narrow shelf road. They were all on horseback and Skharr retreated immediately from them and ducked as more blasts of magical power followed his attempts at evasion.

"It's time for a show!" the DeathEater shouted as he hunkered behind a few rocks for cover.

The priests pushed forward, sure that the advantage was now theirs. Instead, their target left his bow and bounded over the rocks with only his sword. It was a longsword, heavy enough for most men to require two hands to use it effectively, but he carried it easily in one. He grasped his dagger in the other as he surged toward the approaching priests. His weapons carved through them without the slightest pause and he used the confusion caused by their horses to press forward harder.

One of the horses tried to rear in front of him and the barbarian caught its reins and forced it down, then simply upended both horse and rider.

That was one way to cause chaos, she conceded. It was a talent she at least matched Skharr in. She grinned, hefted her weapons, and turned to head deeper into the sanctum

Taking the dragon's head with them made Skharr think Cassandra at least had some kind of plan in mind. He could only hope it was a good once since there was no telling what nature of madness she had concocted. Still, he had his share of problems to deal with.

While he had managed to catch the newcomers by surprise, it looked like the effects of his abrupt reversal to attack them outright had already outlasted its usefulness. A searing heat burned across his back when one of them managed to circle and target him from behind. While he could feel the effects, it did appear that the dwarven handiwork had at least some way to keep part of the magic away, although he wouldn't put much faith in it. He ducked under the next salvo and stayed on the move as he focused on the priest who tried to eliminate him from behind.

The man realized the error of his ways and immediately began to back away from what he'd thought was a good position to attack. As the barbarian lunged toward him, he raised his staff in an attempt to block the strike.

Skharr felt a slight pause as his sword sliced through the elderwood but it continued to carve effortlessly through the shoulder, chest, and abdomen of the priest and opened wounds from which he wouldn't recover. His blood flowed both red and black, and the DeathEater had no desire to find out why.

It was clear that this contingent of priests was better prepared for what they faced, and he had a feeling that they likely had a little more experience with violent intruders. Those they had faced earlier were no doubt more used to having a dragon there to do the work for them.

Nine or ten of them approached at once. All had dismounted and seemed to have decided that having horses around would only lead to a faster defeat. Skharr's blood boiled over how they abandoned their mounts to be attacked and torn to pieces by the drakes, but he had a feeling he would be able to take his anger out on them as a group before too long.

The first one stepped forward, extended his hand from his robe, and appeared to grasp thin air before a crackle was heard. Immediately, the nothing he held turned into a sword of sorts and simply emerged from his hand. The blade was difficult to look at and although it looked like it was formed from pure shadows, tongues of flame flickered from the edges. He knew without a doubt that as a weapon, it was more than capable of cutting through his armor.

Even so, it wasn't the first time he'd stood against spellcasters, and he moved to the left. Three or four others of the group drew similar weapons from themselves, while the others still used their staves to launch bolts of blackness at him. These forced him to move or prove that his armor was able to withstand everything they could throw at him.

Those armed with the dark swords followed him but were slower in their approach than they possibly thought they were, and he guessed they anticipated that he would be slower due to his size. It was always Skharr's pleasure to prove anyone wrong in this misassumption, and he circled them to surge at those who still held their staves.

None of them knew what to do other than back away as he lopped the first one's head off. It launched into the others and he impaled a second man as he twisted and used the body of the priest he'd run through as a shield, reached around him, and stabbed his dagger through the throat of a third. Two more stood where they could pose a threat, and one of them dropped his staff to summon a sword before the others could redirect to engage the barbarian.

It seemed unlikely that they would rush in to help their comrades in need either. As he ducked and wove under the priest's strikes, he buried his dagger in his stomach and dragged the blade through to eviscerate him before he shoved him aside. The last one standing looked for something to fight with.

The DeathEater put an end to his dilemma when he leaned forward and delivered a powerful kick into his chest. The force of the blow thrust him over the edge of the cliff and he screamed as he plummeted to land with a thud that echoed through the canyon around them.

More of the priests arrived, although these abandoned their horses quickly when they were attacked by the drakes that assailed them with unbridled fury. Blasts from the newcomers appeared to follow him as he ran from the group and tried to stay ahead of any attempts to trap him. If he was killed or captured by the bastards, he wouldn't be of any help to Cassandra while she was inside the temple.

Skharr paused and his gaze settled on where the drakes appeared to have focused their attentions on another group of priests who had emerged from the temple as well as where the horses were being herded into a position to be more easily attacked. It still angered him to see that, but an idea began to form. It wasn't a particularly good one but the best he could manage now that priests targeted him from both sides.

Before he could question the wisdom of it, he rushed directly toward where the drakes were assembled and darted to the right and the left when he felt the ground shake around him. The blasts of power fell short of striking him as he moved. The attack had caught the attention of the beasts above, however, and a small pack of them banked away from the horses, where it appeared there was already too much competition for them to deal with. They turned their attention to the new arrivals.

The DeathEater flicked his dagger, caught it smoothly by the blade, and judged the distance it would have to travel before he launched it forward with all the power he could manage. His aim was true and the blade sank to the hilt in the chest of one of the closest drakes that appeared to be ready to spit fire at him. The flames pushed from the wound and the flammable liquid it spat spread onto the ground as he moved quickly. He avoided the snapping jaws and severed the head in a smooth motion. The other beasts were suddenly aware that more attackers were present and began to direct their fire at the priests.

Logic suggested that if they lived this close to the temple, some connection must exist between the mages and the drakes. With the beast gone, however, it appeared the creatures had suddenly lost their fear of them and now turned on them as eagerly as they had attacked the four outsiders.

It was interesting to watch as the creatures joined the fight and caught him in the chaos of a three-way battle between himself, the priests, and the drakes, although neither of his enemies was focused on him enough to pose much of a threat. All he had to do was avoid the vicious claws, flames, and blasts of magical power that were exchanged between the factions in the canyon around him.

Even so, he had to beat out a fire that caught on his hauberk as he sliced one of the priests' throats. She stumbled into the path of another stream of fire from one of the drakes.

Skharr leapt aside, hacked through the back of a drake, and drove forward in an attempt to avoid the thick of the fighting. Ironically, it was generally where he wanted to be but in the end, as long as they fought each other, they wouldn't fight him or try to find out what the hell Cassandra could be doing.

He realized that his efforts had brought him considerably closer to the temple. A part of him felt there was a better way to go about this than simply letting their mutual enemies fight each other before they turned on him but for the life of him, he couldn't think of one. He had reached the temple gate when one of the drakes turned to face him. It was one of the larger, more powerful females if he had to guess and appeared to have identified him as an isolated and thus easy target instead of the priests.

The mages seemed to have rallied and attempted to fight the other beasts off as a combined force.

With his feet planted to steady himself, he grasped his sword with both hands and watched the drake approach slowly. Given that she didn't try to breathe fire at him, he assumed he looked like a tasty enough meal for her to carry to her nest.

"While I am generally open to the idea of being consumed by a female," he muttered, "I would draw the line at being chewed on by her young."

The drake snorted, rushed at him, and spread her wings to try to attack him from above. He pushed forward as well, ducked under a sweeping attempt to catch him with the claws in her wings, and drove his sword into her chest.

Although the blade sliced smoothly through a few of the ribs, it caught on something else before he could pull it out. He was dragged across the ground but retained his firm hold on his weapon until he looked down and realized they were closer to the edge of the cliff than he'd expected.

"Fuck me." Skharr released his sword and searched frantically for something to hold onto as the weight of the drake continued to drive them both to the edge and finally, over it.

# CHAPTER NINETEEN

If she was any judge of the matter, the place looked a little more like a dungeon than a temple. Although, given what she'd learned about dungeons from Skharr and Theros, there was very little difference between the two. The difference that came to mind was that temples were built by puny mortals who wanted to show their adoration for the gods. Dungeons were generally built by the gods themselves, although for the same purpose.

Still, she could see signs that humans—or at least some of the various beings that looked and walked like humans–had been in the area she now moved through. This wasn't something often seen in the dungeons she had cleared or heard of being cleared. Then again, most of the those she knew of did not have a dragon guarding their entrance, nor did they have priests guarding the dragon.

This was something entirely new. Perhaps she would be the one to name it in the future.

"What would you call a place like this?" Cassandra muttered. "The hallways are lit, books are displayed along the shelves—anywhere else and I might think of this as some kind of underground library."

And yet something far more sinister pervaded the space. The mist she remembered rising from the Utter-Pit grew consistently thicker, and while she couldn't put a finger on the smell of it, she slowly but surely developed a hatred for it. An odd sweetness pointed toward fruit that was rotting, and it made her want to vomit the longer she moved through the tunnels.

She paused and peered around the corner when light footsteps approached. Since they were accompanied by the light tap of wood on stone, she could only assume these were priests, although their conversation and lack of any haste indicated that they had no idea what was happening outside the temple.

"There's too much to do," one complained. "Why would I want to leave now? I have everything I want here."

"Because you might want to look into broadening your horizons." The second voice sounded a little long-suffering. "If you will be stuck here, wouldn't you want to know if you are missing something else in your life and pursue that while you can?"

"This is a dangerous topic, and no. I don't think I would like to be confused. I have all the power and study material I need here. Aside from a few problems with the freshness of food, it is the perfect place for a humble academic to live. Certainly, there is a notable absence of an angry lord trying to find ways to reverse the fact that he could never bring his rod to full erection."

"You have to put that behind you. Besides, it only happened to you once."

"And it was one time too many."

Cassandra narrowed her eyes and stepped into plain view. They thought of themselves as mere academics. Perhaps it was a subject they were never allowed to fully consider, and while there were many reasons why she would have assumed these people chose to be there, being a student would never have come to mind. Surely a certain amount of sadism and lack of empathy for their fellow mortals must be involved.

Then again, that did not rule most academics out.

All four priests stopped when they saw her, but one was quicker to realize the danger than the others. He pointed his staff at her and unleashed the same blast that the earlier group had attempted. It seemed to confirm that they were all academics. Students of magic were given the same weapons that were fairly easy to use but lacked any kind of creativity.

They all paused when the blast avoided her like the earlier attacks had and pounded hard into one of the nearby bookshelves and shattered it and the books it contained.

"That did not work," she pointed out coldly and hefted her spear to catch their attention. "Try again for a copper?"

The priests took that as a challenge and she charged forward. As much as she appreciated armor that protected her from magical attacks, she was cautious to not strain its ability to keep her alive. For now, the best she could do was ensure that they were not in a position to try to overwhelm her.

She thrust the spear forward and sliced through one of their robes into the young woman. The next priest stepped forward and she grasped his staff and forced it around as the crystal released another blast of magical energy. It ripped into his colleague's lower abdomen and the older man fell screaming in agony.

When she tried to draw her spear out of the woman she'd killed, there was not enough room or time to make any. With a scowl, she released it, drew her sword instead, and opened a gash across the chest of the priest whose staff she'd used to kill another one. He fell back, coughing blood as the last of them stood his ground for the barest of moments before he spun and tried to run.

"Oy!" she shouted. "I can do that too!"

She raised her sword, pushed as much concentration into the sword as she could manage in such a short time, and directed a blast of blue fire at the priest. His robes immediately caught fire and his screams joined those of his fallen comrades when his attempt to flee was brought to a halt by the fire that consumed him.

"I can do that too?" Cassandra snorted derisively as she cleaned her blade. "What the— He wouldn't know what I could do before he caught fire. I'm...uh, I need to focus."

A little irritated, she sheathed her sword again and dragged her spear from the body of the fallen priest before she returned her attention to the hallway. The mist had thickened and the scent grew more repugnant as she approached an area that was not quite as well lit. Fewer torch sconces hung on the wall but a dull green light emanated from the other end of the hallway. For a moment, she stopped and drew a deep breath to calm herself. She wasn't sure if the twins were still close behind and the reality of facing whatever waited for them on her own was more daunting than she would like to admit.

There was no turning back now, though. She tightened her hand around her spear and continued her advance.

Noises could be heard ahead as well. She narrowed her eyes and tried to determine what they were. Cries of pain or possibly fear—or both—came through very clearly. It sounded like chains were dragged across the ground and the cracks of whips explained the cries of pain as well. Her fear diminished rapidly in the face of this obvious distress and she stepped out into a chamber where the mist was at its thickest.

She must be just in front of the Utter-Pit at this point and she could barely breathe through the mist. Quietly, she narrowed her eyes and tried to make out the moving figures ahead.

Two priests dressed in the same garb as the others stood at the back of the line, and they carried what appeared to be whips of fire and darkness that emanated from the crystals at the tips of their staves. In front of them, a group of at least twenty—what looked like a combination of humans, dwarves, and she could make out at least three halflings—was in chains and being dragged forward. Even the whips were not enough to stop them from trying to pull away, but the figure leading the group seemed to instill real fear into the captives.

Through the mist, he appeared almost human but did not wear the same robes as the other priests. Cassandra approached cautiously and attempted a better look. Long, wispy white hair trailed from his skull. He was an older man and wore only what appeared to be tattered black trousers that exposed most of his body to the mist around him. Black veins rippled through every muscle and his skin pressed against his bones. He did not appear to have any eyes, only the eyelids sunk into his skull.

Instead of speaking, he hissed and growled as he dragged the prisoners forward with unnatural strength. His teeth were blackened like his skin and despite his lack of eyes, he appeared more than able to see where he was going as he hauled the captives closer to the pit.

"Like hell," she whispered. Her discomfort over the stench and the mist were pushed to the back of her mind and all she could focus on was her rage. Karthelon likely knew what was happening outside. The new sacrifices, especially in this number, probably meant he was gathering strength to attack.

And Cassandra would not allow that to happen.

Her spear moved almost of its own accord as she rushed forward to thrust it through the chest of the closest priest before they even realized they were being attacked. She didn't bother to try to pull it out and instead, drew her sword smoothly from its scabbard.

The way she hacked at the second whip-wielding priest's neck wasn't the most elegant of attacks but grim satisfaction followed when the blood sprayed from his throat as he staggered and dropped his staff.

Those being hauled to the pit seemed surprised by her sudden intervention. They still tried to fight back but appeared unsure if the new arrival was there to help them or to step in where the two dead priests had failed. She assumed this meant the priests regularly fought each other, which was not too surprising all things considered.

But she would answer their unasked questions by action. Even without the whips lashing their backs, the creature at the front was still strong enough to drag them, inch by inch, toward the pit. It seemed wrong to even think of it as human. She rushed to the front of the group of prisoners and swung her sword onto the chain their captor used to drag them.

Any other weapon would no doubt have bounced off ineffectually, but her sword sliced through the steel that had no difficulty hauling the twenty or so people, severed it, and continued deeper into the stone floor to almost a full inch as the heavy metal fell away.

The creature doing the heaving stumbled forward and fell when all the strength he exerted was suddenly no longer balanced by the weight of the prisoners.

Cassandra lunged forward. She had no intention to allow a fair fight against a creature that strong. As much as she wanted to punish it for trying to sacrifice the people behind her, their safety was more important.

He had barely scrambled to his knees before she reached him, arced her sword up, and screamed as she drove it down again. Whatever had infused the creature with such strength had probably made its bones harder and its skin like boiled leather, but her sword still split its head wide. Thick, black blood oozed out before the being sagged and stilled.

She kicked it over, retrieved the keys that hung from its belt, and tossed them to the captive closest to her.

"Thank you," the dwarf woman whispered and immediately began to undo all their chains. "But there are more of us—in the prison over there!"

With a scowl, she looked around and sighed inwardly with relief when she realized the twins had already arrived to help. They dropped the dragon's head quickly, however, and covered their mouths, possibly afraid of what breathing this mist in would do to them.

Hells, she probably should have thought of that herself.

"You two!" she shouted and waved them closer. "Find the rest of the prisoners and lead them out of here."

"What about you?" Bandir asked.

"I have a god to anger. You might want to put as much distance between yourselves and this place as possible."

"What about you?" Tandir repeated. "We can't le—"

His voice cut off when he realized someone was tugging his hand. The child was smaller than humans tended to be—which made her assume that it was either a halfling or a dwarf—and clutched the barbarian's hand as she looked at him with huge brown eyes.

"Please...can you get us away from here?" The little girl whimpered.

There was no power on earth that would keep the twins from helping the prisoners to leave the temple now. Cassandra smiled as Tandir picked the girl up and let her ride on his shoulders as his brother collected two other children.

"Show us where the others are," Tandir ordered the dwarf who appeared to be in charge of the group.

It wasn't long before the twins were leading three or four dozen captives away from the cages they'd been kept in. They looked like they had been captured from all over and confined with only a handful being fed to the dragon while the others were reserved for the sacrifice.

The twins raised their weapons in salute to their barbarian princess, which she returned to them as she hefted the head by its horns and hauled it in the direction where the sacrifices were being taken.

A small inner sanctum looked directly over the pit and she intended to desecrate it in a manner that would surely bring the bastard Karthelon out to deal with her.

She doubted that the god had anything better to do with his time.

A flimsy lock was all that held the door closed but it shattered easily after her second kick dislodged the door from its hinges.

The walls were lined with dozens of links, probably to hold the sacrifices in place while they were offered one by one.

At the far side of the sanctum was a small, primitive-looking altar. As she approached, she realized that it hung by chains over the dark emptiness of the pit below. Channels had been shaped all along it, and a body was likely placed tilted downward so when the victim's neck was slashed, the blood would flow out in a matter of seconds.

This was a grisly, horrifying place that had been allowed to remain for far too long.

"Well, then, Karthelon." She growled her disgust and lifted the dragon's head. "It would appear that I took something of yours. I am here to return it."

She raised it as high as she could and hammered it onto the altar with all the strength she could muster. The old chains that held it in place shattered under the added weight and the stone swing wildly and broke against the rocks before the damaged altar and the head plummeted into the pit.

Disappointingly, nothing happened but a moment later, the ground shook and a deep, rolling growl or roar rumbled through the area to tell her she had been successful.

"Maybe I have the talent for pissing folk off too," she muttered and immediately beat a hasty retreat when cracks appeared in the wall of the sanctum. Seconds after she left, it crumbled and when she turned, it had disappeared into the pit along with a chunk of the cliffside it had been built on so precariously.

In its stead, the shadows took shape inside the pit and began to push from below. Even the air around her felt like it had thickened as she finally found a position that was not in danger of being dragged into the depths.

She didn't want to have her back turned when Karthelon finally decided to make an appearance.

―――――――

There were many reasons for Skharr to assume all was lost and he would die. The drop that yawned below him was more than enough to kill almost anything unable to at least slow their descent. While there was the possibility that he might be able to hang over the edge of the cliff, he shared it with an angry and wounded drake that seemed as intent on killing him as avoiding the fall.

Still, things could be worse. At least he had managed to free his sword and sheath it. He growled as he hammered his fist into the creature's jaw and forced it up and away from him as he tried to dislodge her from her position. He'd only tried this particular trick once and it had been a long time before, back when he was considerably smaller and more reckless.

In fairness, the drake he'd tried to get to fly with him on its back had been smaller too. Perhaps a larger creature would be able to accommodate the fact that he was larger as well. All he had to do was make sure she wasn't able to fight him off her back when she approached the edge of the canyon.

Once she was in the air, he would be able to guide her to take him to a point that was far enough away from the fight so he could kill her quickly and make his escape. There wasn't much more he could do.

"Stay…still…" He pounded a fist hard into the creature's ribs as he straddled her back and managed to stay away from the claws and the teeth. "We both need to get out of this predicament, you maggot-brained godsbedammed twisted spawn of life-sucking darkness, so you might as well carry me, hmm?"

He had already managed to retrieve the leather strap he used to keep his hair restrained inside his helmet and now, all he had to do was loop it inside the beast's mouth but away from the fangs, which would allow him to guide her like he would with a horse's reins. It wasn't quite long enough to be a comfortable solution, but it was certainly better than nothing. All he needed to do was find a way to open her mouth, fit the strap through, and catch it on the other side—without having any of his hands or fingers taken into her mouth in the process.

"It's not as though you didn't try to kill me before, you misbe-gotten scale fail." Skharr growled in annoyance and waited for his moment before he twisted and drove his fist into her jaw again. "You tried to kill me and now, I'm giving you the opportunity to try again without us both dying at the bottom of the godsbe-dammed fucking ravine!"

She had no answer to that, but her screech of pain from his attack was enough for him to throw the leather strap through, catch it immediately on the other side, and pull as tightly as he could to ensure that the drake would not be able to chew through it.

It fitted fairly well and Skharr angled himself and let her start to climb to the top and pull them both up and away from the drop. He maintained his pressure to prevent her from walking on all fours. Even wounded, it appeared she had more than enough power to lift them both from the ground and after a few attempts, the world fell away below him. There was no need to look down for confirmation and his stomach lurched as the beast flew toward the cliff face where all the nests were.

For a single moment, he dared to look down. It didn't seem like much had changed while they had struggled, but before he focused on guiding the drake to where they'd left their horses, he caught sight of something emerging from the temple. He paused and let the beast catch hold of the cliff wall as he narrowed his eyes and registered that a small group of prisoners had been led out of the temple by the twins.

"Fucking hells," he muttered. "Theros had better keep that

little mercenary alive a little while longer. Come along, you tub of fire-breathing troll snot. It's time for you to help instead of hinder."

The drake hissed and thrashed at him but was not willing to spit fire that would likely burn her as well. Instead, with some insistence, he dragged her around and she spread her wings to swoop earthward. He yanked hard until she flew directly into the largest group of priests where they had gathered to try to provide themselves with some degree of protection from the monsters overhead.

She leveled out before she made impact and Skharr released the strap and jumped off his perch on her back. He doubted that he could reclaim the strap and wasn't sure he wanted it anymore.

He landed more lightly than he thought he would but the sudden stop was still enough to knock his legs out from under him and he rolled as well as he could. His armor prevented anything from breaking or being torn, but he knew he'd have earned more than enough bruises for a healer to look at once they were through.

Still, he was alive and that was never something to take for granted.

"Come on!" the DeathEater roared at the rescuers, drew his sword, and hacked the wing from one of the drakes that swept overhead. It joined the pile of creatures and priests pressed against the cliff wall.

The twins saw their opening but the released captives appeared to need a little push to be able to move again.

Skharr wished he could have saved a couple of the horses the priests had left to be slaughtered, but it appeared they would have to make their retreat on foot and hope that the battle was resolved before the surviving priests could mount a pursuit. He collected his bow from where he'd discarded it and motioned for them all to join him on the road that would hopefully lead them to some semblance of safety.

# CHAPTER TWENTY

"It has been many years since a mortal has been capable of surprising me."

A shiver ran down Cassandra's spine merely from hearing the voice emitted by the shadows. She couldn't tell what affected her precisely, even though there was a hint of the same shiver that came when the dragon had roared. It was like there was a relation between the two, although the voice that spoke now was a little higher pitched than what she expected from a god.

The figure that appeared from the shadows also didn't quite meet her expectations. She had expected something a little like the other gods and even more similar to Grimm—good looks, impressive, powerful-looking, and with the arrogance that came from being young and powerful for hundreds of years.

Instead, the figure that stood in front of her was far less impressive. He was shorter than she was and slighter of frame as well. His skin was pale and contrasted sharply with the dark eyes and refined, almost delicate features. If she hadn't known better, she would have assumed he was a dark elf or one of their many cousins.

"There were four of us," she pointed out and raised an eyebrow. "It can't have been that rare an occurrence."

"No one is surprised to discover that a barbarian is contrary, difficult to control, and even more difficult to kill. On the other hand, a paladin with your particular skill for disruption and destruction is something altogether new. It makes one feel lucky to be alive to see such madness taking over the world."

She took a step forward and let the anger that roiled through her body have some control as she pointed her sword at the god in front of her.

"A pleasure you denied to…how many people did you sacrifice here? Hundreds? Thousands?"

"Thousands, at least. It's not as though I kept count. Do you remember how many animals and plants you've consumed over the duration of your life to maintain your abilities? Don't answer that. I know you don't."

She didn't, but if he thought she would be convinced that it was right by calling her nothing more than an animal meant for food, he had not paid attention.

"As it turns out," he continued and stroked his chin thoughtfully, "I am now without an heir or a champion. You would know since you killed the last one. It took centuries to find the right being to continue my legacy in the world like all the other gods have. Of course, they had more of a choice so they merely called on armies in the form of the guilds. For myself, I wouldn't want merely any mortal to carry my name."

"And you are considering me. I suppose I should be flattered."

He shrugged. "It is not a delicate process. It took time for me to form Grimm into a worthy creature and you would require the same. A slab of marble might be impressive but only once an artist's chisel strikes can it transform from a simple piece of stone into something greater than itself."

"So…you've compared me to food and then called me a rock."

Cassandra shook her head. "Are you supposed to entice me with these?"

"I have no need to debase myself before you." A faint snap of anger was hidden in the calm, chilling voice. "The offer is what it is and I have no need to coat it and make it more palatable to the likes of you. If you are interested in bettering yourself, the difficulties will not stop you. But if you are content with your base form, you will find any excuse to avoid my offer. You would be my champion and my consort. You will be more than merely another foot soldier in my army as you appear to be in the eyes of Theros. But it will not be an easy path. All but one have died in the process of being formed in my image, but since you killed the one who survived the process, I think your chances are better than most."

He was right. If it was something she wanted to do, the difficulties would mean nothing. As things stood, the benefits held no appeal to her and the difficulties were merely another reason why she would not be taken in as his consort or his champion.

"As fascinating as your offer is," she responded and took a step forward, "I will decline. I'd rather be Theros' foot soldier over your bitch any day."

He laughed at that, but she sensed the anger seep increasingly into his voice. He'd attempted to play the diplomat to serve his interest in having her on his side instead of fighting, but she assumed it didn't change the fact that killing his pet and desecrating his temple had made his blood boil.

The laughter made the ground shake and rocks fall, and distracted, it took a moment before she realized that something had wound around her legs. Slivers of shadow caught hold of her, held her in place, and immediately grasped her shoulders and wrapped her arms as well. They effectively trapped her while another slid around her neck, not quite enough to choke her but sufficient to prevent her from being able to move.

Cassandra jerked against the restraints and panic surged

through her. While she couldn't feel the wisps of shadow that entwined her, they were incredibly effective as restraints while Karthelon approached.

"I remember how intoxicating power was when I was a mortal," he whispered and leaned a little closer. "But you must understand by this point that even the world's greatest warrior would pose no more threat to me than the world's mightiest gnat. While you might buzz around me now, as effective an annoyance as you might be, if I even simply watched, you would be dead before I could blink. Assuming your annoyance does not inspire me to swat you away."

She gritted her teeth and continued to fight the all but invisible bonds. There was no question that her fight was in vain but she would continue to try.

"Swat…away, then. Otherwise, I'll continue to annoy the absolute shit out of you until the end of my short, miserable life."

"I don't think I will." He inched away. "Humans were always the more fragile creatures. You've only survived this long because you are adequate at surviving in many areas in the world instead of excelling at one. So much fragility—of the mind…"

His voice faded. It felt like he spoke to her through water and in that moment, she looked over what appeared to be a battlefield. A battle had occurred and despite the destruction, she knew she was looking at the remnants of Draug's Hill.

"No…" she whispered and struggled to reach down to help and stop them from bringing the walls down.

Skharr was still alive, but his hands and feet had been severed and he was naked while he was dragged by a rope around his neck over the rubble of the fallen wall to the laughter of the soldiers. She turned to where the twins were being killed as well. Tandir had a copper pot over his head, and the soldiers took turns beating the fragile metal to crush his skull. Bandir was strapped to five different horses with ropes attached to various parts of his body as the animals were drawn in opposing directions.

Even worse, when she looked at Langven, he appeared to have been given a place of some honor, having been strapped to the wheel of an overturned wagon. Dozens of soldiers laughed as they swung sticks at him while he was still being slowly poisoned by the dragon's venom. They broke his limbs one by one as the wheel continued to turn.

"Such a fragile thing." The voice felt like it was being breathed into the back of her neck as she watched. "I wonder how many of your friends and loved ones I would have to break, piece by piece, before you realize that contesting me is as futile an effort as trying to break free from the bonds I have you in. They would all die anyway, of course. Your life would need to be a cautionary tale with a single lesson to be spread across the world that none should fuck with Karthelon. But if you had chosen to fight alongside me, you would be returned to the world in a form that none would recognize as the pathetic insect that stood against me."

Cassandra jerked at the restraints again when she heard Langven scream in pain below.

"Of course, your mind is not the only realm I have to torment you with."

The battlefield disappeared and she looked around and frowned when she realized they were back in the Utter-Pit, although she had been brought to her knees.

"Torment is one word for it," she retorted and stared into the black eyes. "All I can feel is anger."

"I've seen it before. Those who think they are powerful generally display anger rather than face how insignificant they are. It would be the first lesson you learn from me. It's so much easier to…let it all go and bask in the fear and terror. Folk have a way of accepting the world around them and think all will remain the same. They are shocked when things change. For instance, you seemed to think that your beauty will last forever, but…well, I suppose there are a handful of diseases that humans are prone to that could change that faster than the impending doom of time."

Her hands were dragged to where she could see them, and her eyes widened when she saw the small, blotched sores that began to cover her skin. It looked like the pox but it spread faster than anything she had witnessed before, burned across her skin, and left it marked and scarred even before the blisters and sores healed.

She screamed and tried to put her hands on her skin to heal it, but nothing happened. No magic was summoned. She burned with fever and the sores erupted in her mouth to make it difficult to make any sound but a gurgled cry of pain as the blood seeped down her throat.

"So fragile."

"You...wouldn't...happen to be speaking about...your ego, now, would you?" she whispered. Every word made her feel like someone put hot coals in her mouth. "You should merely kill me. Fragile though I might be, it's easier to withstand...all you have in store for me when I know you need my fear and anguish to...survive..."

Cassandra saw the placid, calm look vanish from his face as the shadows holding her took physical form. They wound tighter around her and made her gasp as they tore through the pain she was already experiencing.

But when she grew more used to the agony, she forced a laugh.

"Honestly, if there was the option, I might wonder if you are unable to take women in other ways so you have to bind them and injure them to feel like a real man." She smirked at him and ignored the pain when the rage warped his face. "There is nothing like an immortal life of impotence to turn a man into a pathetic sadis—"

She was cut off when his hand swung into her cheek and

upended her with the violence behind the blow. The shadows tightened and held her down again.

"Interesting," he said before he stepped into her vision again. "Know that you have caused a great deal of pain for those you love and admire, but I will not give you the satisfaction of being the mortal who defied me."

His hand was wound in shadows, which were immediately wrapped in dark purple flame. They formed what appeared to be a sword of pure darkness that sucked in all the light around them when he held it out to press it against her neck.

"About...fucking...time." Cassandra growled her defiance and leaned upward as she felt the heat radiating from his sword.

"Your legend ends here, as so many others have," he whispered and raised his blade to strike. "In the end, you were only human."

# CHAPTER TWENTY-ONE

She wasn't sure if she should keep her eyes closed when the weapon swung or watch. Theros was meant to have stepped in to help long before now, given that Karthelon was directly involved in holding her down and torturing her, but there was nothing more to be said other than the fact that she knew the dangers of what she now faced. She'd made her peace with the fact that it was likely that a god would not intercede on her behalf.

The sword should have struck her by now.

Her eyes opened again, and Cassandra frowned and looked around for any sign that she was possibly dead. She'd heard many theories about what happened when the body died but decided to not make any assumptions about what came next. Her body was freed from the restraints and when she looked up, Karthelon backed away slowly. He seemed confused and even a little angry as he stared at someone who stood over her.

Theros had abandoned his disguise as an old man. Instead, he wore full plate armor—not unlike the suit she wore—and carried a spear that she guessed was what he'd used to block the strike aimed at her, judging by how it raised slowly to point at her captor.

The dark god hissed and tried to attack again but this time, instead of blocking, the spear was thrust forward into the darkness that was wrapped around his hand. The whole area flashed and Karthelon was hurled off his feet. He scrambled across the ground as he looked at his hand. Twisted and bleeding, it looked like it belonged to a marble statue and had been cracked down the middle.

"This is none of your concern!" he all but spat as he finally regained his feet.

"You were breaking the rules agreed upon by all of us," Theros replied, stood over Cassandra, and offered her a hand to help her up. "That is very much my concern, especially as it pertains to the life and death of my finest paladin."

"Paladin?" The dark god scowled at her as he clutched his injured hand to his chest to hide it from prying eyes. "She's run around like a half-dressed whore and not once did I hear her call on your name for help."

"Well, we all have a little growing up to do sometimes," the lord high god answered with a smirk and a wink directed at her.

She realized that her hands were still covered in the blisters and sores Karthelon had given her, but Theros placed his hand over the injuries and they began to fade. The heat, pain, and fever that came with them were quickly pushed aside as well, which confirmed that he did have some skill in the art of healing humans. It was certainly better than almost any other healer she'd ever heard of.

"She...invaded my temple!" their adversary insisted. "Killed my priests and the guardian of this place—and all on your orders, it would seem. Was I supposed to let that kind of attack stand?"

"Not unless you sent priests, guardians, and others to attack her and hers beforehand," Theros retorted sharply. "You wouldn't have...attacked her first? Sent your son and then drakes and dragons, or nothing at all that would show you as the aggressor in this situation?"

The dark god gathered his power for another attack. Even she could see that but knew there was no need to warn the lord high god. He raised his spear, which suddenly glowed with a pale silver light that seemed to physically drive the mist around them back. Their powers suddenly crackled and surged forward to meet each other in the middle. If both had been at full strength, she assumed it would have been an even match, but with his temple destroyed, his priests dead, and his sacrifices gone, Karthelon was visibly weaker than the god he stood against.

Well, perhaps not quite as even as their adversary would have wanted, assuming the title of Lord High God meant something other than merely Theros and Janus patting each other on the back.

The silver light drove forward, split the blackness, and turned it to dust as the dark god retreated step by step until the light wrapped around him. It looked similar to how the darkness had wound around her and it squeezed, tightened, and enveloped every inch of him until a scream echoed through the whole temple, followed quickly by a blast of the silver light. Cassandra closed her eyes, but all she felt in the aftermath was a gentle gust of wind that brushed her hair a little.

Of course, the same could not be said for the temple they were in, and cracks began to shiver along the walls. The earth shook as rocks began to fall from the ceiling.

"Come along, my paladin," Theros muttered and extended his hand for her to take. "I think it is time that we leave this place."

"You think so?" she asked but still put her hand in his. "And here I was thinking we could bring friends and make this a place for folk to relax in when the winter months grow too cold in the north."

He chuckled softly. "You did well."

"I know."

Startled, he stared at her for an instant before he nodded. "Well...good. It's best you know that."

The world shifted from where they stood and in the blink of an eye, they reappeared at the beginning of the narrow shelf path leading toward the Utter-Pit. She couldn't see it but the cloud of smoke that began to rise from within was difficult to miss and she turned to see that the horses were exactly where they'd left them. Those the twins had ridden looked like their sudden arrival was somewhat unsettling, but neither Horse nor Strider appeared affected by it and instead, browsed a few dry patches of grass.

"A handy trick," Cassandra muttered and looked around. "But what about Skharr? The twin—"

She stopped when the sound of footsteps approaching from the path caught her attention. Skharr and the twins led a group of some forty or so prisoners who had been liberated from the temple.

"She asks about Skharr before she asks about us," Tandir muttered and shook his head. "It is disrespectful."

"Oh, shut up," she all but snarled, immediately raced to them, and pulled them into a warm embrace.

It was shared by the massive figure she knew could only be Skharr and for a moment, she closed her eyes and enjoyed it. They all smelled of sweat, blood, and battle, but that could be complained about later. All she cared about was that they'd all made it out alive.

"I would not want to interrupt this moment of reunion," Theros said calmly to do exactly that, "but I would not want to be anywhere near the Utter-Pit as it undergoes…that kind of trans-formation."

She looked back as the ground shuddered gently and she noticed a massive, mushroom-shaped cloud rising from the pit.

"I think he might be right about that," the DeathEater declared.

"How did you know the fang would provide her with the antidote for the poison?" Cassandra asked and shook her head. "I thought you were taking it to…uh, I don't know. Steep your arrows in it to make them deadlier."

Skharr raised an eyebrow. "What makes you think my arrows need to be deadlier?"

He made a good point and she paused and frowned as she took another sip of the koffe he had prepared for them. She knew drinking too much of it would leave her wanting more when it ran out, but it also meant she should enjoy it while the stocks remained.

"I guess not. Still…it seems like you were thinking much further ahead than I was. But we still could have had Theros heal Langven."

"That would be him intruding on the natural order of things. I've heard that would lead to the end of the world, but I think it merely means he feels he worked hard enough for one day and he would prefer it if we did what he was unwilling to."

She rolled her eyes and glanced to where the twins paid no attention to the conversation. It seemed inconceivable that they'd had the time to recover trophies from the drakes they had killed, but they had even managed to collect a claw each from the dragon while they beat a hasty retreat. She had a feeling they would boast about it for years to come. They were entitled to that much, at least, and they had a plethora of scars to prove they had earned those trophies the hard way.

"Well, it's a good thing you have such an intimate knowledge of how gods tend to think," she said finally. "I think."

Before Skharr could answer, her face lit up when Langven finally pulled the curtains away from the window of the room he had occupied in the Draug's Hill hall. He still looked weak and his wounds continued to heal slowly, but all signs of the venom were gone, as was his pallid, feverish look from the night before.

"What is that I smell?" he whispered as he approached the fire they were gathered around. "I swear, I will never forgive you for hooking me onto this...koffe stuff."

The DeathEater nodded. "I believe I can bear that burden for the rest of my days. How do you feel?"

"Like a day-old fawn that was somehow rolled on by a falling tree. But...alive. And better than yesterday, I have to admit."

Cassandra smiled and squeezed his hand gently. "I'm glad to see you on the mend."

"Well, I needed to be up and about before you left for Verenvan." He scowled when he pronounced the name of the city. "Having your last memory of me as a sickly, wheezing, dying man on the bed would be horrifying to think of."

"You could always simply leave him wheezing and dying on the bed," Skharr said and raised an eyebrow. "Metaphorically speaking, of course."

"Are you jesting?" The mercenary captain took a slow sip of the warm koffe. "I do believe that a good fucking would kill me."

"Another time, then," she replied with a smile playing over her lips. "I'll have to find my way back here for us to spar again, although you'll have to play your part. It would be a shame to spar with you as a fat and comfortable lord over these lands."

"I'll try my best."

His smile was matched by his eyes widening in shock as she leaned in, pressed her lips tenderly to his, and held him for a moment longer than was necessary.

"I'll hold you to that promise," he whispered when she finally drew back.

"Good. Now get some more rest. Seeing you sitting makes me think that you'll keel over at any second."

"We'll help him back to his cot," Tandir volunteered.

"We wil—ow!" Bandir bounded from his seat when his brother kicked him and both helped Langven up and walked him carefully to where he had been resting.

"That was...unexpected," Skharr commented around a mouthful of sausage.

"Feeling a little jealous, are you?"

"Why would I be jealous? I'm the one you're riding to Verenvan with."

"That was my plan, yes."

He finally allowed himself a grin as he took a sip of his drink. "Then I suppose I am a little jealous of the little guy. And not only because he's staying here with a nice bed and good food."

"Don't act like you don't love the road, oh Savage One."

"That depends entirely on who I happen to share the road with, Your Grace."

She rolled her eyes, stood slowly from her seat, and stretched to ensure the blood pumped through her limbs. "Well, I'll meet you at the horses. We'll leave whenever you're ready to start your travels again."

# AUTHOR NOTES - MICHAEL ANDERLE

WRITTEN DECEMBER 22, 2021

Hi there, this is Zen Master Steve™, hijacking Michael's author notes today.

If he were here, he'd thank you for reading the book (thank you!) and tell you he was in Mexico preparing for Christmas while trying to arrange furniture in the new house.

He undoubtedly would have several funny stories about how that process is going.

Since he's not here, I'll tell you about a secret game that Michael, Lynne (our queen of editing), and I have played for the past few years.

It's the "make the other person on the Zoom call spit coffee on their keyboard" game. (Perhaps that should be trademarked as well, hmmmm….)

The object of the game is probably clear from the name. It's the techniques that vary.

Sometimes it's a well-timed joke, other times it's a *look* that offers an unspoken commentary on something that's been said, and sometimes, when it's Michael, there's a subtle hand gesture he makes to try and trigger the desired reaction.

With that as background, I received a gift in the mail from Michael the other day that he and I will try and use on Lynne. Since I don't make the hand gestures that Michael has perfected, he got me this perfectly innocuous cup.

As you can see, the message is uplifting, which we believe will lull Lynne into a false sense of security. The moment she says something I don't like, I'll drink from the cup instead of debating the point, which changes the message every so slightly.

Wish Michael and I luck as we try and win the game in 2022.

Thanks for reading our books and Happy New Year to you and yours from all of us at LMBPN!

# CONNECT WITH THE AUTHOR

**Connect with Michael Anderle**

Website: http://lmbpn.com

Email List: http://lmbpn.com/email/

https://www.facebook.com/LMBPNPublishing

https://twitter.com/MichaelAnderle

https://www.instagram.com/lmbpn_publishing/

https://www.bookbub.com/authors/michael-anderle

Made in United States
North Haven, CT
30 May 2022

19646684R00162